ASANAS

a novel in four postures

Stephen Brooke

Arachis Press 2018

Yesterday is but a dream,
and tomorrow only a vision

ISBN 978-1-937745-52-3

Arachis Press
4803 Peanut Road
Graceville, FL 32440
http://arachispress.com

POSTURE I

halasana
the plow

One

SPARSE TRAFFIC PASSED on Third Street. A ghost, a reflection of Lynn's own oval face, was superimposed on the low pastel-colored buildings, the palms waving in the afternoon sea-breeze. Enough day-dreaming. Turning from the window, the young woman picked up the check, looked it over, and replaced it on the Formica-topped table.

"Why don't you come to my yoga class with me?" she asked her companion. "You have far too much stress in your life."

"Yoga?" replied Karen, toying with a cigarette. No lighting up in here. "I'm not into that New Age crap."

"It's just relaxing exercise. You could use some of that."

"There's only one relaxing exercise I need right now and I'm not getting any of that!" Karen's laugh came as a short bark.

Her friend gave her a disapproving look. Karen should know it well; she would know also that Lynn would nag her until she gave in. "Okay, when is this class?"

"This evening, six o'clock. Bay Park."

"The rec center, right?" asked Karen.

Lynn nodded. "So don't work late again!"

"Yeah, I have this overwhelming urge to do accounting after hours. I'll try to be there." She considered the smoke in her fingers, turning it over, and then slipped it into its pack, and that into her purse. "Need to get back right now."

"Wear something comfortable," advised Lynn, as she counted out her share of the lunch check. "And you'll love Pat, our instructor."

"Oh, sure."

The air was warm for March, even in southern Florida. Lynn looked to the empty sky, deep blue from the lack of humidity, as the pair parted at the entry to *The Compass Rose*. That was typical for spring, the dry season. For a moment more, she watched Karen, already halfway up the block, stride purposefully north in the athletic shoes she always slipped on before heading out for lunch. There would be heels waiting in her office at *Fairfield and Fairfield*, though she would kick them off under her desk as she worked.

Karen was unusually sardonic today, wasn't she? Lynn asked herself. Her friend wasn't always like that. She turned south, herself, walking at a more leisurely pace. There was no hurry. Sammy was away on a buying trip and she could open up when she felt like it.

No one was in a hurry today. It was that time of year, tourists and winter residents already heading home. After Easter, Tamarind would again become the slow, sleepy southern town of summers past. Lynn crossed with the light at the corner of First and continued eastward, toward the bay.

She could smell the bay on the onshore breeze. It was not a smell Lynn minded. It was the smell of her home, the smell of the tides, rising and falling in their own slow-paced rhythm but as steady as an heartbeat. Two blocks and then south half a block brought her to the wide front windows of *Bayside Art and Antiques*, canvases displayed to the left of the door, curios and

4

furniture to the right. Might as well leave the door open on a day like this, she thought, unlocking and swinging it wide.

It would be a slow afternoon, a good time to catch up on the business side of things. The owner, Samson Ibarra, left that more and more to her these days. How much of that was his trust in her and how much his tendency to laziness, she was not quite sure.

And it was only the promise of eventual partnership in the gallery that kept her at it. Lynn would rather be painting pictures herself. Wasn't that why she had the art degree? Inertia was keeping her here, she feared. Inertia and uncertainty.

Well, that and the fact she liked old Sammy. Lynn could not deny that. So she took care of the shop management and the publicity and all the little tasks of running a gallery, while Ibarra went on buying trips for antiques—the end of the business for which he truly cared—and charmed customers and artists alike.

One of those little tasks was dusting the merchandise. A professional cleaning service came in a couple nights a week, a competent man-and-wife team, but they had strict orders to touch neither art nor antiques. For this chore, Lynn trusted only herself.

It was the sort of thing one could do between customers, a few minutes here and there, as able. There were not many customers coming into the *Bayside* shop this Monday afternoon. Lynn retrieved her blue feather duster from beneath the counter and began with the paintings hanging on the north wall, not hurrying but thoroughly attending to each frame and picture in its turn. She noted dull glass on some of the watercolors, hiding the natural brilliance of the medium. Those could be cleaned tomorrow, if she had the chance. First thing, maybe, before Sammy came in. He would be back, wouldn't he? Yes, he should be.

Lynn paused before a large oil, a sunlit landscape replete with bravura brushwork, almost drowning in it. She was not sure she liked the piece, at once virtuosic and overdone, both vulgar and vital.

Like the artist himself. His signature was in the lower left corner, 'M Stone' in stylized red letters. She lowered her duster, dangling it at her side, and stared at the painting.

An older couple, in matching yellow Bermuda shorts, wandered in. Lynn sighed, tucked the feather duster into her back pocket, and turned to greet them.

Two

"THAT IS PAT? I was expecting some skinny old hippie woman."

"Sorry you're disappointed. Should I tell him?"

Karen ignored that. "No wonder you enjoy your yoga," she whispered.

"Behave yourself," her friend whispered back. "If you scare him away the whole class will want your blood. Including me."

"Why didn't I wear a leotard instead of sweats?" wondered Karen.

"Hush. We're starting." Lynn seated herself on her mat.

Karen had to make do with one of the well-worn, navy blue mats provided by the rec center, being sure to spread a towel on it first. She plopped down beside her companion.

"Bring your own next time," advised Lynn. Karen only nodded.

Pat did not call for attention or announce the beginning of the class. He simply started talking. "We will prepare by taking a complete breath. I'll demonstrate for our newcomers." His glance glided across Karen. She was definitely a newcomer and felt a bit conspicuous.

It did not take long for that to fade. Karen could see she was not the only neophyte in the group, a group consisting in large part of older women. She did not spend much time looking about at them, nor at the large, beige-walled meeting room. Pat was much more interesting—it was rather easy to keep her focus on him.

Fifty minutes of asanas, yoga postures, followed, Pat with his slim muscular body leading the willing but mostly out-of-shape group. After a closing meditation session, he sat, lotus position, on his mat and said, "Thank you for coming. Class will be the same time on Wednesday." He remained where he was, smiling at them for a moment, before continuing. "We will continue to meet for ten weeks, Mondays and Wednesdays."

A slightly stocky woman—more muscular than fat, but some of each—in tan shorts and a sandy pixie cut came forward to announce, "Hi folks, I'm Jen Carter. I, uh, am the director here at the center." She paused, seemingly needing to think her words through thoroughly before going on. "If you haven't paid for the class yet, you need to come and see me." She turned her eyes toward the young man sitting beside her. "We also need to thank Pat here for taking on another class for us."

Karen smiled inwardly. Her first thought had been 'lesbian' on seeing this woman but, from the looks she had seen her give their instructor through the session, it was pretty obviously not so. She suspected a lot of the class was giving Pat those sorts of looks.

Karen looked about as they stood. Three men in the class, it seemed. No, four. A teenage boy at the back of the room, already slipping out. Probably here out of curiosity. She suspected the kid would not return. "I think I'll stick with it," she informed Lynn. "Let me go pay and I'll be right back."

Lynn watched her friend write out a check and exchange a few words with the director before returning. "You were in his last class, right?" Karen asked.

"I was," said Lynn. She glanced toward Pat, who was still seated and acknowledging greetings from some of the other class members. "He teaches out at the Springs, too."

Karen's eyes had followed her friend's and rested a moment on their instructor. Then, she turned and asked, "Does he have a girlfriend? Does he *want* a girlfriend?"

Lynn laughed; it was a laugh that came readily. "No girlfriend that I know of. Some of the girls think he's gay but I've seen him taking looks. I'd say he's just shy."

"Introduce me to him."

"I have grave doubts as to the wisdom of this." Lynn shook her head with mock seriousness. "But okay, let's go."

Karen knew her friend was not entirely joking. She'd been putting her in these sorts of situations since they were teenagers. As they approached, Pat rose to his feet in one easy motion. He said nothing; the smile remained on his face but the man seemed a bit anxious. His eyebrows came up questioningly, a silent invitation for them to speak.

"Hi, Pat."

"'Evening. Need anything?" He faced Lynn but his eyes kept shifting to Karen.

"This is Karen. She signed up for your class."

"Oh." He held out a hand. "Welcome. Is this—ah, ever do yoga before?"

"No," answered Karen. "Will it give me a nice body like yours?"

"I hope not!" The instructor laughed, then immediately blushed.

Lynn gave her an exasperated look. "You promised to be good."

"I only complimented him," she replied. "Can't I pay you a compliment, Pat?"

"Anytime." Then Pat smiled that sweet, shy smile of his she would come to know so well, and shook back his long hair. The gesture seemed natural; there was no self-consciousness in it. "Thank you."

"Good, then. I'll think up some new ones for Wednesday!"

"Bye, Pat," added Lynn, as the pair headed for the exit.

"Do you need a ride?" asked Karen.

"Nope, I drove today. It's a bit far to walk home from here." Lynn, more often than not, walked to her place of employment at this time of year. The weather was good for it. "And Sammy had the truck so I needed my car to run errands."

"He's back tomorrow?" They stopped next to Karen's deep red Lexus. It reminded Lynn of the jewel-like tones of the old Flemish masters.

"With a load of antiques to sort and catalog and price," she answered. "We'll be busy."

"All right. Lunch tomorrow?"

"I'll try."

Lynn watched Karen's taillights as she exited the parking lot, and went to her own not-so-new Escort. It was white but that was not her choice; it was just what was available at the time, and at the price she could afford. Minutes later, she was pulling in at the *Neptune Apartments*.

Once a motel, before all that business went to the chains over on Forty-One, first, and then further out by the interstate, it now contained studio apartments arrayed in a horseshoe around a small pool. That pool had been the reason Lynn chose to live here. The evening air felt a little too cool to go in right then.

It wouldn't be long. Seasons change. Maybe it wouldn't be long for a lot of things.

She checked her phone for the first time since before yoga class. Nothing. Not the most popular girl, are you? she asked herself. For a moment, she considered calling Matt.

But no. Lynn shook her head and went inside.

Three

SAMSON IBARRA, AS Lynn, was that relative rarity, a Floridian born. The state is a place where most have come from somewhere else, come to seek sunshine and opportunity. His grandfather had come seeking work in the cigar factories of Ybor City.

"Unloaded already?" asked Lynn, surveying the cluttered store room. Lots of crockery among the new arrivals, wasn't there?

"Last night. I didn't want to leave anything outside in the truck." Ibarra nodded his head in approval of his own statement. "Some heavier pieces will be delivered later."

She suspected that Sammy had been there all night. "Here, look at this one," he said. Item by item, Ibarra proudly showed off his acquisitions, removing the taped newspaper that had protected them. Lynn found his enthusiasm contagious this morning.

But she would never have quite the same passion for antiques. They both knew that. "Do you have a list?" she asked. The scribbled notes he handed her were about what she expected. She could probably figure them out and get all of this organized.

"You should go home and get some sleep," Lynn told her boss. Or you might start to look your age, she added, only to herself. Samson was a little too thin-skinned for her to say such things aloud.

Ibarra grimaced. "I know, my dear. I suppose I must leave my new babies with you." The light tone could not completely hide his reluctance to part with his treasures. The man ran neatly manicured fingers through his hair. That he dyed both hair and mustache black, Lynn was quite certain.

His eyes lingered on the new pieces for a moment more, before he said, "I'll try to get back this afternoon." Without another word, the antique dealer disappeared out the back door. Lynn could hear the vee-eight of his old Impala—a veritable antique itself—roar to life a moment later. Good, he was leaving the truck with her.

Not that she needed it at the moment. Lynn had chosen to walk the four blocks from her apartment this morning. It was nice at this time of year to stroll up Bay Street in the morning, and not yet too warm to walk home in the afternoon nor face the likelihood of summer rain. She glanced at the round-faced clock hanging above the door into the showroom. Nine-thirty—an half-hour yet until she needed to open up. Time enough to get the coffee-maker going. She began the process of cataloging the new items, as the machine wheezed and chugged on the counter.

Some of these vases and curios were likely to end up in Sammy's own rambling old house, out in the Springs. Some would be resold to other dealers if they sat around *Bayside* too long, or exchanged with their friendly rival, the *Antiqua Gallery*, up toward the river. *Antiqua* was a bit more tourist-oriented, with no pretensions of being a dealer in fine art.

A group of paintings, still wrapped in Kraft paper, leaned against the wall by the back door. A new find or just something picked up at an estate sale? Lynn would have to look at them later. It was time to open up now. She filled her coffee mug and headed for the front door.

She must go back there later and continue getting things into some sort of order, gathering up the paper and tape strewn on the floor, making sure there was room for the items yet to be delivered. Lynn silently chided herself for not asking when they would arrive; she couldn't take off for lunch if they might show up while she was gone.

And she was curious about the paintings. It was slow that morning—not unexpected. At her first opportunity she began their unwrapping, tearing away the brown paper. The first five had a 'Highwaymen' look about them but she doubted they were authentic. Sammy would have bought them as a lot. Two more. Hmm, interesting, somewhat expressionistic Florida scenes, but the young woman couldn't place the signature. It did seem familiar, though, didn't it? The same name on both. She could try looking it up later. By noon, everything was tidied up in the storeroom, though she had made no attempt to document any of the merchandise.

No delivery yet. Lynn took a moment to call up Karen and tell her she wouldn't be getting out of the gallery. If able, the pair showed up at *The Compass Rose* at Twelve-thirty each day. The restaurant lay about as close to halfway between their workplaces as was possible. This was both coincidental and convenient.

The two friends tended to be zealous about having this time together, the one time they could count on. Lynn felt a small pang of guilt about missing it today, not that it was really all that uncommon for one or the other. Did Karen feel the same when she had to cancel?

Despite the woman's seemingly cool, almost uncaring, persona, Lynn suspected she did. Maybe more than Lynn did herself.

Karen had always been needy.

Four

"I DIDN'T STUDY with her," explained Matt. "Before my time. But *my* teacher did." He turned his eyes again to the two modest canvases.

Samsom beamed. "I knew it was a find."

"Her house is not far from where I live. The studio and grounds are kept by her family as a sort of museum now."

"I know the place. I visited it when I was in high school." Lynn attempted to squelch an embarrassed giggle as she said this. It sounded so inconsequential. She often felt that way when Matt and Sammy conversed, like they were the only adults in the room. "Maybe the family should know about the paintings," she added.

"Definitely," agreed Ibarra. "If only for further authentication."

Matt Stone shrugged. "Her name's on them, isn't it? What more do you need?"

Sam ignored the hint of disparagement in the man's voice. "Probably nothing. It would be courtesy to contact them." Lynn knew he didn't like Stone very much, even if he did show his paintings. He would like it even less if he knew she was involved with the artist. The dealer picked up one of the oils. "It does say Horley," he stated and then squinted at the signature. "Thirty-six?"

"Both of them," said Lynn, smiling. Samson was being obstinate about not wearing his glasses again. She thought his vanity a bit endearing.

"Very early," offered Matt. "I don't think she lived in this area then." Lynn knew she didn't. She had researched Doris Franklin Horley online earlier in the day. No point in saying it, though.

"And they have stayed together," said Sam. "Almost certainly bought at the same time."

"I bet that's your delivery, Sammy," Lynn said, noticing a panel truck pulling up on the street. "I'll send him around back." She hurried out the front door without waiting for a reply.

There was not exactly a parking lot for the buildings along Bay Street, but a narrow alley provided access for deliveries and a few spaces for vehicles. Customers would park on the street, those that hadn't walked from somewhere. Lynn directed the young man behind the wheel to go down half a block and come around. He would have to come from the south as the alley was one-way, not that it ever mattered much and certainly not this late in the day. The driver nodded and u-turned in Bay Street. That was easy enough with most of the parking spaces empty on both sides.

She turned back to the brick building, built an half-century ago. The brick was, in fact, fake, carved into stucco, and long since painted over in a coral tone. Lynn wondered why Matt had dropped by this afternoon. Had he intended to talk to her before getting sidetracked by Sammy?

By the time she reached the back, both men were helping the driver unload. "You're the last on my list," he told them. "Everything in here is yours." It was nearly Four. He would certainly be glad to be done and able to head back to wherever. Lynn hadn't noticed any name on the truck nor had she bothered to glance at the license plate. It didn't matter much.

A desk. Ornate—Lynn did not think it the sort of thing that would sell well here. Some lamps, a chair. Two chairs, make that. She watched the pair carry the items in, the slight Samson, who did not at all live up to his name, the tall and tan, golden-haired Matt.

Though Matthew Stone's hair wasn't really golden, but sun-bleached. He had the look of an athlete gone to seed, a man who still half-heartedly attempted to retain his youth. Lynn knew well that the artist allowed self-indulgence to sabotage the effort.

"Help me get the desk in my truck, will you, Matt?" asked Ibarra. "It's going home with me."

"Do you have someone to help you unload it?" wondered Lynn. Samson lived quite alone in his big old house.

"You should have had it delivered there," was Matt's opinion.

15

"And that would have cost more," replied Sam. He clearly felt that was reason enough. To Lynn, he said, "I can find someone to help me with it. My neighbors mostly like me. Lock up here, will you?" He and Matt muscled the desk into the pickup and he set off for home, leaving his Impala parked.

Although Sam told her she should feel free to drive it and left a set of keys with her, Lynn had never felt comfortable with the idea. Ibarra trusted her too much, she sometimes thought.

Matt casually wrapped an arm around her as soon as the truck disappeared. "Wanta get some dinner?" he asked.

Lynn could not resist replying, "Are you sure you want to be seen out with me?" She regretted it at once, but Matt didn't seem to mind.

Rather, his answer came bluntly honest. "We'll go someplace no one knows either of us."

Lynn, for a moment, thought he joked. It was hard to tell with Matt, hard to tell how serious anything he said might be. She only nodded and looked up at the clock. "I'll close up in a few minutes. Will you drop me by my place so I can change? I didn't drive today."

"Those clothes are okay. And can't you close early? It's only like half an hour." He immediately chuckled and answered himself. "Of course not. I know how conscientious you are about things like that."

Lynn was not positive whether that was a compliment or an accusation. She didn't feel like figuring it out either.

Five

THERE WERE MANY things Lynn couldn't figure out about her life, about her relationship with Matt. He had gone with the dawn, leaving her alone in her small apartment.

Gone back to his studio out in Leawood, out by the beach. He had his classes to teach today, too, in Sarasota. Matt needed that extra income; the man was not willing to live the life of a starving artist.

Nor had his estranged wife been willing. Lynn would rather not think of her. She wiped the steamy mirror in her tiny, green-and-gray tiled bathroom and peered at her face, an oval face that seemed serious even when she wasn't.

She looked okay, she thought, more youthful than most women her age. Lynn had done the 'oh no, I'm thirty, where am I going?' bit last year. Nothing had actually changed, of course.

Well, maybe her weight but she worked on that. Her walking was a part of that effort but today Lynn would drive, to the gallery and then to yoga class. She arrived at work well before Ten AM opening time. Before Sam showed up, too. That was normal enough but she had thought he might be there early to sort through the new merchandise.

She was fond of Sammy, even if he could be sometimes petulant, even tyrannical. And, certainly, he liked her and always seemed sorry for his occasional lapses of temperament. Samson Ibarra had given her a job right off when she had hesitantly approached him.

But it was nearly five years now, five years of the gallery struggling along and her career, her life, doing the same. Lynn unlocked the front and turned the 'open' sign over.

The black desk telephone behind the counter jingled. Ibarra insisted on retaining a land-line here; the man was decidedly old fashioned in many ways. Perhaps that was reflected in his affinity for the antique. It was Sam himself on the phone.

Not coming in today. Catalog the new merchandise as she saw fit. She suspected that his weekend trip had caught up with him and Sam needed a day to recuperate. He was not so young and abhorred exercise.

Samson's presence was not necessary to the running of the shop but Lynn knew well that he connected better with the customers. He became their friend in a way she never would. Never could. She attempted to seem blandly professional when anyone came in, to hide her own shyness behind a mask of competence.

Few did come in this morning and Lynn found plenty of time to finish sorting through the new arrivals, matching them up against Sam's scrawled notes. The vases and other knickknacks were lined up in orderly fashion on the shelves, the larger pieces arranged on the floor below, ready for Sam to decide on prices before they went up front. She could pretty closely estimate those prices by now, it was true, but would not think of trespassing in Samson Ibarra's realm.

Lynn finished in plenty of time to meet Karen for lunch. In this pleasant weather they could sit at the docks across Bay Street instead of in a restaurant. She should suggest that to her friend. But Karen didn't have the love for the water she did.

The rich scent of the bay hung in the air here. It faded as she walked east, or perhaps she just became accustomed and noticed it less. Karen was already at a table, the window table they always tried to take. And as always, Karen faced south and Lynn north. Lynn suspected her lunch companion preferred to be able to see the door but never asked her of it. Everyone had their oddities.

A waitress came immediately. Jan. She knew to wait for both to arrive. "Mushroom is the soup of the day," she informed Lynn. "Served in a scooped-out French bread roll." Jan also knew that Karen didn't go for that sort of thing.

"That sounds fine. Iced tea too, please." Her friend across the table went for her typical burger and fries. She won't always stay so skinny eating like that, thought Lynn. It was not the first time she had that thought.

"Your boss is back?" asked Karen, stirriing sugar into her tea as they waited for their orders.

Lynn had told her so over the phone the previous day. No matter. "Yes. He isn't coming in today, though. I think he's tired himself out."

"Maybe he has a new boyfriend out at his house," Karen suggested.

Lynn frowned at the remark. "I've told you he doesn't do that. I think Sammy is pretty much celibate most of the time." She knew Karen had trouble believing anybody would willingly choose that sort of lifestyle. The discussion went no further as Jan brought their lunches and the conversation turned to other subjects.

Six

THEY HAD BEEN right about the teenager. The boy did not show for the second class. The other three male students did.

One middle-aged man came with his wife. Or girlfriend; she didn't know them. There could be any number of reasons he chose to accompany her. Two older men seemed to be together.

Would Karen show up? She had said she would but that was never a guarantee. Lynn surveyed the rest of the group as they began to settle into their chosen spots. As before, mostly older women, mostly white. All but one white, in fact. Ah, there was Karen, arriving with seconds to spare.

At least she had remembered to bring a mat this time. And, not surprisingly, she wore a leotard. Was that a good choice for Karen? It showed off her long slender body but also the beginning of a pot belly. That was what happened when naturally skinny people started to get out of shape.

Karen slipped off a wraparound skirt and unrolled her mat next to Lynn's, as Pat entered and walked to the front. He offered no greeting but, as before, went directly into the complete breath. Maybe it helps calm him before starting in, thought Lynn, as much as it does the class.

"Welcome to all," said Pat on the completion of this opening exercise. He spoke then for a few moments about yoga and the purpose of the class. Lynn had heard this particular speech before and did not pay much attention, letting her eyes wander. Her spot was far enough back and far enough to the side to allow her to see much of the class without turning her head.

The man over at the other side of the group was not disguising his own attempts to look over the class. That was the guy who had come with a female companion. Lynn couldn't see the other two men, positioned directly behind her, without making it obvious. But this man, a rather ordinary looking sort in sweats, definitely was checking out the women in the room.

They moved on to a series of yoga poses, easy ones for the most part or Pat would demonstrate an easier version. They finished with their instructor introducing the Sunrise Salute, and then a brief meditation period.

As the session ended, Pat announced, "I lead a more advanced class at the Springs. If anyone is interested, come see me."

"Here or there?" someone asked.

The young man smiled. "Either would be fine. Thank you all for coming this evening."

"That's it, right?" came a deep voice. Lynn turned to the two older men behind her.

"It is," she informed them, not sure which had spoken.

The shorter of the pair, a somewhat paunchy individual with a head of wavy brown hair, nodded and asked, "So what's a nice girl like you doing in a place like this?"

"Don't be an idiot, Joe," rumbled his companion. "That doesn't even work in bars." He held out his hand. "Roger," he said. "Roger Bernhard." Nodding toward the other man, Roger added, "This is Joe Gill."

"U.S. Army, retired," stated Gill. "Both of us." He glanced toward the front of the room. "Your friend ran away." Karen was conversing with Pat. Or talking to him, anyway, with Pat putting in a word now and again, or nodding his head.

"That's Karen," she told him. Roger's oversize hand engulfed her own. "I'm Lynn." She shook Joe's more average one.

"Good to meet you, Lynn," said Joe. To his friend, he said, "I'm gonna mingle," and abruptly left.

"Off to scout out the single women here." Roger grinned. "Probably thought you and your friend were too young."

Lynn wasn't quite sure how to respond to that. "But he's got it backward," the man continued. "Actually Joe and I are too old." Was Bernhard blushing slightly? He was fair, and reddened easily, Lynn guessed. "Nice to meet you, Miss Lynn," he said and wandered off in the direction of his buddy.

Karen did not look entirely happy when she returned. Frustrated, thought Lynn. She must not be making headway with Pat. Lynn suddenly felt a bit protective of her yoga instructor—all the more since she had introduced Karen to him. She would not let that boy be hurt.

Boy? Her age, and Karen's, she suspected.

"Flirting with the seniors?" asked Karen.

"They think we're too young," Lynn informed her. She looked at the pair, talking with a group of women across the room. "They don't look that old, do they? Fifties, maybe."

Her friend shrugged. "I would have taken them for a gay couple." She gathered her bag and mat. The skirt was already fastened around her waist. "I'm out of here. Won't see you tomorrow, will I?"

"Maybe. I'll call."

Seven

Fairfield and Fairfield read the brass sign, and below that 'Karen Fairfield, CPA.' It had been two years since the other Fairfield, Karen's father, had passed but she had seen no reason to change the firm's name. Lynn pushed open the heavy oak door. Its solidity suggested similar solidity from the accounting firm, and an air of privacy. Glass doors would not have the same effect; Lynn readily recognized that.

Allie raised her eyes from the computer screen before her. "Miss Fairfield is waiting for you," she said. Allie's accent was definitely southern but Lynn had never been quite able to decide on its place of origin. She could have asked, of course, but that would have taken the fun out of it. "Go on in."

The twang suggested Alabama, didn't it? Lynn entered her friend's small private office. The rich tones of her mahogany desk could scarcely be seen through the clutter of manila folders. A cigarette smoldered in a green glass ashtray, already filled with butts. "I'll be ready in a moment," Karen told her. "Do you want to eat at the *Rose* or somewhere in Leawood?" She gave a last look at the paper she was holding, nodded, and set it aside. "With tax season right around the corner, I fear I won't be able to take another afternoon off for a while. Everyone will want to meet with me, whether they need to or not."

"Let's have lunch at the beach," decided Lynn. "Your car?"

Karen only nodded. The question had been for the sake of politeness—they always took Fairfield's vehicle. "Close up at Four," she told Allie. "I don't think I shall be back."

They descended the rear stairway of the stuccoed office building to the parking lot. "So Ibarra has you running errands on your day off, does he?" Karen asked.

"I volunteered. Those paintings interest me."

"What was the name?" Karen's key chirped as she unlocked the Lexus.

"Horley. Doris Franklin Horley," replied Lynn. "We can stop by there after we eat."

Karen's office was located on Fifth Street—also know as Tamarind Road—the main thoroughfare through town. Further north it crossed the river; to the south, it curved out toward Leawood and the Gulf of Mexico. That was the shortest and simplest route to the beach.

A low bridge took them across the marshy southern end of the bay. Through the gray-green grass ran a labyrinth of channels, the brackish water rising and falling with the tides. Here and there, a spot of white could be spied, a feeding egret. Cormorants perched atop any handy piling driven into the mud.

"Too bad it's still too cool to swim comfortably," remarked Karen. "I hate going to the beach and not going into the water!"

"There will be northern visitors out in it anyway. And surfers, if there are any waves."

"Don't they mostly go to Venice if it's any good?"

"Uh-huh. At the jetties." Lynn remembered surfer boys from their school days. Were any of them still in the area? It didn't matter—there was always another generation to take their place.

Much of Leawood was empty lots, down here, with the occasional house sitting among them. They were scattered, two rarely being found side by side, as if no one wanted a neighbor. Little but saw palmetto and scrubby pines grew from the white sand, with a live oak attempting to take hold here and there, its dark green foliage standing out against the general drabness of the season.

Karen steered her Lexus straight west, toward the Gulf. "*The Hot Dog Stand*?" asked Lynn. *The Hot Dog Stand* was not exactly a hot dog stand, but a small beachfront restaurant.

"Yep. I think I want a flounder sandwich." In that it was Karen's car, Lynn made no objection to her choice. It was like Karen. She wouldn't mind a fish sandwich herself. Mullet, maybe. The odor of deep-fried fish greeted them in the parking lot. That and the smell of salt water, for the sea breeze had come up as it oft did by the late morning.

"I think we beat the lunch crowd," remarked Lynn, as both approached the worn wooden counter. She turned to the gray-haired woman standing ready to take their orders. "Are there still plenty of visitors out here?"

"Fair number," came the reply. "I reckon there'll be plenty over this weekend." But not so many after that, they all knew. "What would you young ladies like today?"

Both ordered. "I think we'll eat outside," said Karen.

The woman nodded. "I'll bring your food out when it's ready. Would you like your drinks right now?"

"Sure," Lynn replied, and her friend nodded in agreement. A minute later they were sitting at a picnic table under a yellow and white striped awning, sipping iced tea. There were many holes in the awning, not large, but allowing tiny beacons of sunlight to play upon the tables.

They gazed out toward the Gulf, beyond the wide white sand beach. A pair of limestone jetties extended into the calm clear water. Fishermen would be out on those in the morning and evening, but not when the sun was high overhead. Now only a few tourists splashed in the shallows around them.

Their sandwiches and baskets of fries were brought, and coleslaw for Karen. Lynn had never been fond of it—too sweet, usually. "Too bad they don't serve beer," she remarked. "It would be perfect for washing this down."

"So would a nice Riesling," laughed Karen. "But tea will do." Despite being a northern girl—born and mostly reared in Ohio—she took her iced tea southern-style, with plenty of sugar.

"They are expecting you at this studio?" Karen asked.

"Yes. I sent them phone snaps of the pictures and they were very interested. Um, *she* was, Joanne was the name. The artist's grand-daughter. Joanne seems to run the place." Lynn finished off her last French fry. She felt vaguely guilty about having eaten them—she was usually good about sticking to her diet. "I promised to send high-res pictures when I get the chance."

"Sam will hang them in the gallery, I assume."

"That he will, and with a substantial asking price." She shook her head. "If only he had come across the paintings at the beginning of the season instead of the end. The prestige of exhibiting them could have done wonders for us."

Eight

THE ROAD RAN parallel to the beach. A collection of older beach houses and motels was arrayed down its length, with newer, taller apartments rising here and there. Those were a promise of things to come, the inevitable development, the growth that was always a part of Florida.

Think of all the people who will want art to hang in their new homes, Lynn told herself. To Karen, she said, "Right at the next corner." The Horley studio lay out to the east of the downtown strip–such as it was–on two or three acres. Would development mean its eventual bulldozing as well?

"It's nice out this way," remarked Karen. "Oh!" She put on her brakes and peered out the side window, past her companion.

Lynn followed her eyes. Horses. That came as no surprise. Karen did have a thing for horses. A couple of them gazed back at the women from beyond a white board fence. Lynn had no idea what sort of horses they were, other than brownish. She did not even know if they were good-looking.

Karen sighed and started forward again. After a moment, she said, "I should use the long weekend to go up to the farm." There was no point in commenting on that. Either she would or she would not, and Lynn was busy counting down the numbers on the mailboxes.

"The next drive on our left I think–yes." There was a sign welcoming visitors to *Painter's Paradise*. That helped.

"This has been here a while, hasn't it?" asked Karen.

"At least half a century," Lynn replied. "We can ask Joanne." A handful of low wooden buildings lay before them, surrounded by a lush tropical garden, palms and elephant ears and a huge banyan.

"I hope they have a good well" she went on. "It must take a lot of water to sustain all this through the dry season." Karen nodded in agreement and parked next to the only other vehicle there, an older Ford pickup. Bags of fertilizer and pine mulch filled the bed.

A short, deeply suntanned woman wearing ragged-cuffed and dirt-stained jeans, and a plaid shirt in little better condition, greeted them. "Miss Devinne?" she asked, looking uncertainly from the one to the other.

"That's me. Call me Lynn," she told her, stepping forward and shaking her hand. "This is my friend, Karen Fairfield."

"Pleased," the woman said, taking Karen's hand. "Joanne Horley-Baker, but I go by Jo." She turned back to Lynn. "Wherever did you find those paintings?"

"My boss, um, Samson Ibarra, bought them at an estate sale up in Ocala. Mr. Ibarra owns *Bayside Art* in Tamarind."

"I know the place. Some of the locals show there, right?" Jo didn't wait for an answer. "Come on in." She led the way toward the barn-like building marked 'studio.' Would that I could have a studio that size, thought Lynn.

"Ocala, eh?" continued their host. "My grandmother spent the early part of her career up that way before settlin' here in the Fifties." She chuckled. "There are artists here now and they still call it an art colony, but nothin' like how it was in the middle of the last century. I've got scrapbooks I could show you."

"Do you paint, Jo?" asked Karen.

"Nah. I didn't inherit any of Grandma Doris's talents. Instead I ended up growin' stuff like my Grandpa." Jo waved an arm at the vegetation around them. "He planted the better part of it."

"A forester, I understand," said Lynn. She had researched all she could about Doris Franklin Horley.

"That he was." They entered the building. It looked even more a barn inside, with high ceiling and open rafters. "Grandma got famous enough that he didn't have to work so hard anymore and retired to spend all his time on fixin' up this place for her." Jo winked at the pair. "My husband has to have a real job so I can be the one takin' care of 'Paradise.'

Lynn had immediate studio-envy when she looked about the room. Large and airy, plenty of natural light—and big fixtures overhead for night painting sessions. Counters and cabinets and a pair of easels. A few framed paintings and drawings hung on the walls. A larger number of photographs of the artist and her friends accompanied them.

"We have a few of Grandma's paintings here and some out to loan. Most are owned by someone else, naturally." She turned her eyes to Lynn. "And now there are two more we didn't know about. You're gonna sell 'em, I suppose?"

Karen laughed before she could answer. "That's what they do. For a good profit too!"

"Undoubtedly more than our foundation could afford. But we would love to have some clear photos for our files."

"You'll get them," promised Lynn. "You must let me see those files someday."

"You're always welcome. If I ever find the free time, I intend to get them online."

"If there is one thing I have learned," announced Karen, "it is that time is never free."

Lynn chortled. "I know how much you charge for yours."

"Be thankful I'm not charging you now." Karen gave the studio a perfunctory looking-over. "Would it be okay if go outside and wander, Jo?"

"As okay as it gets. We get just about as many visits from garden enthusiasts as we do from art folks."

"I can believe it," spoke Karen, and slipped out the door.

This woman was about their age, wasn't she? thought Lynn. She must not have grown up locally or she and Karen would have know her. Joanne gave her the tour, showed her files and scrapbooks; there was enough here that Lynn could have spent days, weeks, rather than the hour or so she had. It also made her ask herself once again why she was not painting.

"Matt Stone has his studio out here somewhere, doesn't he?" asked Karen as they headed homeward.

29

Lynn did not answer for a moment. She didn't really want to talk about Matt or even think of him. "Yes. We passed by earlier but no one was there."

His home and small studio was up in this north end of town—still the 'art colony' Joanne Baker had mentioned—a couple blocks back from the beach. "It's right over there," she said, pointing toward a nondescript clapboard house to their left. Lynn rather disliked the pastel coral color it had been painted, and the white trim. It seemed a caricature of a beach house.

"There are cars there now," observed Karen.

Matt's auto and that of his estranged wife. "Yes," agreed Lynn. "There are."

Nine

"WHEN I MAKE you a partner you won't be able to take any days off," declared Sam Ibarra.

Lynn could not resist saying, "It doesn't stop you from staying home."

Her employer chuckled. That was good—she was never entirely certain how he might react to a jibe of that sort. "That is all too true, Lynn." Then, more seriously, he went on. "You know you will not take home as much money if we do this. I feel like, ah, like I would be doing you a disservice to take this step."

"I would make sure Karen looked over the books first," Lynn deadpanned.

Sam again became serious. "I would insist upon it." He returned to his original thought. "We both will have a couple of days off. We won't open on Monday, or Sunday either, of course." He glanced at his watch. "I shall leave as soon as you return from lunch."

Church, no doubt, thought Lynn. There was a Good Friday afternoon service of some sort. "But you will be here tomorrow, right?" she asked.

"I think so, at least for the morning. Not that anyone is likely to come in!"

"If it is slow, maybe I can set up the new acquisitions and get some good photos." The gallery did have a web site—maintained by Lynn—and also printed up a catalog now and again. "Especially the Horley paintings."

"I am thinking it might be a good idea to keep them under wraps until Fall. What do you say?"

The question surprised Lynn; she had already thought along these lines but Sam usually made such decisions without asking her opinion. She had to agree his plan made sense. "I say it is a good idea. Letting them hang through the slow summer months is a waste of their publicity value."

"Exactly. Now off to lunch with you." It was a few minutes earlier than she usually left but Lynn didn't object.

Neither she nor Karen had much to say at lunch that day. Sometimes it was just that way, their minds elsewhere, maybe, or simply nothing new to talk about. At last, Karen asked, "There is no yoga class on Monday, right?"

Lynn only nodded.

"Three days open. I think I'll leave early in the morning and go to the farm for the weekend. It's been ages and this is my last chance before the tax deadline rush. That will tie me down the next couple weeks." She sipped her tea before adding, "It's kind of late to ask but would you like to come?"

It seemed a casual question but Lynn doubted her friend had just thought of it. "I need to be in the gallery tomorrow," she answered. "Well, maybe I don't *need* to be but I should show up."

"And there is Matt."

"Yes." She didn't want to talk about that and Karen didn't pursue it. Lynn wasn't even sure she would see Stone this weekend. He did have a family, after all.

"Have fun," she told Karen, as they parted outside *The Compass Rose*. More than I'm likely to, she told herself. It had been long since Karen had visited her country place, the little farm her father had bought with an eye toward retirement. That never happened.

Lynn hurried back to the gallery. She had no reason to; she simply felt impatient this afternoon, like she needed to get going, to get things done. Sammy was still there but more than ready to leave her in charge.

"Are you going to Leawood?" she asked him. Lynn knew there was a Catholic church in Leawood.

"The cathedral in Venice," came his reply and then, clarifying, "Epiphany Cathedral." He could have given it any name and she would have been none the wiser. Ibarra gave himself a looking over in an ornately-framed mirror hanging in the showroom. "You should come on Sunday."

Lynn had to smile at the invitation. She might not have any other plans but couldn't see herself at Easter mass. "I'll see you tomorrow."

"Most likely," replied the gallery owner and hurried out the back. A moment later, Lynn heard the Impala's engine roar to life.

Ten

WHERE WAS THE turn? She didn't want to miss it in the dark. If she reached the spa, Karen would know she had gone too far. Pat lived at the spa. Lynn had told her that. He didn't just teach there but acted as a handyman of sorts.

Small businesses lined the way here, interspersed with wooded vacant lots, dark trees silhouetted against an overcast predawn sky, before one reached Consonante Springs, proper. Here and there a security light provided stark illumination of a parking lot. An all-night convenience store, empty of customers, and the lone clerk out smoking in front, was passed on her right. Karen turned onto the cutoff that would take her out to the interstate, while Springs Road curved north and crossed the river.

A traffic light and a rival pair of filling stations, both closed, marked the crossing of Highway Forty-One. On to the east she drove, toward a promised sunrise. Karen felt she would like a cigarette but she had made it a rule never to smoke in her car. The odor would cling forever.

There was the interstate. She had not decided before starting out whether to turn south or north on Seventy-Five. Either would get her there. Well, it was decision time. Karen pulled onto the southbound ramp.

Dad would have gone the other way, she thought. He would have stuck to the interstate as far as he could before cutting off to the east. It was the quickest way, he claimed, and at the speeds he drove, she believed him.

She left the highway, turning back to the north and east at Port Charlotte. The horizon was growing lighter before her, a peach-tinged smudge on the low sky. The swiftly moving clouds were like a river, carrying its load of flotsam away to the northeast. Who was that surfer boy who drove her this way once, back in high school? She could see his face but couldn't come up with a name. Skip? Yeah. He had turned east at Arcadia and headed straight across state to the Atlantic. God, it had been a long time since she had seen the ocean.

Karen was tempted to head there instead of the farm. No, make it some other time. The motels would all be full over there. Flat land, farm land, lay on either side of the road. Now, cattle could be seen here and there, the humped backs of Brahmas, and the white cattle egrets stalking after them, hoping to nab whatever treats their passing might stir up. It was a part of Florida most people didn't know, perhaps a part most wouldn't want to know.

A tedious drive, as well, wasn't it? And too far. She should put the property on the market; Karen was finding no more time for it than her father had. She could get an acre or two closer to home, maybe keep a horse. On she drove, into morning and the lake country of central Florida.

Yes, she did stop for a smoke, and for coffee, too, not far from her destination. It was nice here. She thought she liked it better further north, though, up toward Ocala. That was the area to have a farm. Her father's place—her place—wasn't really a farm at all. They had just gotten used to calling it one.

A decade and an half later, she still did. There was no longer even a sign at the dirt road. It didn't matter; Karen remembered the way. She'd been here often enough as a teen, almost every weekend it sometimes seemed, though she was sure that was wrong. A lot less since. The road was a bit wet but that was good. It firmed it up.

If she had arrived earlier, she could have watched the sun rise over the lake. Singer Lake, they had been told was its name, but she and Dad just called it the lake. The sluggish creek on the south end carried its outflow down through swampland to the Kissimmee and, eventually, Lake Okeechobee. Under a tarp behind the house still sat the canoe they had bought to someday explore it.

Dad's big fishing boat she had sold after his passing. Karen could not see ever using it, of ever going out on the lake and casting for bass. But that had been the idea of this place. These twelve acres–almost twelve–could be developed into a fishing camp, a project to keep Dad busy when he handed the accounting firm over to her.

That was her father's dream. She would never go through with it, though from time to time she thought she liked the idea. Yeah, best to put this property on the market.

Karen sat for a few moments in her sedan, looking the place over. There was work to be done. If she wanted—it didn't matter much. She could just sit on the dock the whole weekend, watch the sun rise on other mornings. No, it didn't matter at all.

Eleven

No ONE WOULD buy anything major this morning. These were last-minute shoppers, looking for art or knickknacks they could carry home with them, take north when they abandoned Florida at season's end. Many snowbirds had already gone back to Ohio or wherever to celebrate Easter.

Lynn gazed out toward the bay across the street. "It looks like more rain," observed Samson, coming to stand beside her. "We can use it."

Rainy weather was somewhat rare at this time of the year, the end of March, in this part of Florida. This wasn't the beginning of the rainy season; no, wait a couple months for that. A late-season cold front was responsible for the drizzle this morning and last night.

"I hope it doesn't ruin Karen's weekend," she said, to no one in particular.

"I heard there were some heavy winds overnight. Up north of here."

Lynn had heard that on the morning radio as well. Trailers had been damaged and that sort of thing. "Not where she went, I think," she replied. But she wasn't certain about it.

Ibarra checked his gold-banded wristwatch. He wore it with the dial turned inward. Less likely to damage it that way, he told the curious. "I believe I shall leave the place to you. Close up when you feel proper. I would not expect anyone much this afternoon." He seemed to think on that for a moment. "Maybe we should start off-season hours this weekend."

In other words, begin closing at Two on Saturdays. Lynn only nodded. "Enjoy your weekend," she told him.

"Weather permitting!" he responded and headed for the back room. A few seconds later she heard the door close. Maybe she would close early. She could skip closing for lunch then; it wasn't a good day to walk to the restaurant anyway.

Samson had seemed fidgety, as if he wanted out of the gallery as soon as possible. Maybe it was just the rainy weather. Lynn didn't mind the drizzle. It wasn't like she had anyplace to go.

Not today. Not tomorrow nor Monday either. She wouldn't see Matt. He might be separated, his wife might be in Saint Pete these days, but he still had his little girls and would spend time with them this Easter weekend.

And he still needed to be circumspect about spending time with Lynn. There was no reason to give Anne any sort of advantage when the seemingly inevitable divorce came.

What then? She was uncertain. Would they marry? Would she even want to marry Matt?

Business picked up more than she or Sam had expected. But what else was there for folks to do on a rainy holiday weekend than shop? Or loiter in shops, really—no one bought much of anything. Lynn didn't have the opportunity to go into the back and set up the camera as she had hoped.

Maybe she should just pop in tomorrow and do that. She had nothing else to fill her day.

"Can you deliver?" asked a young woman looking over a writing desk.

"Not before Tuesday," Lynn had to inform her.

Not before Tuesday. Everything was on hold for a few days.

Like her life. She smiled inwardly at the thought. No self-pity, girl. You're doing well enough.

By Three, she had the door closed and was in the back, photographing everything she could. It was good to get that accomplished, to get anything accomplished on a day like this.

Twelve

THE HOUSE WAS old enough to have a fuse box, rather than circuit breakers. Nineteen Forty—when it was built, there wasn't even electric available here. Karen switched the power on and opened the can of fresh coffee she had brought along. It would take a minute or two to get enough water pressure from the pump to fill the coffee maker.

The place looked okay inside. Outside, too. A man came and mowed from time to time, not that a lot of that was necessary through the winter months. There were branches down, maybe from the blow last night.

The house was dusty, of course. Lots of dead roaches from the last time it was sprayed. Probably live ones lurked now.

There was sediment in the first coffee pot she filled from the tap. She dumped it and filled again. That was better; the water looked reasonably clear. The well water tasted pretty good here, certainly better than what came out of the pipes at home.

A squall passed through, momentarily hiding the lake behind gray curtains. There should be less of that as the day went on. As the weekend went on. She could do some tidying up in here now.

But coffee first. She poured the hot fresh brew into a mug. Her mug, bright yellow, the one she always used when she came, washed and put away for the infrequent visits. Sugar? Damn, she should have brought some. Maybe milk too, now that the fridge was cooling down. Go out later and stock up, she told herself. There's a little store just up the road.

A fast-food place, too, if she didn't feel like cooking, and a bar beyond it. A red-neck bar on a Saturday night? Hmm, maybe not. She would be too tired anyway. Pictures of cowboys did pass through her mind, and pictures of her with them.

Karen spent the remainder of the morning rolling an oversize industrial canister vac from room to room. "I don't think I'll need to do that for another year," she announced, with a fair amount of self-satisfaction, and went to take a look outside. It was breezy and the air was damp, but there was no rain, at least for the time being. She wandered down to the lakeside and lit up a smoke.

It was nice here. And, yes, she should put it on the market. Karen could see a boat now, out on Singer Lake. Some people would try to fish in any weather—they would enjoy themselves even if it made them miserable.

Maybe that was what she was doing, visiting this place.

She would run to the store later. Relax now. Another cigarette? No, no, she shouldn't smoke so much, or at all, really. It was starting to sprinkle rain again.

Instead Karen sat down just inside the open French doors and watched the changing sky for a couple minutes, before hesitantly going through the yoga asanas she had learned in class. I'm probably doing these all wrong, she told herself. Her mind drifted to the instructor of that class.

Stop daydreaming, she told herself. The water should be hot enough for a shower now. Get cleaned up and get out of here.

By the time she drove to the little grocery store, the sun had broken through. Tomorrow should be nicer, and Monday too. She should make the most of this weekend; there would not be any more chances to relax for awhile.

She looked up the two-lane road, past a blinking yellow traffic light. A pair of motorcycles sat in front of *The Corner Bar*, and a single faded blue pickup truck. Karen shook her head. Not the way she wanted to spend this evening and, after all, if she wanted to go out it wasn't far to Lake Wales or somewhere like that.

Tonight she would take it easy, get to bed early, Karen decided, and went on into the store.

Thirteen

"MISS LYNN!" SHE looked around. Ah, the two men from yoga class. "Are you alone?" asked the smaller one. That was Joe, right?

"I am," she admitted.

"Come sit with us," he invited. His big companion nodded an agreement to the idea. It *was* crowded. She should have expected that at an Easter brunch.

"Okay," she said and slid into the booth, next to Joe. More room on that side. She asked the waitress for coffee and French toast as soon as she made it to their table. It was what she always ordered here.

"We're having mimosas," Joe informed her.

"Fake ones," rumbled Roger. "They don't serve alcohol here."

"Oh. How do you fake a mimosa?" she wondered.

"Ginger ale," was the answer. It didn't sound that appealing to Lynn, not that she liked real mimosas.

"Are you a local girl?" Roger blurted out. "I mean, grew up around here?"

"I am," Lynn admitted. "Mostly, anyway." Both men gave her inquisitive looks so she went on. "My family moved here when I was ten. Dad worked for the city."

Now Clearwater employed him, in their planning department. No point in adding that. No point in talking about herself at all. "You guys were military, right?"

"Yes, ma'am," responded Roger. Was there a trace of a southern accent in that deep voice? "We put in our time and retired with full pensions."

Joe nodded agreement and looked to his friend. "Rog and me have been friends for twenty years and more, even when we weren't stationed together. So we figured we might as well stay that way and retired to the same town."

"The same house, too," Roger said. "Saves money."

"Yeah, we might as well be married!" Joe laughed, perhaps a

little self-consciously. "We've actually considered it for the legal benefits, now that it's okay here in Florida."

"But it would cramp our style, so to speak," was Roger's thought on that.

"Yeah. We joined your yoga class to meet women."

"Any luck?" asked Lynn. She tried not to giggle. Perhaps that was as good a reason as any to come to class.

"Well, you're here!"

Roger shook his head. "Out of your league, Sergeant Gill."

"It's best to aim high, Sergeant Bernhard," replied Joe. He winked at Lynn. "But I'll bet this lady already has someone."

That was a statement Lynn did not even wish to acknowledge, much less respond to. Rather, she deflected. "Maybe I should point you at my friend, Karen. She's unattached."

Joe shook his head. "Too skinny."

"Like you can be choosy, Joe," his friend told him.

"No reason not to be," came Gill's amiable reply. He chuckled and turned to Lynn. "Anyway, I can tell she makes too much money to be interested in anyone like us. Well-off girls go for well-off guys, always."

"Not too mention that both of you are way too young," added Roger.

Lynn laughed outright at that. "I though you told me that you were too old."

He gave her a sheepish smile. "Yeah, that too."

"Are you going to stay with the class?" she asked, pushing her empty plate out of her way, toward the edge of the table.

"Sure," Joe told her. "Beats sitting at home."

Roger nodded his agreement. "Or in a bar."

"I can certainly agree with you gentlemen on that," said Lynn. She held out her cup for the waitress to refill it. I've done enough sitting, she told herself. More than enough.

Fourteen

"I'm putting the farm on the market," announced Karen. "I talked to an agent this morning."

Lynn was not completely surprised by this. "The real estate market has been getting better. For sellers, I mean." So she had heard, so she had read.

"Yep. I'll overprice it, of course." Karen laughed. "I have extremely mixed feelings about this."

Jan appeared, order pad in hand. "Iced tea?" she asked. That was what they always ordered; she would have been safe bringing it without asking.

"Yes, please," responded Karen, "and, um, a grilled cheese." She looked up. "That comes with chips, right?"

"Yes'm. Slaw, too."

"Okay." She looked across the table to Lynn. "I ate too many burgers over the weekend."

Her friend nodded. "I'll have the chef's salad," she told the waitress.

"I should eat more salad," mused Karen as they waited for their orders.

Lynn ignored this, knowing there was no real answer to it. "So you called someone upstate to list the place?" she asked.

"I did. A local agent—you know I don't like dealing with the big companies." Lynn did know. Karen had rather strong ideas about supporting small businesses, operating one herself. "You'll have to go up with me one last time before it sells."

If it sells at all or you don't change your mind, thought Lynn. "Sure," she said.

"I didn't do much but hang around the place," Karen continued. "The rain kind of put a damper on things. So what did you do all weekend?"

"Hung around too," admitted Lynn. No point in mentioning her unexpected encounter with Joe and Roger on Sunday. After that she had seen pretty much no one. "Swam some."

"Beach?"

Lynn shook her head. "Pool."

"Sounds like you were as bored as I was."

Jan brought their tea and Karen went through her ritual of adding three packs of sugar. She took a sip, nodded her head, and said, "I may be working through some of my lunchtimes the next three weeks. Or two and a half now, I guess."

"The Fifteenth is when we'll go to shorter hours at the gallery," said Lynn. "Slowing down already, of course."

Their lunch arrived and the conversation went to other things, impersonal things. Lynn found herself gazing out onto the street again. Should she mention what Samson Ibarra had told her first thing this morning? No, better to wait until everything was sure; she would want Karen's assistance then.

"I don't suppose you saw Matt over the weekend," she heard her friend say. Had their conversation been moving that direction?

"No. He was busy."

Karen snorted. It wasn't loud but it was assuredly a snort. "With his wife."

"And family." Matt had an obligation to his little girls, at least.

"He needs to make up his mind about divorcing, um, what's her name?"

Lynn didn't really like talking about Matt's almost-ex. "Anne," she said.

"Anne. He seems a little too comfortable having the both of you."

Maybe so. It was a thought Lynn had entertained before. She chose to treat it lightly, joking, "You think he's cheating on me with his wife?"

"I wouldn't put it past him but I suspect this Anne has enough sense to keep him at arms' length." Was there an implication Lynn should do the same?

Lynn sighed. "With Matt's ego, I'm not sure I'd put it past him, either." Did she really believe that?

"He feels entitled, yeah. Bob had too high an opinion of himself to cheat on me." Karen gave her a half-smile, crooked, almost a grimace. "He just got tired of me." She almost never mentioned her former husband.

Lynn had no idea how to respond to that.

"And he had good reason," continued her friend. "All I do is work!" She rose. "Time for more of that."

Fifteen

BOB HAD NEVER really seemed a part of her friend's life, only a presence that came and went on the edge of their relationship. When he and Karen divorced it had made almost no difference.

Lynn didn't want to think about any relationships at the moment but all this was in her head now. A couple was browsing in the shop, separately. Some would split up like that, some would make their rounds of the merchandise side by side. She had no idea why.

Karen had married Bob while Lynn was working in Orlando, at the commercial art firm she had joined straight out of college. She might as well have been up north somewhere, as she never got to the beach. Karen had stayed on at the University of South Florida to get her Masters degree. By the time Lynn came back to Tamarind, her best friend was working with her father and her marriage was already in trouble.

Karen's workaholic ways certainly had played a part. From what she had heard, Bob was not much different. She idly wondered, for a moment, where the ex lived now. Ah, it didn't matter.

She heard the back door close. Not Samson, Lynn was sure—he had taken off mid-afternoon and would not be returning today. Matt, most likely. He might prefer to park out back and not have his van seen in front of *Bayside Art*. She had somewhat expected him to drop by. It would have been nice if he had called first.

It was like Matt to assume that spending Tuesday evenings together was a given. She should tell him she would be busy tonight. But she wouldn't. Wouldn't tell him, wouldn't be busy.

Where was he? She stepped into the back room to find him crouched in front of a rack of paintings, casually looking through the canvases.

"You break it, you've bought it," she told him.

He nodded absently, barely acknowledging the joke, and straightened up. "These are all things Sam picked up, right?"

"Yeah. Junk, mostly."

"Agreed. I hope he didn't pay much."

"Samson Ibarra *never* overpays," she stated. "They're mostly stuff he found at estate sales."

"I have to attend a reception tonight," Matt said, with no further lead-in. "I won't be able to see you."

"Oh. Okay." Lynn wasn't sure she cared that much, knew it was not all that important, yet part of her was bothered that Matt only now let her know. Rather than address any of that, she asked, "How was your weekend?"

He shrugged. "It was just a weekend. I had the girls with me at my place yesterday, and on Sunday." His tone became wistful. That was rare for the man. "I do miss having them around, even if I get more painting done now." She thought Matt would say no more but he added, almost an afterthought, "And how was your holiday?"

"Boring. I didn't do much of anything." Lynn hated to ask, hated to sound needy, but she said, keeping her voice as even as possible, "When will I see you?"

"Why don't you come out on Thursday? We could make up for tonight, and for this past weekend, too." He looked at her a few seconds, as if considering a decision, before saying, "Or tomorrow night."

Matt had never before invited her to spend the night at his place. It seemed reckless. "What about Anne?" she asked.

"She found a job in Saint Pete. Anne won't be coming around on weeknights." The next words carried a tinge of self-mockery. "Another step closer to splitting completely."

Did he regret it? Well, of course, she told herself, even if it was inevitable. No one came to the end of a relationship without regrets. Lynn knew this. Lynn had gone through it. She had her own disappointments.

"Okay," Lynn decided. "I'll drive out after my class."

He cocked his head at her. "Class?"

"Yoga. You know that."

"Oh, yeah." He could not completely conceal his disinterest, but he did ask, "Didn't that end a few weeks ago? I remember you saying something about it."

Lynn had to laugh. "So you *do* pay attention sometimes. A new class started up last week."

He gave her a wink. "Well, anything that keeps you flexible is good with me. I'll be waiting for you." Matt glanced up at the clock. "I need to go clean up and head to Sarasota." He leaned in for a perfunctory kiss and was out the back door.

Sixteen

THE MAN WITH the roving eye was here again, accompanying his wife. Definitely his wife; she could see the wedding rings from the vantage of the entryway. Roger and Joe, too, in the same spot as before. She didn't mind taking a place right in front of them. If someone had to get a view of her backside they were as good a choice as any.

Lynn moved over to let someone else through the door. The black woman, the only one in the class. She didn't know her name. Young, as was the guy with her. Husband? Whoever he was, he left her and headed back outside. The man didn't seem overly pleased to be there.

Probably going to sit in the lot and wait for her. That would disgruntle a lot of men. Lynn went on into the high-ceilinged room and claimed her spot. It was almost warm enough to turn on the fans overhead.

"Hi, Miss Lynn," came Roger's greeting. "Your friend coming?"

"She said she would," Lynn replied, unrolling her mat. "She could be sneaking a last minute smoke." Both of the former soldiers laughed at that. They weren't all that old, really, were they? Fifties, she would guess. Despite Roger's claims, they were not 'too old.'

As Pat entered, stage left—which Lynn knew to be the kitchen—Karen slipped in the back and settled down beside her. She nodded a greeting and turned back to their instructor.

"Namaste," he greeted the class. "Welcome back. Let's begin with our complete breath." He went on to introduce a standing version and then an abdominal exercise based on it, snapping the abdomen in and out.

"That hurts," whispered Joe.

"Good," came Roger's barely audible rumble in reply. The big man probably had good abs already under his tee, Lynn thought. She pegged him as the morning calisthenics type.

Little else new was introduced in that session. It had been a week since the last class and Pat's pupils needed to be reminded of what they had already learned, practice the simple asanas he had already shown them.

"I'll be back," murmured Karen as class came to its end, and headed in Pat's direction.

"She's going to flirt with that boy, isn't she?" asked Joe.

"It seems likely," Lynn allowed. She watched her friend, standing close to Pat, laughing at something. Would she touch him? Yes, there was the hand, lightly, casually, on his arm and lifted after the moment's contact. There was no discernible response from the yoga instructor.

Lynn wouldn't have expected any, not from the guarded Pat. There was mingled disapproval and admiration in her as she watched her friend's performance. One thing Lynn knew was that she could never emulate her without feeling far too self-conscious.

A couple minutes later Karen found her way back. The sergeants —as Lynn had come to name them in her head—had wandered off somewhere. Oh, over there with the recreation director, Jen. The woman was making rather extravagant gestures, waving her arms wide, apparently in explanation of something or another, while Roger nodded sagely. Joe, on the other hand, was letting his eyes wander elsewhere about the room.

"He seems like a nice guy," stated Karen. "Definitely shy."

"Reserved," was Lynn's assessment.

"I'm not sure there is a difference. It's just presented differently." She rolled up her mat and stood. "Are you going to be around tomorrow?"

Lynn shook her head. "Spending the day with Matt." She gathered up her own mat and towel, and the pair started toward the door. "Heading straight out there now."

Karen did not hide her surprise. "Oh. Well, I promise not to tell you again what a horrible mistake this whole Matt thing is."

"That's good." Lynn sometimes felt that way herself. Not right now though. She wouldn't allow it. "I'll see you on Friday if you're not too busy."

A noncommittal "Okay" was Karen's response. "Can't promise. We'll be back to normal in a couple weeks."

Lynn laughed. "When were we ever normal?"

Karen joined her. "That's why we're friends."

Yes, thought Lynn. Still friends, best friends, long after finding each other in high school. "I'll be on my way," she said, and climbed into her small sedan. A bag was packed, resting on the back seat, and even some art supplies. There might be time for those.

She followed Karen's Lexus out of the parking lot, but turned south four blocks over while her friend continued toward her house out east of town. The streets were nearly deserted, even this early. Lynn rolled her window partway down and let the cool air flood through her car. My hair will be a mess when I arrive at Matt's, she told herself, and then decided she didn't care.

Down Tamarind Road, curving westward around the bay, she drove. The road was even emptier here. She hit the brake as an armadillo scuttled across the pavement. Why was she hurrying anyway? Lynn drove more slowly the rest of the trip out to Leawood, through marsh and then the sandy subdivision lots, a light in a house here and there along the way.

She slowed at the turn north toward Matt's house and then, instead, drove straight ahead, to the beach. For a while, she stood there in the dark, beside her car, listening to the Gulf, breathing in the salt air.

Lynn smiled and reminded herself that in a month the sand flies and mosquitoes would be so bad at night she wouldn't be able to do anything like this. She got back into the idling Escort and drove on.

Seventeen

MATT STOOD OUT at the end of the limestone jetty, taut, poised to throw his cast net. The rough, refrigerator-sized blocks were a mix of brown shades, some almost a straight ocher, other more rust-colored, siennas and umbers. The tops, exposed to the sun, were somewhat bleached out; around the waterline could be seen red and green mossy growths, some above, some below the saltwater. Lynn assumed they would all be submerged at high tide.

Her boyfriend cast, a bit clumsily. Matt hadn't used the net in months, he had told her. The hope was to scoop up some bait fish for surf-casting. It was really too late in the day for that but they hadn't managed an early start this morning.

It felt odd to wake up in the bed he shared with Anne, to have slept in that bed, made love in it. The bed, the house, said "Anne" in many and varied ways; it didn't seem like Matt's personality was on display at all. He probably didn't care. Matthew Stone had other ways of expressing himself.

She turned her attention back to her sketch. It was boring, wasn't it? Just a bunch of rocks and a little figure out on the end of them. Too bad there weren't any clouds this morning. It might be fun to sketch over at *Painter's Paradise*. If they had time, Matt had promised to visit Horley's studio with her this afternoon.

He cast again and seemed pleased with the result this time. Little flashes of silver were shaken from the net into his white plastic bucket.

"How are you going to surf-cast when there isn't any surf?" she asked, as he approached. An ankle-high swell was whispering onto the edge of the white sand beach.

"I'll have to pretend. There were waves over the weekend," he told her. "Came with that cold front." The reddish-brown line of cast-up seaweed above the high tide mark attested to that. He picked up his fishing rod. It was a spinning rod, Lynn knew, and looked a little stouter than most, but she had little knowledge of fishing in general. Nor did she wish to learn.

Rod in one hand, bait bucket in the other, Matt ambled down to the water's edge. He reached into the bucket and then fumbled for a moment with something he had pulled out; Lynn knew he was putting the hook through one of the little shiners but didn't want to think about it. She gazed out on the blue-green expanse of the Gulf of Mexico. A sailboat would be way more fun. It had been ages since Lynn had sailed.

Matt waded out to knee-depth and cast his line near the lime-stone groin. Even Lynn knew that the fish tended to loiter about structures such as that rather than out on the barren sand bottom. Maybe a snook would take his bait. Karen's father used to catch those, and sometimes Karen too. Hmm, wasn't there a season on them? She had no idea when it might be.

The pair had tried to make a fisherwoman of her but she had resisted, both here and at their farm. That lake would have been fun to sail, too, wouldn't it? Darn, she really should get a little sailboat one of these days.

The sun was glaring on her paper, making it hard to discern the pencil lines she had just drawn. Lynn put it away; that was sign enough to quit sketching for the morning. That and the fact she wasn't particularly happy with her efforts.

She went down to the water, rolled up her jeans to mid-calf, waded in. Still pretty cold. That would change quickly over the next month—by May it would be like bathwater. Mid-May, anyway. Her feet had an amber tinge to them, seen through the shallow water, thanks to the outflow of the bays and of the tannin-filled rivers. My toes look like they belong in a Rembrandt, she told herself, and smiled at the thought.

For a couple minutes, Lynn stood watching Matt cast and slowly reel in his bait. "You should be painting," she called to him.

He did not even turn his head to call back, "So should you."

There was no good answer to that. Lynn hadn't painted in—oh, she didn't know. Too long.

"I'm not sure where my easel is anymore," she admitted, wading closer to Matt so she wouldn't have to yell at him. There was no room for it in her tiny apartment. That was the excuse she told herself. "Maybe with the stuff Karen is storing for me."

He turned to look at her. "Isn't it at the gallery? I've seen one in the back room." Matt pulled back his arm for another cast. "Sam will never know if you abscond with it, even if it isn't yours."

"No, mine is aluminum," Lynn stated. "We use that wooden one for photography." Was this the time for her news? Why not? "It *will* kind of be mine soon. Samson is finally making me a partner."

She was surprised that Matt did not seem particularly pleased. "You'll never paint then," he told her. He reeled in his line and splashed in to stand beside her. "Is that what you really want?"

"I have to make a living, Matt." She tried not to sound defensive.

That brought a short laugh. "Yeah, me too. That's why I teach." He shook his head and put an arm around her. "Just make sure it doesn't take up your whole life. Let's head back, okay?"

They rode in silence for the first minute or two, Matt driving. "You know," he spoke, glancing sidelong at her, "you could get your MFA and teach."

She had to smile at that. "Like you?"

"Hey, there's nothing wrong with it," he objected, with mock seriousness. Some real seriousness underlay it, she was sure. "You went for a BA, didn't you?"

"Yeah, my folks insisted. They thought it gave me more opportunity than the BFA."

"Probably true." He turned the van east from the beach road and back a couple blocks to his house. His and Anne's house. Lynn wondered if she had chosen the color scheme. Anne was no artist.

She idly wondered also what sort of job Matt's estranged wife had taken, before they came to a stop in the crushed-shell drive.

"Let's get cleaned up and go somewhere for lunch," her companion suggested. "And then, whatever. Over to the Horley place, if you want."

"Sounds good. First on the shower!"

First didn't make much difference as Matt slipped in with her a minute later. "This is going to make us late for, um, wherever we were going," she told him.

"And you mind?" he asked.

Lynn had to admit she didn't.

Eighteen

"I LEAVE EARLY on Friday mornings," Matt informed her, "so I can get the studios open for anyone who wants to work."

Lynn nodded. "That's just mornings, right?" And was it a hint she shouldn't spend the night?

"Usually. I sometimes switch off with the other instructors." The sound he made lay somewhere between a chuckle and an harrumph. "I'm pretty much the only one willing to get up early." She knew Matt didn't teach any classes on Fridays but supervised the workrooms for any students who wanted to come in.

"Here it is," she said, spying the *Painter's Paradise* entry sign. Returning to their topic, Lynn told him, "The studios were open twenty-four hours a day at South Florida. We could come in and work anytime."

"Same at FSU," Matt responded, turning onto the lime-rock entry road. "We don't have enough bodies to keep an eye on the place at night."

They pulled up to the studio building, beside a couple of sedans. Lynn couldn't see Jo's truck anywhere. Was the place even open when she wasn't there?

Apparently so. A gray-haired woman was conducting another couple around the room. She gave them a wave and turned back to her charges.

"I know her," Matt whispered in her ear. "One of the members of the local art association." He turned his eyes toward her again. "Maybe she volunteers here."

That seemed likely to Lynn. Joanne wouldn't be able to run the place all on her own, keeping up the grounds as well as attending to guests.

"Let's go out and wander the grounds," she suggested. "I hadn't the time for that on my last visit."

"Sure." He nodded a farewell toward the attendant as he held the door open for Lynn. "Deb," he said. "Her name is Deb some-thing."

"Cooper," Lynn replied. "She's been in the gallery more than once."

"Ah. That's not surprising. Which way?"

The stepping stone walkway wound around a spreading banyan, the centerpiece, in a way, of the grounds. Prop roots dangled from the branches but only a few had attached themselves to the earth below.

"It would take over the whole place if we let it," came a cheerful, southern-accented voice. Joanne Horley-Baker, again in rather disreputable work clothes, had rolled up behind them with a mulch-filled wheelbarrow. Most of its red paint had been scraped off.

"Hi, Jo," Lynn greeted her. "This is Matt Stone."

"Painter, right?" asked the woman. "I hear your name mentioned from time to time." She snickered. "Sometimes even favorably!"

"Sometimes beats not at all," came Matt's dry response. He held out his hand, "Pleased to meet you, Jo."

She stripped off a dirt-caked glove and shook. The hand wasn't all that clean either. "Been in the studio yet?"

"Just poked our heads in," Lynn told her, "and saw Deb Cooper. So we decided to look over the grounds first."

Jo nodded. "She'll talk your head off if ya let 'er."

"I know," admitted Lynn. "That's why I got us out of there."

"She's one of the volunteers who sometimes watch over the studio. They're not all that reliable but better than me sitting in there all the time. I'd rather be working out here. Oh," she said, "thanks for sending the files."

"You're welcome." Stone's face barely betrayed his puzzlement. Lynn could recognize it. "The pictures I took of Samson's acquisi-tions," she told him.

He nodded and turned to Joanne. "In a way, Mrs. Horley could be considered my grandmother too. Artistically, that is—I studied with one of her students."

"There are a surprising number of people around here with connections like that," came the reply. Then she laughed. "We're one big family, Cuz!"

Jo pulled her glove back on. "Need to get back to work. Y'all wander around as long as you want."

"We thank you," replied Matt. "Would you mind if I brought my easel over here sometime?" He looked around. "Lots of subject matter."

"Don't mind at all." She grinned. "Of course, it's always nice when our visitors leave a donation for the upkeep of the place."

He answered quite seriously, "I pledge right now to give a cut of anything I make from the paintings." He glanced at his companion and added, "So does Lynn."

Lynn immediately resented Stone's statement, not so much his presumption of speaking for her but the fact that he was goading her to start painting again. She would do that when and if she wished! Yes, she could tell his tone implied it was a joke but she knew he meant more.

They never did get back into the Horley studio that afternoon after wandering through the gardens. A tour under the guidance of Deb Cooper did not appeal to either.

And then, there were other things they would prefer to be doing with the time they had, back at Matt's house. As they pulled out, Lynn asked, "You belong to the Leawood Art Association?"

"Yep," said Matt. "I don't attend the meetings very often but it is a good idea to be a member." He frowned and stopped at the end of the drive, turning to look at her. "You knew I exhibited in their annual show, didn't you?"

"You never mentioned it."

"Hmm. I should have. I'll bet Sammy knows." He pulled out onto the blacktop and headed west, faster than he should have.

Yes, Samson Ibarra probably did know. People told him things.

Lynn had to admit she didn't really care where Matt showed his paintings.

They made love again that afternoon, there in that house that did not really belong to either of them, the sun shining in on them through the tall windows. Lynn drove home before that sun set.

Nineteen

KAREN LEANED BACK in one of the two chairs for clients in her office, both upholstered in a coarse salt-and pepper fabric. There was no room for a meal atop the desk. Too many papers, too many folders, and even some old-fashioned ledger books covered its top. Along with Karen's computer, of course; that was where most of the data she dealt with lived these days.

She scraped the last spoonful from the bottom of her yogurt container. Mango, Karen's favorite, though she made sure to have some other flavors on hand. Another? Nah, save it for later. It was a good thing she had stocked the fridge here with them. There would be evenings eating at the office over the next couple weeks.

But she should make sure to get out to lunch with Lynn tomorrow. If only to hear the details of her trip to Leawood! Her dislike of Matt did not preclude listening to gossip about him.

Hmm, another hour and she would call it a day. And part of a night. She had sent Allie home two hours ago, at Five; Karen didn't expect her secretary to stay all the hours she did, but did give her a little overtime during this season.

Karen might not even have to stay this late again herself. She had caught up pretty well, not that clients wouldn't come in with last-minute woes for her to solve and salve.

The hour swept by. I said one hour and I meant it, the young woman told herself. She stubbed out her cigarette, stood and stretched. Yes, anything else could wait. Where were her shoes?

The heels were under the desk, of course, where she customarily kicked them off. She gathered them up and stuffed them in her bag. There were her running shoes, already in there. Karen slipped them on and slipped out of her office, dowsing the fluorescent lights. Only a desk lamp burnt in the reception area.

Good enough. She turned it off and locked the solid oak door behind her. Dim, brushed aluminum and plastic sconce lights illuminated her way down the hall to the rear stairs, the parking lot, her automobile.

Damn, she was tired! It was a good thing the drive home was short, to an older subdivision just east of the downtown. If she did buy a larger place, further out, it wouldn't be so convenient. But if the farm sold—yes, she should look around.

It might not be a bad idea to put this house on the market, as well, Karen told herself as she pulled into the drive of her modest ranch. She wasn't really fond of it. It was just a place where she slept.

Her father had snapped it up during the recession, eight years back, when property prices plummeted. Karen was still attending college at the time, working on that Masters in accounting he had insisted she needed. Dad had been right, of course.

She had liked the little cottage by the bay, their first home in Tamarind, better. It had been demolished a couple years ago to make way for upscale apartment buildings.

Tired but not sleepy—it would take a while to unwind from the day. She plopped down in the recliner in the living room and turned on the television, idly flipping through channels. Two minutes later she pushed the remote's 'off' button. Maybe she should just go to bed. Or go get some ice cream from the kitchen.

The clock read past midnight when she opened her eyes again. She had been dreaming, hadn't she? A few lingering images. What were they? Horses. Well, maybe horses.

Karen got up. She might have just stayed there in that comfortable recliner and gone back to sleep if she didn't need to use the bathroom. Her legs felt stiff.

Horses. That wasn't unusual. Horses frequently galloped through her nights. And had she dreamed about Pat Janson?

Why shouldn't she? Karen asked herself, as she dowsed the bedside lamp in her small, simply furnished room, slipped between the cotton sheets. She preferred to sleep in the same single she had since a teen, leaving the king in the master bedroom made up but rarely used.

It took her a while to fall asleep again and, again, thoughts of

Pat drifted through her mind. She should—oh, she didn't know. Don't make any plans the next couple weeks, she decided. Then, who knows?

As far as she could tell in the morning, Karen had no more dreams.

Twenty

"WHEN YOUR WORKLOAD lightens up a bit, I will want you to look over the books for *Bayside Art*."

Karen looked up, immediately interested. "So Ibarra is finally making you a partner?"

Lynn nodded. Too solemnly, she told herself at once. "He is. I've waited for this and now—well, I'm not sure I want it."

Her friend took a long sip of her tea before leaning back and giving her a thoughtful look. Staring at her, really. "You certainly don't want to be an employee the rest of your life."

"I know, I know. But I should be painting. Or doing something creative, anyway." The statement sounded so inadequate, not at all what she meant.

"Ah, Matt's been in your ear."

Lynn didn't answer. Yes, Matt had helped give voice to the misgivings she had already felt.

"You hated commercial art," Karen reminded her. "No one knew it, did they? You always keep up that chipper appearance of yours."

It was true. A bit humorous too, when she thought about it, enough so that Lynn gave her friend a lopsided smile. "No one but you."

She recognized pretty much everyone saw her as the optimist, the go-getter, but she felt like she was constantly failing. Karen understood. She had always understood. Neither woman said much else through the rest of their lunch, each dealing with her own thoughts.

"I'll walk with you," said Karen when they stepped out of *The Compass Rose*. Lynn only nodded; if her friend wanted to walk, she would. "I need to get my muscles moving before I go sit for another eight hours."

"Do your yoga postures," suggested Lynn.

"I do, I do." Karen actually giggled. "And I imagine Pat while I do them."

"Whatever motivates you." They ambled south to the corner and turned toward the bay. "You've been working late?" Lynn asked.

"Way too late. All work and no play." She sighed, somewhat too dramatically. "Did you get to play yesterday?"

"Several times." Both giggled now. But Lynn certainly wasn't going to elaborate about the sex, even with her best friend. "We went to the beach for a while and out to the Horley place."

"I should visit again. Maybe look at property out that way too. I'm thinking of selling my house." She suddenly laughed. "It only occurred to me last night!"

"It's not cheap out there."

"Can Matt afford to stay after the divorce? Assuming there *is* a divorce."

"Anne never held a job while they were together, so I imagine so. Even with alimony and child support."

"You may have to sell a lot of his paintings to keep him solvent," remarked Karen. "Even so, he still doesn't seem in any hurry."

"No, he doesn't and, honestly, I don't care. I have too many other things to think about!" Lynn halfway believed herself. Perhaps Karen did too.

They had reached the corner of Bay Street. "Let's go over and look at the water," suggested Karen. Lynn was willing.

There was a grassy spot by the seawall, where they could gaze out across the bay. A light breeze played with the surface. Lynn plopped down, only to see her companion gracefully lower herself into a lotus position.

"You can only do that because your legs are so skinny," she accused.

"It helps," Karen admitted, "but it took practice too."

"You've thrown yourself into it, haven't you? As usual." Karen was quick to become passionate about things and, sometimes, as quick to lose that passion.

"I guess so, but I haven't had much time for yoga." She turned to Lynn and asked, "Do you know Maddie?"

Maddie? She had no idea who that might be. "I don't think so."

"Madeline Fry. She's in our yoga class." That still told Lynn nothing. "Young. Black."

"Oh" She did know there was a young black woman in the class.

"Pat was telling me about her. It seems she confides in him." Karen gazed out over the water for a moment before saying, "I think a lot of women feel they can confide in him."

Lynn wouldn't but she could see how his presence could invite it. His position as a teacher, too.

"He says she feels out of place," Karen continued.

"I don't think her husband approves either." Or boyfriend. She wasn't sure which.

Karen nodded. "Then you have noticed her."

"Sure. Just as I have noticed you flirting with Pat."

There was Karen's bark of a laugh. "Not that it did me much good!"

"Did you expect him to ask you out?"

"No, no." Karen seemed unusually subdued as she answered. "I think I'm going to have to do the asking." Her eyes again focused somewhere across the bay. "I think he likes me."

Lynn allowed herself only the slightest of smiles. "I think so too. You know he checked out your ring finger as soon as you walked up that first night."

"Really? You always notice details like that, don't you? Maybe that's the artist in you. I just barge in without looking." She sighed. "The story of my life."

Lynn rose. "I'd best get back to the gallery."

"Yeah." Karen's ascent was not quite so graceful as her descent. She doesn't have enough muscle to pull it off, thought Lynn.

Before parting at Bay Street, Karen said, "I'm going to be working right through the weekend. I don't know if I can make Monday lunch but I'll definitely be at the evening class."

"To continue the pursuit of our instructor?" It was spoken jestingly but both women knew it to be a serious question.

"Maybe after tax day, when I have time to think about things like that."

Lynn felt obliged to mention something else. "Yoga instructors don't make much money, you know." Would Karen take this wrong? "And I suspect that Pat doesn't care."

"I was married to a hard-working, high income guy. A lot of good it did me!" Karen took out her cigarette packet, then put it away, saying, "I think I'll quit these things."

"Again?"

"Again."

POSTURE II

virasana
the warrior

Twenty-One

HE DIDN'T KNOW that women thought him sexy. No, Pat had no clue.

Inside, hid the awkward boy he once had been. When that boy, residing now in a sculpted body, unleashed his shy, sweet smile, it was a potent force. Yet Pat Janson remained unaware as life carried him toward middle age, rarely dating, leading a solitary existence. Some would say a lonely existence, though he might have denied that.

He was just what Karen needed. Or what she thought she needed. Is there a difference?

She had made time for his yoga class all through her busiest season. Karen was perhaps a little proud of that. She felt better for it, too, didn't she? If only because it took her mind off work for an hour or so—otherwise she would have been at her desk every evening, eating wrong, smoking too much.

Instead, she did that only five nights a week! No more, though. She slipped into her leotard in the dark, locked office. Allie was gone, out and headed home at the normal closing time. It was time she got going too. Yes, in more ways than one.

She wrapped a short, batik-printed skirt around her waist and headed down to the parking lot. Hers was the only car left. The older gray minivan pulled up to the rear entryway—in a restricted space but no one would care after hours—she recognized as a janitor service that cleaned one office or another. These past weeks, Karen had most certainly been in the way of the woman who came into *Fairfield and Fairfield*. She should add a little something to her check to make up for the inconvenience.

Soon, there would be light enough even after class to walk over to the rec center and back, she told herself as she pulled out onto First Avenue. Not that she was likely to; Karen couldn't see herself strolling up and down the streets of Tamarind in this costume, even when they were mostly deserted.

Ha, she had beaten Lynn for once, Karen realized, stepping into the recreation center. If she had been paying attention she might have noticed her friend's car wasn't here yet. Maybe she had time to talk with Pat before class, wherever he hung out. Or maybe she'd best not bother him now.

Maybe she shouldn't bother him at all. It wasn't like she intended to pursue the boy, just get to know him better and see where that went. Boy? Her own age, at least, but thoroughly boyish, none the less.

She could go check out one of his classes at the Springs, sometime. Ah, there was Lynn. Her hair looked wet. "You've been swimming," she surmised as the woman unrolled her mat beside her own.

"I have," admitted Lynn. "We're closing an hour earlier as of today so I have time to jump in the pool." She turned to her companion. "Come on over sometime and join me."

"My new house will definitely have a pool," announced Karen. "At least twice as big as the one at your apartment."

"That still wouldn't be very large. Ah, here we go."

Pat had entered, quietly, a slight smile on his face for no one in particular and everyone in general. He led them through the usual introduction, the complete breath, and then announced, "This evening we are halfway through our time together. Miss Carter will have an announcement for us at the end of class."

The recreation director was nowhere to be seen and the lesson continued, revisiting some of the postures the class had learned already, a new asana being introduced, virasana, the warrior pose. "The name really means simply the 'man posture,'" explained Pat, "but women can usually achieve it more easily."

"That's just a plumber's squat," came Joe's voice from behind them. "I don't bend that direction."

"Me neither," agreed Roger. "Miss Karen doesn't seem to have any problem."

"Skinny legs," whispered Lynn, turning her head partially toward the pair. She was not able to go down all the way either, a couple inches of air persisting in remaining between her rear end and the floor. Karen ignored all of them, smiling serenely with her eyes fixed on their instructor. "Showoff," said Lynn.

At the end of the session, Jen Carter did come forward. "Our summer yoga class will start on June Thirteen," she announced, "and we are going to an afternoon schedule." A murmur rose and subsided at this news. "Yes, I know some of you will find that inconvenient but there are too many other programs that need to use this room in the evenings." She turned toward Pat. "Anything else I should add to that?"

"Three in the afternoon," he said. "Mondays and Wednesdays, as now."

"Oh, right!"

"And," he continued, "I do teach classes at the Springs for any who find the new time inconvenient."

"Sounds okay to me," Joe said. "Better'n now, in fact."

Lynn shook her head. "That's fine for you who are retired. Some of us have to work."

"I might manage it in the summer," felt Karen. "It may not hurt to leave work a little early two days a week. But not if you can't make it." She glanced toward Pat, conversing with a pair of older women who had approached him. No sense in butting in now, she decided.

Lynn had followed her eyes. "We should check out the Springs," she said. "They do have an Olympic-sized pool there."

Twenty-Two

"I'M NOT IN any hurry, Samson," she assured her boss. Soon to be former boss.

"Oh, I know, my girl. You've been patient." Ibarra's eyes went from Lynn to the showroom and back again. "I've made you wait long enough."

Lynn recognized they both had some misgivings. "So a few months more won't matter. Would it simplify things if we waited till the year changes? Make the transition official on January First?" That did seem like a long time but she was willing to wait.

He frowned, not in displeasure, but in thought. Samson's face never seemed to hide anything. "I don't think it matters. I'll ask my lawyer." That resolved satisfactorily in his head, the man confided, "You should have a lawyer of your own to look at things. Your Ms. Fairchild may give you good advice but, officially, she is impartial in all of this."

The accounting firm had been hired for an independent audit of their financial situation. Lynn expected no surprises there; hadn't she been pretty much taking care of that herself?

Samson went on. "I think maybe it would be good to do this before the season picks up again. By Fall."

"Okay, Sammy. I don't think I know any lawyers." But Karen would. She would ask.

And she did and got some names, as well as advice that it probably wouldn't be worth the money. "I shouldn't say that, I know," Karen told her. "Not as a professional. But I'm your friend too."

She went on. "I might recommend switching over to a partnership on October First, just for tax purposes. But Ibarra's right, it doesn't matter much."

Yeah, the quarterly state tax reports. That made sense. The start of July would work for that too. They might be ready by then. Enough of that topic of conversation. None other came to her mind right then and Lynn found herself staring out the window.

"Are you taking Thursday off this week?" Karen asked.

Lynn nodded. "No reason not to. Did you have something in mind?"

"I think it is time we went out to Consonante Springs. Make it a spa day." She laughed at her own words. It was not the sort of thing either would normally think of doing with free time.

"And a spy-on-Pat day?"

"Why not?" Both had to laugh at that. But Lynn felt a sudden apprehension, a slight tightening inside. What if Matt wanted to spend the day with her? "Do we need to make reservations?"

"I wouldn't think so. You know, I haven't stopped there since I was a teen."

"Me neither," admitted Lynn. "In fact, I believe we went together." She brought up the memory. "Yeah, with your father."

"He was checking it out as investment property, I think," said Karen. "It was on the market. I've heard it may be again." She sipped her tea before adding, "Some developer will tear down the old place and put in a golf course one of these days."

"Like we need another one of those." Lynn sighed. "It would be nice if the county could take it over. Make it part of Prima Park." That piece of land lay just east of the old spa, along the Tamarind River. "Or even the state."

"Not going to happen with the current politics in Florida," was all Fairfield had to say about that. Lynn wasn't even sure whether her friend approved or disapproved.

Karen's father would have surely disapproved, she reflected as she walked back to the gallery. Despite seemingly being all business-and-profit, and a thoroughly old-school Republican, he had become one of those zealous Yankees who were passionate about preserving Florida. Once he had his own piece of it, of course.

Those who chose to live in insular golf course communities didn't get that. They didn't see beyond their gates. But then, how many people really did see beyond their own gates?

Twenty-Three

The stream had been renamed the Tamarind River decades ago at the request of developers and local government, but there remained locals who called it Sawmill Creek. The number of those dwindled as more and more former northerners took up residence in the area. Their road paralleled the river between Tamarind and Consonante Springs.

"Samson lives around here, just a little off Springs Road," said Lynn. She felt, and probably sounded, a bit hoarse; Karen had her air conditioning running a little too cold for her. "An older home. Um, back there."

Karen only took a cursory glance at the blacktop lane on their right. "Close to the spa."

"Uh-huh. One of the houses built back when the Springs were first developed." Maybe even before that, she thought. Lynn had never really paid much attention to the dates but knew the spa—then called a hotel—preceded the Second World War. It was a stuccoed two-story building in a more-or-less Spanish style, now coming into view on their left. The color was somewhere between pink and orange, long faded from whatever the original shade might have been.

A small bridge, barely noticeable as such, was crossed, and they turned into the circular drive that brought them to the front door of the *Consonante Springs Resort and Spa*, as it was officially titled. The springs that gave it and the neighborhood their name were on the other side of the highway—the little stream they had just crossed flowed from them down to the river.

"Not supposed to park here," muttered Karen, spying a sign. She circled and pulled into a parking lot on the east side. As impatient as ever, thought Lynn, always peeved by anything that seemed to waste her time.

A woman, not really old but gray haired, stood behind the reception desk, a desk that reminded one of the hotel this had once been, welcoming northern visitors a half-century and more before, who came for the springs and the beach. Guests still stayed here, Lynn had heard, some long-term through the winter months.

"Welcome to *Consonante Springs*, ladies," she said. "Can I help you?" Her name tag read 'Verna' but gave no further information.

It was Lynn who said, "We were thinking of having a day here," but Karen took it from there, asking about the rates.

A mandala hung on the wall to the left of the desk, an ornamented circle inside a square inside a circle, in greens and golds and violets. Words in some script appeared above and below. Sanskrit? That would be her guess. Lynn gazed at it for a few seconds.

"The words mean, *Yesterday is but a dream, and tomorrow only a vision*," the woman told them. "That's from some Hindu text or another. I don't know which one!" Her laugh sounded slightly artificial. "Our yoga instructor made it."

"Pat?" asked Karen.

"That's right," she said. "Pat's been with us for some time. Even before my husband and I took over the management here. That would be Carl. Carl Fell, and I'm Verna. Anyway," she continued, after all that gushed out, "Pat has a class at Eleven. It's included in the day visitor fee. Or if that is all you are interested in, you can pay just for the class."

Karen turned to her friend. "Well, I bet you didn't know he was an artist. Maybe you need to sign him to the gallery!" Returning her attention to the receptionist, she asked, "Day visitor? Do we get to wander around the place if we pay that?"

"Pretty much, ma'am. It includes almost everything except a massage. And food. Those are both extra." Her smile looked as artificial as her laughter had sounded. "Any classes are open. There is an aerobics—" She looked up at the yard-long wrought iron hands of the clock behind them, above the entry. "Hmm, no, that's nearly over."

"And the pool?" asked Lynn. That was really why she had agreed to come.

"Very much included." Mrs. Fell's attitude actually seemed genuine for a moment, perhaps catching some of Lynn's own enthusiasm. "We have monthly and seasonal passes for that, if you are interested."

Lynn nodded. Too far to come, wasn't it? But a pass for today was a good idea and both paid. "She seemed kind of phony, didn't she?" she whispered to her friend as they walked up a wide hall, floored with rust-red tile. The pool, Verna had told them, was this direction. They could search out anything else later, if they felt like it.

Karen shook her head. "Just the nervous sort, I'd say, and not so comfortable around people." She let out a sharp, single laugh. "And tired, maybe!"

"Yeah." She shouldn't have judged. Who knew how people who came into the gallery saw her? The pool lay ahead and Lynn dismissed such thoughts. Not crowded and, indeed, Olympic-sized, it was partially under roof but open to the Florida air on two sides, with sections of screen above and between creamy-tan limestone columns.

"I don't think I'm going to make it to Pat's class," Lynn announced. "I could stay right here all day."

Twenty-Four

"PAT LIVES IN a trailer across the road, back a way, beyond the springs," Karen reported. "The lifeguard told me."

The lifeguard looked to be a teenage girl. A bored teenage girl sitting on a high director's chair out of the direct sun. Maybe a college student, thought Lynn. High school kids would have classes today. Not much longer—vacation was only a month or so away.

"We did miss his class," she said. "Do you think you'll come out here during Summer?"

Karen settled back on the wood-slatted lounge. "Don't know." There was little noise around the pool, few swimming in this hour just past noon. "I do know I've had too much sun already."

"Then let's get out of here." Lynn tanned easily but her friend was fairer. And Karen's bathing suit exposed rather more skin than Lynn's. "There are showers inside. Or we could use that." She pointed to an outdoor shower head by the pool

"That'll work. Probably cold."

"Definitely cold." Lynn didn't mind. A quick rinse, towel off and use the changing rooms adjacent to the pool. They would still have some hours free if either felt like doing anything.

"Pat alert," hissed Karen. Lynn took that as a warning to slip away. No. Karen was waving to him.

Why should she feel self-conscious? She had been here a couple hours already in a suit that revealed little more than the tights she wore to class. Oh, yes, her bare and a little too thick middle was on display but so what?

Pat wasn't interested in her, anyway. Not that his eyes didn't glide across both of them as he approached.

"Hi," he said, and then, almost apologetically, "you missed my class."

"We were enjoying the pool too much," Lynn told him.

"Yes, we're planning on coming all Summer," added Karen. This was the first Lynn had heard of it. "Maybe for your class too."

"I'd be glad to see you. Um, both of you." He purposely turned his gaze to Lynn.

He doesn't want it to look like he's focused on Karen, Lynn told herself. But he was, pretty much. Her slim freckled body was a little too close for his eyes not to stray to it from time to time. He made an effort.

"We're going to dry off and maybe wander the place a little," Karen went on. "Are you free to be our tour guide?"

"Um, oh, yes, I could do that." Pat did not look completely certain. Maybe he had some other job he should be at. Didn't he do odd work around the spa?

As Lynn slipped into the changing room, she whispered to Karen, "We should mention to Verna or someone that we were monopolizing Pat's time. We don't want her to think he was goofing off."

Her friend laughed. "But he *will* be goofing off—with us!"

"True. I've never seen him in civvies before. It seems odd, somehow." Pat was in shorts and a polo shirt, but not with the 'CS' insignia on it, as did the staff's shirts.

"Hmm, yeah. I wouldn't mind seeing him in some other outfits." Karen went into one of the stalls to change before suddenly giggling and adding, "Or out of them."

Well, Lynn could hardly fault her for that. After all, she had a relationship, had been in one for months now. Karen deserved someone. But she'd better not hurt Pat.

She shoved her damp towel and suit into her bag and stepped out into the concrete-floored room. Why did she feel protective toward the yoga teacher? Was it just a—well, vulnerability he seemed to project? Lynn expected a great many women who knew Pat would share her attitude.

"Do you want the history?" he asked, when they rejoined him. "Or should I keep my mouth shut?"

"We'll save the lessons for later," came Karen's immediate answer. "Let's just walk."

The trio followed an arched passageway to the rear of the complex. "That's the Kuenst house," Pat said, pointing out the large and somewhat shabby building. It lay about halfway between the hotel and the river. Banyans spread before it; big oaks behind. "Mrs. Kuenst doesn't stay here much anymore."

The owner of the resort was a widow. Lynn remembered that. Hadn't her husband unexpectedly died right there in the house, years ago? Something like that. Well, no history today they had decided. Or Karen had.

They continued down the shallow slope toward the river. There were a few mosquitoes in the shade, buzzing about their ears. "You should have canoe rentals," she told Pat, as they stood at the top of the sandy bank.

"You can do that at the park," he replied, nodding toward the east. They followed him westward, along a dirt path by the stream. Someone must occasionally rake the fallen oak leaves out of the way to keep it open. The ground all around was littered with them; their musty, slightly sharp odor was more than noticeable. "Here's where Springs Creek joins the river." It was narrow. Lynn thought she could probably jump it, with a running start.

Once she could have, anyway. "Want to see the spring itself?" Pat asked.

"Sure," came Karen's answer. "Don't people swim in it?"

"They used to. No one is interested anymore." He shook his head before continuing. "Unless a spring stinks of sulfur, no one thinks it's good for their health." There was a more sarcastic tone to his voice than Lynn had ever heard from him before. In fact, she had never heard sarcasm from him at all.

They had to cross Springs Road, beside the bridge, to reach it. The spring itself proved a bit disappointing. An old bathhouse, seemingly no longer in use, stood next to the clear pond where the outflow welled up. It was an artificial pond, most likely, and smaller than the pool they had just left. Some effort seemed to be made to mow around it but little else. "There have been offers to bottle water from here," spoke Pat, not very loudly. "Agnes has turned them down. Mrs. Kuenst, that is." He turned to the girls. "But sooner or later she is bound to sell this place." He shrugged, smiled a bit sadly. "Or her heirs will."

Then he brightened up. "I'll bet neither of you has eaten! Come on back to the spa and I'll find you something, even if it is past lunch." He chuckled. "Vegetarian, of course."

"We would expect nothing else," said Karen.

Twenty-Five

"So, YOU HAVE a date?"

"One could call it that."

Was Karen going to explain? It seemed not. They pulled out of the spa's circular drive and west onto Springs Road.

Lynn had felt it proper to inform the balding middle-aged man now at the desk—Verna's husband, Carl—that they had been monopolizing Pat's time. He only laughed easily. "We certainly don't mind Pat spending some time with a girl or two. He does a lot around here."

She couldn't help wondering if he spent time with a girl very often. Or with two, for that matter. But while she had been talking with Carl, apparently Pat and Karen had decided to spend more time, sometime.

Thinking of two— "Well, maybe you should double-date with Matt and me." Lynn tried to say this seriously but didn't quite succeed.

"Your boyfriend would be a bad influence on Pat," Karen answered, not even attempting to sound serious. But, of course, she really did dislike Matt. Karen had never hidden that from her friend.

"Ask him about his art," she said. The thought of Matt had brought that into Lynn's mind. Maybe Pat actually was someone the gallery could work with.

"Eventually. If we run out of other things!" They were following the curve into Tamarind, where Springs Road became Seventh Street. "Want to go straight home?"

"Might as well." She hoped Karen wouldn't extend an invitation to stop at her house. Lynn was too tired for that now. And it wasn't even all that late, was it? Maybe a couple hours rest would get her in the mood to do something this evening.

Not with Matt. She hadn't even spoken with him for a couple

days. Karen said no more but took her straight—well, yes, there were a couple turns—to her apartment.

"Lunch tomorrow?" she asked, slipping out of the car.

Karen popped the trunk where her bag of wet things was stowed. "Sure. Unless something comes up." They both knew how that could go.

Almost four. Really too late to plan anything, Lynn decided. She tossed her wet clothes into the bathroom tub. They could be sorted out later. The clothes she wore went in after them and Lynn slipped into a somewhat worn fuzzy pink robe herself. That felt better. She went to the kitchenette and peered into her fridge. Half a bottle of Chablis. Good enough. A small glass, only.

A buzzing noise? Oh, the phone, in her purse and set to vibrate. Hmm, Matt, and already gone to voice mail. She didn't feel like finding out what he had to say. Let it wait till morning.

If she went back to the Springs sometime, she should take some art supplies, paint and canvas, maybe. And perhaps even Matt. He could certainly find subject matter out there. Oh, Lynn told herself, there are subjects everywhere. She just needed to sit down and work. She might be more inclined to do that if Matt were not there.

Did she have anything worth saying in paint, these days? Did she have anything to say at all? She'd been using pieces of herself so long to patch the holes in her life, Lynn wasn't sure anything was left.

And now the gallery was going to demand even more, with her as a partner. She took another sip of her wine and considered fixing some sort of meal. No need, still early, and Pat had fed them not so long ago.

The young woman looked about her tiny apartment. Her life was just as small, wasn't it? There was no room to expand here. Maybe it was time to find a new place, even if she did like the pool, the convenient closeness to work.

Why, she could go live in a trailer out near the Springs, like Pat!

That would be a change, for sure, a real shakeup. Lynn got up, poured another half-glass of Chablis, and considered dinner again.

Twenty-Six

"To COME UP with an apt cliché, my wife doesn't understand me."

"Neither does anyone else," Lynn couldn't resist telling him.

"Ah, the fate of the true artist," sighed Matt.

Samson looked from one to the other. Does he suspect that there is anything between us? wondered Lynn. She had wondered this before. Ibarra never gave any indication that he did.

"You know, Matt, I am not big on divorce," said the older man. "But you and Anne should decide something one way or the other." He held up his hands. "I just say this. It is not truly any of my business, I know."

"I brought it up," came Stone's amiable reply. "That made it anyone's business. Open to discussion!" His brief, wry smile gave way to introspection. "And you are undoubtedly right."

He was still uncertain about a final break with Anne. Lynn had always known this and had chosen not to think about it. Maybe Matt was as uncertain about his life as she was about hers. Oh, maybe everyone was. But they all handled it differently.

Samson looked at the inside of his wrist. "Why don't you leave for lunch, Lynn?" he asked. "When you get back I'll take off for the weekend." To Matt he said, in explanation, "Buying trip. A short one and maybe my last for a while."

"Good luck with it," replied the artist. "I'll be on my way then, too." He stepped out the front door with Lynn, stopping on the sidewalk to ask, "Like any company at lunch?"

"Oh, Mister Stone! Are you actually willing to be seen walking and eating with me in broad daylight?" It probably came out a bit more sarcastically than she had intended. In fact, Matt looked a little hurt, but he only shrugged. "Really," she went on, trying to sound soothing, "it's not a good idea. And Karen would not at all approve me bringing you along."

"Karen. Yeah, right. Okay, I'll call later." He went to his van, parked across Bay Street, as Lynn turned north on the sidewalk. He and Karen would have to learn to get along, she told herself.

Or not. Who knew where she and Matt Stone were headed? One thing she did know was that her best friend would have priority if Lynn ever had to choose between them. Yes, that was for certain.

That didn't say much for the relationship, did it? Lynn arrived at *The Compass Rose* before Karen. She had known she was leaving the gallery too soon, but Sammy had said to go. He'd better not expect her to come back earlier because of that!

Cool inside. The restaurant had its air conditioning going. That would be pretty much the norm for the next several months, until some time in October, maybe. She took her usual seat at the usual table.

Karen looked a bit sunburned when she came in a few minutes later. "Already sipping tea?" she asked and took her place across the table. "Same for me," she told the waitress. Not Jan today. She didn't work Fridays, usually.

"Plans tonight?" asked Lynn, trying to sound as casual as possible. Not that it fooled Karen.

"You mean with Pat? Nope." She stopped to order a sandwich before going on. "The date is Sunday night. Yeah, that's an odd sort of time to choose but it works better with his schedule."

Lynn asked for a salad and turned her attention back to her friend. "Sunday. Hmm, I guess that makes sense. The spa probably keeps him busy tonight and tomorrow."

"That's what I surmised. He doesn't like to talk about himself." Karen finished adding her customary three packs of sugar to her tea. "How 'bout you? Any plans tonight?"

"Not yet." Oh, admit it, she told herself. Matt isn't going to suggest anything. Not on the weekend.

"We should go to a bar. Like in the old days."

Lynn laughed. "Which old days were those?"

"Oh, I guess I mean when we were in college. Hey, do you think we could still pass as students?"

"Not a chance. Too old for college girls, too young to be cougars." Lynn shook her head. "We seem to go from one awkward age to another."

"Well, at least we won't get carded." Karen nibbled at her tuna salad. "And we still look hot. Maybe that's the perfect age!"

"Hot?" Lynn's snicker ended up sounding more like a sigh. "I'm sort of homely," she said, gazing at her reflection in the window.

"With that body, the guys aren't going to notice," Karen told her.

"Yeah, I'm sort of dumpy, too." She couldn't help laughing after saying that, and Karen joined in.

"I know you're half-kidding when you say things like that but half of you isn't!"

"Maybe so," admitted Lynn. "Anyway, I don't think I feel much like going out tonight."

"Me neither, I guess."

Twenty-Seven

IT FELT DIFFERENT, somehow, knowing she would soon be part-owner here. All the more so with Samson gone, off on his tour of estate sales. Lynn felt a new sense of responsibility. No, things wouldn't actually seem to change much in the day-to-day operation of the gallery. But they had changed.

She unlocked the door at Ten, opening it to the warm morning. Nearly warm enough to leave it closed and turn on air conditioning. That cost money. Lynn had always tended toward frugality. Ownership is going to make you worse, she told herself.

Matt had called last night but they made no plans. Lynn was grateful for that. She had felt tired. Better this morning, though. It was quiet. She could see boats out on the bay, locals, most likely, getting a start on the weekend. There wouldn't be many visitors to the gallery. That would give her lots of time to think—but Lynn didn't feel much like thinking.

Mindlessness would be better today. She should get busy on some chore or another, stop brooding on all the questions that would come and go in her mind. Lynn got the spray bottle of ammonia and water and began a careful cleansing of the glass in all the picture frames, the watercolors and graphics that needed protection from the elements. Both she and Sammy agreed that the mixture was a better choice than commercial glass cleaner. Cheaper, too.

Of course, much of that protective glass wasn't glass at all but some plastic or another, acrylic or plexi. She should know more about that, probably. Some stuff came in already framed from the artist; what didn't, they took to a framing shop in Venice, and trusted their judgment.

A yellow pickup truck stopped out front. Not right in front, but a little to the south. Something was lettered on the door but Lynn couldn't make it out. She could see the driver looking over the place for a minute or so, as if making up his mind whether to come in. Then he got out and went around to the passenger side to retrieve something. A man, she could tell now, in neat casual clothes, chinos, a polo shirt.

Paintings, it appeared, so he was almost certainly an artist looking for representation. An amateur, of course, or he wouldn't be coming in on a weekend. The artists who made a living—more or less—from their work would choose a weekday, a more normal business hour than a Saturday morning. They might make an appointment first, too.

Lynn wondered if Karen would say anything to Pat about showing his work. Maybe she should handle that herself. She turned her attention back to the would-be artist, a thin guy in glasses, middle-aged, tan. And very nervous.

"Um, good morning ma'am. I'm Jay Bruce." He shifted the black plastic bag holding his artwork to his left arm and extended a hand. "Are you, um, the owner?"

She shook. "Lynn Devinne. Part-owner." Might as well say that even if it wasn't strictly true, yet. "How can I help you this morning?"

"Yes, ma'am, you see I'm a painter." He self-consciously glanced at the package under his arm. "I'm looking to show in a gallery. Would you be interested in seeing my work?" The question rushed out, as if held back a long time and suddenly unleashed.

Why not? It was unlikely to be good, but Lynn had nothing better to do. "My partner would have to see it too," she told him. "But I could look it over right now." She probably shouldn't take a stranger into the back, especially with no one around. It wasn't safe, was it? She glanced at Bruce. Nah, he was harmless but it would be better to stay up here. "Let's see."

A pair of paintings. Acrylic, weren't they? But painterly enough to make one think they were oils at first glance. 'Jason Bruce' was signed in the lower right corner and '2015.' Last year. She was glad he hadn't brought in something old, but what he probably felt was his best recent work. Or his most presentable work.

"Let me guess, a Stuckist?" she asked.

"Not really," he murmured. "But I kind of agree with their, um, philosophy."

Lynn nodded. They were not bad, not bad at all. Indeed, there were worse hanging on the walls around them. Might not appeal to their typical clientele, however. Maybe the landscape? "Do you think you could come back some day next week?" He looked uncomfortable with the request. "Or you could leave these here and I'll show them to Mr. Ibarra. We could get back to you then."

He hesitated only a second or two. "That would be fine, Miss Devinne. Let me—" He fumbled in his pocket and pulled out a slim pack of business cards bound with a rubber band. Bruce slipped one out and handed it to her.

A lawn service? Then he could probably fit time in during the week—but he wouldn't want to come in his work clothes, driving a truck filled with his equipment. "If we are interested we can set up an appointment," she told him.

He nodded. "Thanks." Bruce glanced toward his two paintings, leaning against the counter. "Usually easiest to get hold of me early or late. I don't even carry my phone when I'm working."

He gave her another awkward handshake and headed for his vehicle. Lynn heard the engine turn over, a bit balky at first, and then returned her attention to the paintings. Best to put those in the back for now. She might be inclined to take one and see if it attracted any attention. Or maybe it would be better to wait until fall to introduce a new artist. No sense in worrying about any of that until Samson took a look.

Once again, she had to ask herself why she was not painting. If this Jay Bruce, who apparently spent his day on a lawnmower found the time, why didn't she? It was a question she could not answer.

But Lynn did decide to go out to Karen's house and collect her easel. She would make space for it.

Twenty-Eight

"It's in the garage. All your stuff is."

"A couple boxes, right?"

Karen snickered. "More than a couple. Some paintings, too."

"Oh. Yeah, I forgot about those. Or hoped to."

"We should go through all the stuff in there before I move." Karen sipped her iced tea and stared idly out the window for a few seconds before continuing. "I need to sell either the house or the farm before making a deal on a new place."

"So you definitely intend to move." It was mostly a statement of fact, rather than a question.

"You should move too. You need more space."

Lynn knew this was true. "It's convenient to the gallery," she said. "That's going to take most of my attention for a while."

"Don't let Ibarra dump all the work on you," said Karen. "It is a partnership, remember."

"It's far too late to worry about that!" Both women laughed; it was true that Samson had handed over much of the day-to-day operation of the gallery long ago.

"Is he back?" asked Karen.

"No. Should roll in this afternoon or evening. I met a local artist this weekend I think we might represent. Sammy will have to look at his work." Lynn hesitated before asking, "Are we likely to see something from another local artist?" She had avoided bringing up the subject of Pat until now.

"I didn't ask about it," came her friend's response. "Maybe you should do that."

Lynn shrugged. "Okay." If Karen didn't want to discuss art with Pat Janson, so be it. She decided to pry no further, but Lynn was definitely curious about the date. Ha, I shouldn't live through other peoples' lives, she told herself.

It seemed, however, that once the subject came up, Karen was willing to talk about it. "We went out for dinner. Vegetarian, of course." She briefly smiled at that. "Some place he knew across the river."

"And then?"

"And then nothing much. We talked." Karen frowned. "He's a bit hesitant about, mmm, extending himself. Maybe that's not the right word. He didn't initiate anything."

"He's not pushy, you mean."

"Like me? Yeah, that's about it. But I could tell he might have wanted to." She finished the last bite of her sandwich. "I'll have to encourage him, maybe."

"I've dated too many guys I needed to *discourage*," said Lynn. That was an exaggeration, of course, but it sounded good. She liked the idea of being witty even if she wasn't—or came up with witticisms well after they were relevant, like in the middle of the night.

"We did kiss goodbye," Karen told her. "I think we will go out again." A slight smirk came to her freckled face. "Or stay in."

Lynn was not going to comment on that remark. "I may go out on Thursday and approach him about his art. Um, do you want to come?"

"Probably shouldn't. But maybe we should all go someplace on one of your days off." Karen's eyes went to the window and the quiet street beyond. "I should go back to the office right now."

Lynn nodded. Time to return to business, to work. "I could stop by your house on the way over to the Springs and look for the easel." She had long been entrusted with a key.

Karen rose. "Sure. If I think about it, I'll try to set it out." She headed for the door. "See you tonight."

"Right." Lynn followed her outside into a bright Florida spring afternoon. "I'll talk to Pat then about meeting. If you don't monop-olize him."

"I'll try to be good," came Karen's mock-serious answer. The two parted outside the *Rose*. Lynn did not hurry back to the gallery. No need.

The answering machine was flashing when she entered. That was not unusual. Most often, people were inquiring whether they were open, when their hours were, that sort of thing. That was why Lynn made sure the message on the machine included information on their hours and location. Still, there were those who left a message asking anyway.

Hmm, the first was a hangup. Heard what they needed, she hoped. The next was Samson. Just left Stuart, might or might not get there before she closed up. Okay. Stuart was a pretty direct drive across the state. He shouldn't take too long, even if the truck was loaded up.

It was a little after three, the winding down of an uneventful afternoon, when he pulled up in the alley. "No extra deliveries this time," he informed her. "Everything I purchased is in the truck." Samson stopped and thought of what he had said. "Everything *we* purchased. I shall need your approval on things from now on, no?"

Lynn had to laugh. "It's not like I know anything of antiques, Sammy. I'll need to trust you."

"Always a mistake! Let's get this unloaded. Nothing here is too heavy for us to handle."

It was not too much after closing time when they had the last of the furniture, the bricabrac, inside. Not one painting this time, Lynn noted, though some small statuary was among Samson's acquisitions. She could mention Jay Bruce's paintings to him tomorrow.

Plenty of time for that. Plenty of time to get off to yoga class, too. They went their separate ways before Five.

Twenty-Nine

"ANOTHER MAN? WE need more women showing here," said Samson Ibarra. He stepped back and looked at the paintings again. "But they are not bad."

"Maybe not right for *Bayside*?" wondered Lynn. What would he think of Pat's work if she brought some to him?

"Hard to say, my dear. There would be no risk to hanging one, I suppose. And maybe," he added, "we need to expand on what is right for *Bayside*."

"Yes." Lynn had been forming an idea since yesterday, and especially since speaking with Pat last night. Was it too soon to mention it? "There are other, ah, little-known artists in the area. I was thinking perhaps a show in the season if we could find enough suitable work."

"That is ambitious. I like it." Samson looked again to the two paintings, both propped against the shelves in the back room, and nodded. "And I shall leave it all up to you."

Lynn had to smile at that, knowing Samson as she did. "With your final approval, of course." Maybe that sounded a tad sarcastic. She always had to be careful with that around him. Immediately, she added, "I think you should meet with Mr. Bruce before anything else."

"Of course, of course. When it is convenient." He returned to cataloging and pricing his new acquisitions, and Lynn went back to the show room. Maybe this was ambitious, she told herself. *Bayside* was more an antique shop than a true gallery. There was little open exhibition space, no room for the sort of receptions and openings the upscale places held.

Should she call Jay? He said he didn't answer during the day but there was always voice-mail. Lynn found his card and punched in the number. Why, it was an old-fashioned answering machine, just like Ibarra stuck with here in the gallery. The man must have a land-line at his house. *It's Lynn Devinne at Bayside Gallery,* she said. *We'd like to talk to you when it is convenient.* What else? *Give me a call first.* That was enough. There was no hurry on any of that—not for her and Sammy. Jason Bruce might be a little more eager!

Ibarra was right, she thought, hanging up the phone. We should represent more female artists. Maybe she could scout some out. Matt might know names or, if absolutely necessary, she could talk to Deb Cooper. The thought that she herself was a female artist flickered through her mind. Used to be one, Lynn told herself.

Matt—she hoped he didn't want to make plans for the two of them on Thursday. There were too many things she wanted to accomplish. She was turning her day off into another work day! Lynn suspected that was the way things would go from now on. Days off were for employees, not owners.

It wasn't so different from Samson's weekend trips. Working vacations for the antiques dealer—that's what they were, and the man thoroughly enjoyed them.

Whose voices were those? Someone was conversing with Sammy in the back room. Not—no, it wasn't Matt. For that, Lynn was grateful. She felt the need to avoid him right now. Tom Merriweather, one of the artists they repped. The oldest one, too.

"I know Jay," he was saying. "He has a couple acres in my neighborhood." That neighborhood was out Springs Road, beyond Consonante Springs and north of the river. It was an area that was once mostly black, and the workers at the old sawmill had lived there. "Did know the boy painted but never saw none of his work. He's kinda private."

"Hi, Mr. Merriweather," spoke Lynn. "Do you have something new for us?"

"Well, I reckon I do, Miss Lynn. My granddaughter dropped me off here while she does her shoppin'." He nodded toward a cardboard box containing several panels. "She thinks I'm a foolish old man but she brings me anyways."

Ibarra went over and peered into the box, then pulled out a

picture and held it at arms' length. "You're getting too good, Tom. People won't think it is folk art anymore."

"Oh, I guess I'll just have to find me one of them big city galleries then, eh?" Both men laughed at the joke. It looked like all his other paintings to Lynn, which she did not consider a bad thing. Those paintings sold well.

Tom Merriweather had been with *Bayside* before she ever began working at the gallery. She couldn't claim any credit there. "We'd best take his pictures, Sammy," she said. "We wouldn't want to lose our best artist."

Tom threw back his white-haired head and laughed loudly. "You have a smart girl working for you, sir!" he announced. A horn honked out in the alley. "There's Dee. Y'all just hang on to as many of those as you want and sell 'em if you can." He rose, supporting himself on a carved wooden cane. "I'll be back, by-n-by."

Thirty

A LIFE, IN several boxes. It sounded like the title of an installation, didn't it? A stack of storage boxes in the middle of a gallery floor. Lynn, as a rule, disliked that sort of thing but she had to laugh out loud as she pictured it. The sound echoed in Karen's mostly empty garage.

There were certainly paints in one of those boxes. Quite possibly dried up. She should purchase some new tubes. Her easel was sitting out where her friend had told her it would be. How old were those paint drips on it?

She looked over the other boxes. Four. Or was that little one hers, too? It didn't matter. She wouldn't look into them today. Let them sit a while longer. Lynn carried the tall aluminum easel out to her Escort. It was not going to fit easily. She should get a compact one for plein-air painting, one she could keep in the trunk. That might be better for her apartment, too.

She folded it as small as it would go—the wing nuts were hard to turn at first—and reclined the front passenger seat. Yes, it would just fit. Off to the Springs and prospective artist Pat Janson.

Her other prospect, Jay, had called after hours, of course. His message had been waiting on Wednesday morning. She should have given him her cell number, maybe, but Lynn was admittedly private about that. Enough messages were exchanged to eventually set up a meeting on Saturday morning. That was just to work out a few things; Lynn had decided to show his work and Samson approved.

He might not sell. She should prepare him for that fact. There was a back way to Consonante Springs, Lynn remembered. She didn't have to return the way she came, through Tamarind. Hmm, back north to Fourth Avenue—its name changed further out, didn't it?—and then east, and then north again. That should take her past Samson's house and then to Springs Road.

Houses were scattered out here, beyond the more developed

area closer to Tamarind, beyond the golf courses. There were many empty lots, some once cleared and since grown up with scrub, some with the old, spreading live oaks, and tall, spindly sabal palms poking up here and there. Dilapidated trailers rubbed shoulders with sprawling country houses. Dirt roads branched off, leading who knew where? And there was Springs Road and the spa off to the east, on the other side of the road.

Pat would be expecting her. They had made the appointment Monday night, before class started, before Karen arrived. He sat, waiting in fact, on one of the cast-concrete benches before the old hotel building.

He was at her car by the time she was parked but seemed uncertain what to say to her. "Hi, Pat, nice to see you."

"Hi, Lynn. Um, yeah, how are you?"

She locked the Escort, not that there was much worth taking in it. If she hadn't found a spot in the shade of one of the oaks, she might have left the windows open. Car interiors got very hot, very quickly, in the Florida sun. "I'm fine. Karen told me to say hello for her, of course."

Pat nodded, seemingly slightly amused. "I would tell you to say hello back but I may see her sooner than you. We have a date tonight."

"Your second." Lynn had, admittedly, had her doubts about that occurring.

"Third," he corrected her. "We went out together after class on Monday." His smile came suddenly. "Unless we count all the classes she has attended."

"Ah, if we do that, then you were dating me too!"

"Oh. Not sure what she would think of that." He led the way toward the entrance and then halted. "Not sure where you want to go, either."

"I wanted to see your art," she told him. "And then swim maybe."

"Hmm, okay." He turned toward the spa's front doors again.

"Some of my stuff is hanging inside but most is in my own place. If you don't, uh, mind going over there."

He had a trailer somewhere on the grounds, right? "Lead on, Mr. Janson, and I'll follow."

A young woman, a girl really, was at the front desk this morning, not Verna. She glanced up from a pad on which she was writing and asked, "Is this the girlfriend, Pat?"

"No," spoke up Lynn before he could answer. "I'm her best friend and we're cheating behind her back." Pat colored up immediately.

He didn't bother to introduce her to the receptionist but pointed toward the mandala hanging by the desk. "You've seen that one." He started off down the hall without further words.

I shouldn't have done that to him, thought Lynn. He's too self-conscious. She shrugged, smiled at the girl, and followed the yoga instructor.

Two more, similar pieces of art hung along the hallway. "There is some stuff of mine in Mrs. Kuenst's house but we won't go there," he said.

"She's not here?" asked Lynn. Agnes Kuenst was something of a mysterious figure in the area.

"Nope. She goes north in the spring, just like the tourists. Sometimes comes back for a while during the summer, though. And here," he said, pointing out the largest mandala yet, "is the last of them over here. They all belong to the spa. Or Mrs. Kuenst, I should probably say."

She has good taste, thought the young woman. And money. I wonder if I could get her into the gallery sometime.

They circled through the pool area. Lynn was surprised by the size of the crowd. "Mornings are popular," said Pat. "It will thin out shortly. We can go out on this side and cross the road."

"You live behind the spring somewhere, right?"

"Yeah, but we don't need to go the way we did before. There's a road over here."

From this, the east end of the old hotel, one could see the neighboring county park. It was a popular place to launch canoes or kayaks onto the river, beneath the ancient oaks. "Mrs. Kuenst donated that property, didn't she?" asked Lynn, peering toward the picnic tables. A low limestone wall separated them from the spa.

"She did," said Pat, leading the way toward Springs Road. "It's named for her father." The dirt path they followed was too narrow for automobiles but she could see tire tracks. Golf carts, maybe?

They stopped at the edge of the road and she scanned what lay beyond. A handful of trailers, one small concrete block house—very old-school Florida, with a flat roof—and a couple of barns or storage buildings. "I'm in the one furthest west," her companion said, pointing. "The nearest to the spring."

The tiniest too, she noted. "You have room to paint in there?"

Slight embarrassment. "It doesn't take much space. And I don't do much of anything else in the trailer except sleep."

"Okay. Let's see it." They walked across the not very busy road. Lynn could see the worn yellow stripes that marked a crossing spot. The dirt road on the far side was wide enough for normal vehicles, and its margins were unkempt and thick with sand spurs.

Then they stood outside the green and white trailer. She could now see the rust streaks running down its sides, and that an extra room had been tacked onto it. There was a small wood deck. This was a mobile home that would never again be mobile.

"My home," announced Pat, holding the door open. "As much as any place."

Thirty-One

"So," said Lynn, "third date. Anything you need to confess?"

Karen snorted. "Not yet! Pat had to tell me all about your visit. You've seen the inside of his place before me."

"You have missed very little. And you should know he sleeps on a mat on the floor."

Karen raised an eyebrow at that but made no comment. "So, are you going to make him a famous artist? I want to brag about my boyfriend, you know." She looked up as Jan approached. "Usual tea, please," she said. "And, oh—what is really unhealthy? I need to make up for last night." She perused the menu. "A BLT. Bring me a BLT. With lots of mayo."

Lynn ordered a salad before continuing their conversation. "I think we could show Pat's work. It's different, though." She sipped the tea Jan had just set down before her. "Samson liked the picture I brought back quite a lot. I was a little surprised at how enthusiastic he was."

"Thinking sales, maybe," observed Karen.

"Maybe," agreed Lynn. "I don't know if we'll put any of them up right away. I'm still playing with that idea of a show in the fall, and Pat's work would fit right in."

"That would be months yet, wouldn't it? Like September?"

"Or October. Yeah. Maybe too long to wait." She sat for a moment, seeming to frown at her iced tea. Karen knew she was thinking something through. "Nearly half a year. We'll hang them now."

"There's no reason you can't have an off-season show, is there?"

"None at all, except no one is likely to come!"

Karen would have none of that. "If you don't show the work, you can be sure no one will come."

"Okay, okay. You're right. I'll talk to Samson about it." She would want to discuss this with Jay Bruce tomorrow morning. She should get some background information from him. Pat, too. Lynn realized she knew little about him, truly.

"Has Pat told you anything about his past?" she asked her friend. "I'll be needing a few lines for advertising and the web site."

Karen shook her head. "Very little. He's not local, not originally. I know that."

"Hmm. Might be better if I grill him," said Lynn, "so he doesn't think you're nosy." She grinned. "Then I can fill you in with the details later."

"Whatever." Karen seemed distracted, thoughtful. "I like Pat. Maybe more than that. Lynn, I haven't felt this way in a long time."

It was already that serious? "I have to admit I'm surprised. He doesn't seem your type at all."

"No, he doesn't. I guess I needed a new type."

Lynn wasn't sure whether to nod knowingly or laugh, so she did neither. The arrival of their food covered over any awkwardness. "Seeing Pat on Sunday again?" she asked after squeezing a bit of lemon juice on her salad. No dressing; Lynn was avoiding the calories again.

"Um-huh. This is good." Karen was devouring her sandwich. She swallowed and asked, "How 'bout you and Matt?"

"Maybe," was all Lynn had to say of that. Matt had made some mention of getting together that night, after his kids went back to their mother. "I should get him to look at Pat's stuff. Jay Bruce's, too."

"Get him out to the Springs sometime," suggested her friend.

"I've been thinking of doing that," Lynn admitted. Maybe a painting expedition. There were going to be plenty of slow afternoons coming up for that sort of thing, and a swim after. "He could see Pat's work there."

Karen nodded. "And Pat would be on his home turf. Matt tends to push people around, so he needs an advantage."

There was no point in arguing that. Lynn recognized the truth in it and her mind was already elsewhere. "I'm going to tell him to bring his little girls out to the spa to swim on Sunday, and meet him there." She looked up from the few scraps of lettuce left in her bowl. "Come too, will you?"

"Why not?" laughed Miss Fairfield.

Thirty-Two

"STOP SPLASHING YOUR sister," called Matt.

"I don't mind," Carole called back, not very loudly. Rebeka giggled and splashed her again.

"I do," said their father. "It's time to get out for a while. Miss Lynn is here." He glanced toward Karen. "And her friend. Come and say hello to them."

The two little girls clambered out of the wading pool. "And don't run," added Matt, holding out a towel for each of them.

"Runs a tight ship, doesn't he?" Karen whispered in her friend's ear.

Like your father, Lynn was about to whisper in reply but, no, not like the late Bob Fairfield, really. That man had often seemed distant, cold, even; Matt Stone always openly demonstrated affection for his daughters. But both were demanding, in their ways.

The dripping girls took their proffered towels and stood looking at Karen and Lynn with something between suspicion and curiosity. The younger, Beka was probably brunette naturally but the sun had bleached her hair nearly a light as her sister's.

"Hi, Miss Lynn," said six-year-old Carole. Her eyes went to Karen. "Hi, Miss Lynn's friend." This gave Beka an immediate fit of the giggles, which proved contagious.

"This is Miss Karen," Matt told them. "Now get dried off." He turned his head to the women, without rising from his lounge. "Going to swim?"

Nothing more than that? wondered Lynn. Oh, of course the man was not going to show any affection toward *her* with the little girls there. She knew that. But still! "Sure," she replied. "Let's go change." Karen followed her to the changing room.

"Cute kids," murmured Karen as they went in, and nothing more. Cute kids—sure. A cliché, just something to say to have something to say. Her friend had been waiting in her Lexus in the parking lot when she arrived, with air running and stereo on high.

Lynn had needed to knock on the window to get her attention. Separate cars because Karen might head off somewhere with Pat, while Lynn—well, she would probably just be going home.

Where was Pat, anyway? "Your boyfriend knew we were coming, right?" she asked Karen.

A laugh. "Boyfriend? I'm not completely sure of that!" Karen's voice became muffled as she stepped into one of the stalls. "He might have a class or something. He fills in for other people here sometimes."

Lynn slipped into a more revealing suit than the one she wore the last time she swam with her friend. Was that because Matt was here? She wasn't certain and didn't really want to consider the question. It was what she had stuffed into her bag before leaving the apartment and that was that.

She did cover up with a loose shirt before stepping out into the common area. The cracked concrete floor was damp; other swimmers must have come and gone already.

Karen pushed back the curtain on her changing stall. "Pat teaches a sunrise yoga class on weekends," she spoke, continuing their conversation as though there had been no break in it. "Followed by leading a walk around the grounds."

Lynn nodded. "I suppose a lot of the overnight guests want to get out of here by the middle of the day." Probably not so many of those now, with the season winding down. Even fewer through the summer.

"Mm-huh. Ready to go?" Karen picked up her bag and headed for the door without waiting for a response. Matt looked up and nodded, perhaps in approval, as they emerged; his daughters were sitting cross-legged on a beach towel, sipping cold drinks. Beyond, the pool sparkled. It would feel good to plunge in.

"How did your meeting with the new talent go?" he asked as they settled into a pair of lounges. "What's his name? Bruce?"

"Jay Bruce," responded Lynn, half-wishing she hadn't mentioned any of it to him. "He came in yesterday morning and

Sammy liked him, so I think we'll rep him. Lots of time to work out the details yet."

Matt's laugh was curt, almost scoffing. "Not that Sam liking someone is necessary. I know he doesn't think much of me."

Karen looked like she might have wanted to say she agreed with Samson Ibarra, but held her tongue. She let her eyes go to the little girls instead, gazing at them for a few seconds, before turning back. The woman's smile hinted of a certain self-satisfaction, "Lynn's other new artist should be along soon."

"The yoga guy. Never met him either."

"Jay does show," Lynn informed him. "He's been hitting the outdoor circuit on weekends for some time. His stuff doesn't really seem well suited to those sort of shows." She frowned, just slightly. "He seems a bit private. I hope I can get him to socialize some in the local art scene." Matt could help there. She was not about to ask him but it wouldn't hurt to introduce the two sometime. "And there is our other artist now."

Pat was hurrying through the arched main entry, a towel under his arm. "Hi," he called, heading toward the outdoor shower. "Let me rinse off and I'll be with you." He stripped off his sweat-soaked polo shirt and stood beneath the stream of cold water.

"Mmm. I've never seen him without his shirt before," whispered Karen. "And I very much hope I do again!"

Lynn had known the man was muscular. The singlet he usually wore when teaching class didn't hide that much. The wet shorts clinging to him now hid even less. He walked toward them, toweling himself off.

"I needed to fill in on the exercise class this morning," he announced, addressing himself to Karen. "Don't much care to. It's billed as aerobics, but we pretty much end up doing calisthenics."

"Is that where you get those muscles?" asked Matt. "I'm sure yoga won't do that for you."

There might have been a touch of mockery in the man's tone, but Pat didn't seem to note it. "There's a weight room on the grounds. Very old-school. We don't open it to the guests anymore." He shrugged. "Liability, you know? I'm pretty much the only one who uses it."

"This is Matt Stone," Lynn said. "Pat Janson." She spied the little girls, both staring up at this stranger. "And these are Rebeka and Carol."

"Pleased to meet you, young ladies," said Pat.

A solemn nod from Carole, and a question. "Are you Miss Lynn's boyfriend?"

"Over my dead body!" stated Karen, snickering.

Pat seemed a bit unsure how to answer. Lynn jumped in. "He is Miss Karen's boyfriend," she told the girl.

"Oh. Okay." Carole seemed disappointed. "Can we swim again?"

"In a little bit," her father told her, and turned his attention back to Pat. "You paint, I understand."

"You have seen some of his art on the walls in this place," Lynn informed him. "The mandalas."

"Ah." Matt nodded his head. "The one by the front desk?" He did not wait for an answer. "Interesting work."

And the compete antithesis of what Matt did, carefully planned and crafted. Not that Stone couldn't do meticulous work, but he took care to hide it, to make sure his canvases always appeared spontaneous, painterly.

"Something different like that could be good for the gallery," he went on. "I'll have to see more when I have the time. But now," Matt said, turning to his daughters, "we have time for one more swim before we go."

"You're leaving so soon?" asked Lynn. She had hardly arrived and Matt was going to take off?

"Have to get the girls to their mother," he called over his shoulder. "I don't think I'll get back home very early."

In other words, don't expect to see him again today. Or tonight. It was about what Lynn had expected.

And Karen and Pat might be in a hurry to go off somewhere together too. "Let's swim," she said. Nothing better to do.

Thirty-Three

"What do you think of Matt Stone?" Karen asked the man across the tile-topped table. She knew she probably shouldn't put Pat on the spot with a question like that.

"He's a bit of an ass, isn't he?" He gave her a lopsided smile. "I shouldn't judge, of course."

"But you have eyes, the same as the rest of us. And I agree."

"Is Lynn involved with him?"

Karen was surprised he had picked up on that. She only nodded.

"Again, I shouldn't judge." He picked at the remnants of his dinner, a few stray grains of brown rice. "I should have taken you someplace to eat."

"But they feed you for free here at the spa," she pointed out. "And me, too, I assume."

"Yeah." Pat put down his fork. "I don't eat evening meals here usually. My own cooking is better."

Bragging? No, he seemed to be simply stating a fact, as he saw it. "Vegetarian, I assume."

"Sure, but not vegan like this. I do eggs and dairy and maybe even some shellfish." Pat leaned back, smiled a bit smugly—or so it seemed to Karen—and told her, "I'll have to fry you up some of my own recipe veggie-burgers sometime."

Karen's voice dripped with exaggerated sarcasm. "Oh, sure. I can hardly wait."

Pat laughed with her but said, "Now I'll have to prove they're good." He paused, frowning slightly. "Hmm, my trailer is a little shabby to have you as a guest. No, that's wrong—it's way too shabby."

"Then come cook in my kitchen." Someone should. The idea appeared to make him uncomfortable. "Or I'll try to brave your place," she added. "You could give me a tour if we're done here."

"Okay. I'll bus our table," Pat said, gathering their plates.

Karen grabbed the glasses. She might as well help, especially so if they were eating for free. Her date led the way into the kitchen. They had dined on a patio behind the spa, apparently used mostly by employees. Mrs. Kuenst's big house dominated the view. It might be interesting to take a peek inside sometime—she knew Pat had access.

She remembered something. "Where is this weight room you mentioned?"

"Hang on," he said, scraping their dishes into a garbage bin and stacking them by the sink. The dishwasher, who had been sitting reading a paperback, looked up, gave them a nod, and returned to his book. "I'll add it to the tour."

There was still some light, but little of it penetrated the canopy of old and massive banyans behind the main building. Pat led the way toward the open area to the west, close to the spring-fed stream, where a smallish concrete block structure, painted the same faded pinkish-orange tone as the spa, stood. Karen had noticed it the first time Pat had showed her and Lynn around but he hadn't explained its purpose at the time.

"The solarium," he announced, showing her into an enclosed space. "Once a place to sunbathe in the nude but that's not done here anymore! There used to be separate men's and women's sections."

Karen could see where a dividing wall had once stood, removed to make it all one area. Wooden-slatted lounges were scattered about. "No one uses it much anymore," Pat went on. "Guests prefer to lie by the pool." He chuckled. "Carl and Verna want to knock it down but Mrs. Kuenst won't give her approval. I think she wants things to remain the way they were in the heyday of the Springs."

"Maybe she sneaks out and sunbathes nude," suggested Karen.

"I wouldn't put it past her! Although her late husband was the one who put an end to that sort of thing here. Here's the exercise room." He pulled out a ring of keys and unlocked a weathered wooden door. Flakes of white paint fell to the concrete floor as he swung it open. "He was trying to make the place more of a, um, mainstream resort. Agnes's father was admittedly something of a crackpot."

"The man the park is named for," said Karen. "He built the place, right?"

"Right. John Prima." Pat flipped on the light, a pair of bare florescents in a ceiling fixture. "The grandfather bought the land originally, and started the hotel, but he was the one who put up most of what is here now." He considered his statement and added, "Not the house. That was Abraham Kuenst."

Karen looked around the room. It was, indeed, very old-school. There were antiquated pulley arrangements attached to the wall— she had seen ones like them in movies but never in real life. A couple of benches, weights, a rack of dumbbells. No mirrors, but holes drilled in the block walls suggested there once had been.

"State of the art, fifty or sixty years ago," Pat informed her. "Seen enough?"

She nodded. The rundown exercise room was depressing. Someone's dream once, now forgotten, kept locked. Karen thought of her own neglected dream, the 'farm.' She hadn't heard much from the agent on it.

Too many things ended up like that. They shouldn't be allowed to slip away. As Pat turned to her from his locking up, she reached out, her hand on his shoulder, pulling him to her and his lips to hers. He responded in what she considered an entirely appropriate manner.

Thirty-Four

"HE OFFERED TO cook for me. I am definitely going to take him up on it."

Lynn tried to picture her yoga instructor standing at a range, sautéing something. She rather liked the image. "Just cooking? Nothing else yet?"

"We did make out pretty seriously." Karen sipped her tea before continuing, perhaps letting that bit of information fully sink in. "And I was right about me having to make the first move. Pat would have taken forever, if I let him."

"As long as it happened eventually," remarked Lynn. "So, cooking—tonight?"

Her companion shook her head. "Not enough time for a real date after class."

Plenty of time for other things, thought Lynn. And thinking of time and the class, and perhaps other things, she observed, "Only four weeks left."

"So there are."

Was Karen purposely being annoying or was she just distracted? Lynn wasn't sure. "I'm going to take the afternoon class when it starts up. I think I am, anyway."

"I don't know if that would do for me," asserted Karen. "I can't just leave my work."

"You could, but you won't."

"Well, yeah." Karen looked out the window for a few seconds before going on. "It's not taking the time off, you know, it's just trying to do it on a regular schedule. Things come up. I suppose Samson doesn't mind you taking the afternoons off."

"No problem there. But I'll stop taking Thursdays, to make up for it. Sammy actually likes that arrangement better."

A slight smile, a knowing nod. "Of course you already talked it over with him. The conscientious Miss Devinne! Maybe I will take in Pat's evening classes at the Springs. Unless I can get him to give me private lessons."

"That would definitely be the best solution," agreed Lynn, swallowing the last of her diluted tea.

There were two older women in the gallery when she got back, both being charmed by Sammy. She knew them, didn't she? Yes, from yoga class. Lynn didn't think she had ever spoken to either and certainly did not know their names.

The taller one leaned in and whispered something to her companion as she came in. They seemed a bit surprised to see her. "Ah, my partner," announced Ibarra. It was nice to hear him say that, wasn't it? "Lynn, I would like you to meet Georgia and Sandy."

"Pleased to meet you," spoke the shorter, plumper woman. Was she Georgia or Sandy? "We didn't know you worked here."

The other stepped forward, extending her hand in a businesslike manner. "Sandy Wiedermann," she said. "We've seen you at class."

"Roger and Joe are always ogling you and your friend," added Georgia.

Sandy laughed easily. "And Georgia would rather they would ogle her." She wouldn't be so bad to ogle, Lynn felt. Cute—that's what she was, and probably always had been. But she knew she was no expert on what guys liked.

"Well, they shouldn't be chasing after young girls!" Georgia stated. "Roger's taken up with that Jen Carter now."

"I doubt she's that much younger than he is. Or we are," replied her friend. "Ten years or so?"

"At least fifteen," claimed Georgia, and turned to Lynn. There seemed an air of the mischievous about her but maybe that was just her natural look. "And now your friend seems set on stealing our instructor."

Lynn wasn't surprised that people had noticed. "She does, doesn't she? We are going to exhibit some of Pat's artwork here."

Might as well turn the conversation away from men and toward art. And sales!

Sam approved of the new direction. "That we are," he said. "Mr. Janson will join our family of fine local artists."

The pair seemed indifferent about the news. "We are more interested in your antique furniture, Mr. Ibarra," said Sandy. "Could you show us some more?" She sounded almost coy. It was a bit jarring from this tall and broad-shouldered woman.

"Certainly. And it's Samson, my dears, call me Samson."

The women followed Ibarra as he pointed out various pieces, entertaining them with a nonstop monologue, description, history, provenance, and the occasional unrelated anecdote. Sam was in his element. Lynn could see they were perhaps more interested in the man than his antiques. Undoubtedly, Ibarra could see it as well but he wouldn't mind. She went into the back and left them to it.

So Roger and Joe 'ogled' her? Lynn thought that was amusing. Of course they did; that was inevitable. She was probably guilty of ogling the physically impressive Roger. It didn't mean anything. Or not much of anything.

Samson was writing up a sale when she returned to the showroom. "We need to deliver that hutch—" He nodded toward the piece. "To Ms. Wiedermann's house. Tomorrow?" he asked, looking up at Sandy.

"Anytime after noon," she replied. "No need to call." Sam nodded and finished his scribbling. Apparently Georgia was making no purchases today. Her eyes wandered disinterestedly about the gallery as she waited on her friend.

Lynn accompanied them to the door. The weather had warmed up enough that it was now kept closed and the air conditioning turned on. She vaguely resented having to spend money for cooling; left to herself, Lynn might well have kept the door open right through the heat of summer.

As they paused, Sandy took a quick look toward Sammy, still

fussing over his papers at the counter, and whispered, "Is Mr. Ibarra taken? I didn't see a ring."

Lynn almost felt guilty about puncturing whatever daydreams the women might have conjured. And perhaps she took a little guilty pleasure in it too. She leaned in and told her, "Sammy is gay. Sorry."

"Oh. Well," said Sandy, shrugging, "it doesn't matter. I've done fine without a man for years."

Georgia nodded in agreement. "One thing I really love is men don't bother me anymore. I hated being ogled and looked at when I was younger. I hated dating. I hated men lying to me."

"And having to care about the way I looked all the time. Now, I love that they just leave me alone. I don't have to please anyone!"

"Yeah, they hardly bother me at all now. It is a huge relief."

"It is a relief! It really is!"

This was the last Lynn heard as the two passed out the door.

Thirty-Five

"THAT 'TREE' POSTURE was supposed to be difficult?" wondered Roger. "I do that every time I pull on my socks."

"It's true. He doesn't sit down like a normal person," Joe said.

As most of the rest of the class, Lynn had encountered some difficulty with emulating a tree, standing on one leg. She should practice it at home, she told herself. Near something she could grab if she lost her balance.

"Waiting on your friend?" asked Roger.

Karen had gone to talk with Pat at the end of the session. No surprise there. "No, we came separately. But I might want a few words with our instructor also before I go."

Roger nodded. "I'm waiting for someone too." Joe gave him a sour look but said nothing.

Lynn could guess who that might be. No need to say anything of it. "So you were both career army?" she asked, mostly to have something to say.

"We were," said Roger. "Thirty years, each of us."

Joe nodded, grinning. "From the look of us, Miss, you'd think Bernhard here was the boots-on-the-ground combat guy, wouldn't you? But it was the other way around."

"It's true," rumbled Roger. "I was in the logistics end of things most of my career." The big man gave his companion an amiable smile. "Joe was out being shot at."

"First war in Iraq. We were both there." He squinted at Lynn. "Were you even born yet?"

"I'm not that young!" she laughed. But she was just a little girl. Her memories of the event were pretty vague.

"That's where we met," Joe continued. "Been friends since, whether we were stationed together or not."

"Joe saved my life but he doesn't like to talk about it." Roger gave his comrade a sidelong look before saying more. "So I won't either."

A glance toward the front of the room showed a knot of women around Pat. Even Karen couldn't get the chance to monopolize him, as much as she might wish to. Lynn turned back to the men. "So how did you end up in Tamarind?"

Joe chuckled. "We just started driving south from Benning and when we saw a place we liked, we stopped."

"A place we both liked," added Roger.

"And this was it. We found a little place close to the water, down at the south end."

Near her apartment. Lynn hadn't known that. "And you bought a house together."

"That's right." Roger laughed. "Just like an old married couple."

Lynn laughed with him. "Didn't you make some joke about getting married?" she asked.

"Yeah, not serious about it, you know, but there are legal advantages. It's not like either one of us is actually gay," said Joe, seemingly wanting to make that quite clear.

"We would both have to be gay," Roger pointed out. "At our age, it could be a good idea to have someone there officially. In case one of us gets sick or something."

"Right. And neither of us will complain if the other chases after one foxy old lady or another."

Roger snickered. "You can chase the old ladies and leave the younger ones for me."

"Like they are going to give you a second look."

"Don't need a second look. One does the job!"

Lynn smiled at their banter. "I thought you and Ms. Carter were a couple now, Roger."

The big man gave her a sheepish expression. "That's so, ma'am. I'm hanging around waiting for Jen."

"Even though she doesn't leave work until late," remarked Joe, "and you're going to see her in the morning." Lynn wasn't sure whether it was amusement or disgust in the man's voice.

115

"Just for a moment," murmured Roger. "Wouldn't be right to go without saying something to her."

Joe shrugged, perhaps exaggerating his expression of resignation. The crowd around Pat had thinned. "I think I can get to our instructor now," said Lynn. "See you later, guys."

Was that too familiar? she wondered, as she walked toward the front of the room. She barely knew the sergeants, really. Pat was speaking in a low voice with Karen now and acknowledged her only with a quick glance before turning back to her friend. His girlfriend. Yes, definitely his girlfriend.

It was Karen who broke off their conversation. "You're going to see Pat about his art tomorrow, right?" she asked. Lynn had mentioned it at lunch.

"Yes. I'd like to pick a few pieces to show, if it's okay with you," she said to Pat. "Maybe you should choose some you think are your best work." He only nodded, so she continued. "I'm going to bring my easel and paints too, and Matt and I are going to set up and make a day of it." All this last part had sort of rushed out.

Karen narrowed her eyes but said nothing. She knows I'm headed out to his place in Leawood right now, thought Lynn. She momentarily resented her friend's disapproval.

"I'd like to see your painting," came Pat's even voice. "Your friend's too."

Her brief mood passed as quickly as it had come. "And I'd be glad to show it to you," said Lynn.

She could not speak for Matt, however.

Thirty-Six

IT WAS ANOTHER clear morning, expected in spring. Rainy season would show up soon enough, the hot humid mornings broken by showers before noon and thunderstorms later, great piles of dark clouds building out over the prairies and swamps of the interior before marching to the coast.

But it was clear and even a bit cool today. Lynn had half a mind to call off their trip to the Springs, to spend the day there in Leawood, on the beach and at Matt's place. It felt like a chore to go anywhere else, to load her easel and folding chair into Matt's Savana. Why bother?

But Matt Stone was up and all business. He probably has a complete schedule for our day in his head, Lynn thought. It was best to just go along with it, or easiest, anyway. The man would not appreciate an attempt at last minute changes.

And she could swim at the spa. There was always that to make up for the beach. She should come out here on her own, maybe on Sunday, and spend some time in the Gulf.

It would be Consonante Springs today. She and Matt had the van loaded and were pulling out onto the beach road before Nine, headed south.

Back behind them was the Horley estate. "We'll have to paint at Paradise someday," she said.

Matt was silent for a rather long time before saying, "I've already gone over and worked. I'll show you the canvases sometime." He kept his eyes straight ahead, on the road. "But I'd be happy to go with you if you want."

Lynn didn't bother to answer. A minute or so later, Matt spoke again. "Sorry," was all he said.

He wasn't thinking about anyone else again, she told herself. It's just how Matt was—and he had recognized it. "It's okay," she replied. "You can go anywhere you want, you know." The absurdity of giving Matt permission brought a sudden laugh. "And you always will!"

He gave her a puzzled glance but did not revisit the subject.

A left onto the road into Tamarind, across the salt marshes. The air was still, the gray-green grass unmoving, the water glass-like. A pelican skimmed its surface, distant. One could see the docks and seawalls of Tamarind from here on a morning like this, faint and far away. Binoculars would help. Didn't Matt keep some in the van? She rummaged through the glove box.

There they were, armored in green rubber. Lynn adjusted the focus, scanned the distant bay shore for a few seconds. Tamarind would not be visible much longer as they moved further east. There were boats in the water up there and that large building—was that the rec center? No, it must be the marina down a way from it.

She put the binoculars away. "A nice day to be on the water," she said.

"You used to sail, didn't you?" The road was beginning its long curve toward the north.

"When I was a kid," Lynn replied. Not since she went off to college, not since she had returned. "Maybe I will again."

"Uh-huh. You ought to. You don't do enough things for yourself." Matt chuckled. "I probably shouldn't be giving you advice on life."

"It's as good as anyone's," she told him.

"Or as bad."

Traffic was light through Tamarind, and no heavier on Springs Road. The sleepiest time of the year, maybe, thought Lynn, after most of the tourists and winter residents left and before school let out, creating an whole different sort of visitor. Then, Floridians from further inland would be flocking to the beaches. Leawood would be jammed with traffic on the weekends.

"Not very crowded," spoke Matt, as they pulled into the spa's parking lot. "I suppose we should check in first, eh?"

Lynn nodded. She suspected they could just wander about the

grounds and no one would bother them, especially now that she was known to be a friend of their trusted yoga teacher. "I'll take care of it," she said. "You can unload."

Pat. Yoga class at Eleven, if she remembered correctly. Maybe she could catch him before then. "Hi, Verna," she greeted Mrs. Fell. "A friend and I are going to spend the day."

"Miss Fairfield?" asked the woman. "I probably wouldn't charge her now that she's Pat's girlfriend."

"I'll have to remember that and bring her along next time. But no, it's another friend." She handed over her credit card. Lynn didn't mind paying. After all, Matt had driven her out and was taking care of everything else. And it helped her feel just a little independent.

She sometimes needed that when she was with Stone.

Thirty-Seven

"YOU NEED MORE colors," observed Matt.

"I know." Lynn had grabbed a basic set of oils at a craft store. She hadn't even bothered to check whether the ones in Karen's garage were still good. Going through those boxes was something Lynn simply did not feel like tackling.

She had allowed Matt to choose their location, a location that somewhat dictated their subject. That was the facade of the old hotel itself. But she had set up her easel at a good distance from his. Now, here he was, checking her work as if she were one of his students.

He made no other comment, however, and returned to his own canvas. Lynn resisted the urge to go look at what her boyfriend had painted. "It's starting to get hot out here," she called to him. "I think I want to go jump in the pool."

"We'll need to find a shadier spot if we paint again later," Matt responded. He methodically began to put away his paints, each in its proper spot. Lynn threw hers into the cardboard box in which she had brought them, and stepped back to take a look at her work. Not satisfactory at all. Too gray. Maybe even muddy.

Matt's work had a grayness about it too, a subdued and subtle tone gradation. Was she emulating him? Maybe she should take a lesson from Jay Bruce's work, full of strong color. Lynn took the canvas down and folded her easel. Time to stow all this in the van and enjoy herself for a couple hours.

Enjoy herself? Hadn't she enjoyed painting? Lynn wasn't sure; she knew she liked finishing a picture but maybe didn't like the actual work of it very much. It was fatiguing, sometimes, making choice after choice, brush stroke by brush stroke.

Again, she avoided looking at Matt's canvas as he packed their gear away. It would be like all the rest of them. "Here's your bag," he said, tossing it to her. "You're meeting with your artist later, right?"

"He won't be free until noon," she replied. Lynn hadn't been able to connect before his class, which was all right. That was time better used for painting. "We can eat here if you want."

"Okay." She wondered if he knew that meant a vegetarian lunch. It wouldn't hurt Matt any. He was getting a bit paunchy and could stand to eat better. As could she! "We could go somewhere else for dinner," he added.

It had been some time since the man had taken her out to eat. They never seemed to have real dates.

A change of clothes and into the almost deserted pool. The same young lifeguard as the first time she had visited gave them a disinterested look from her chair, and turned her eyes back to something in her lap. A phone maybe. Lynn hoped she didn't drown while the girl was texting someone.

Matt took to the diving board. This was a skill she had not seen from him before, yet his grace did not surprise her as he plunged in, leaving barely a ripple. She had no intention of demonstrating any belly-flops into the water herself, but mostly lolled at the midpoint of the long pool, gently backstroking from one side to the other. It was as far across as the length of the pool at her apartment.

Voices. She stopped and treaded water, head up to see what was going on. Ah, Pat had shown up and was in a conversation with Stone. Might as well get out, though she didn't really want to.

"Pat's offering to feed us," spoke Matt as she approached, toweling off.

"Like you did Karen?" she asked. "She told me about your little private patio out back."

"If you'd like. Or carry something down by the river or just take a table in the dining room." Pat paused and considered that. "Lunch time is busy in there, of course, not that we have a lot of guests today."

"The place does seem deserted," remarked Matt.

"I've seen worse. I've taught one person classes on occasion."

"I wouldn't mind a one-on-one class," said Lynn. "Neither would Karen."

Pat gave her and her remark a self-conscious smile. "We'll go change and be right with you," she continued. "And we can look at your pictures after we eat." Lynn headed for the dressing room with no further comments. Matt, she assumed, would do the same.

She could have done all this today without him. Lynn wasn't sure she even liked having her boyfriend along. Oh, sure, she enjoyed being with him out in Leawood. But working alongside him at their easels, sharing her gallery business with Pat, didn't feel quite right. It blurred the lines between her life and his. She slipped into tee-shirt and shorts and rejoined the men.

"Three or four panels would be enough," she told Pat as he led them toward lunch. "A couple of them smaller pieces we can price lower but at least one big showy picture. And maybe you could write a little description of what they are, um, meant to represent."

"Do you want them now?" he asked.

Lynn looked at Matt. No, she shouldn't expect him to cart Pat's paintings about in his van. "Bring them by the gallery sometime," she answered. "This week or next, it doesn't matter that much."

"But you want to look at them today, don't you?"

"Right. We can decide on which ones to show." Sammy would trust her choice there. He had liked the panel she brought to the gallery and that was good enough.

Pat was leading them through the not-very-crowded dining room and on into the kitchen. "It smells like an Indian restaurant in here," remarked Matt. "And like some of it was burnt."

"Something is always burnt," said one of the cooks, a lean, dark man with a gray crew-cut. "Plates for three, Pat?"

"Yes, Jag, please." Pat glanced at his two companions and grinned. "They're meat-eaters, so go gentle on them."

"My specialty. I've taken care of their sort before, you know!" Lynn could detect no accent in Jag's speech, though she assumed he was Indian. Or of Indian descent. The man deftly assembled three lunch trays, varicolored legumes, flat bread, salad, while Pat filled glasses with what appeared to be ordinary iced tea.

"Jagadish heads up the kitchens," the yoga instructor told them as he showed his guests to a table on the patio. "He goes way back here, I think to when Mr. Kuenst was still alive."

"You never met him, did you?" asked Matt. He took a sip of his tall drink. "Good tea."

"You can thank the spring water for that," answered Pat. "We pump a small amount for cooking and drinking. But no, Abraham Kuenst was gone by the time I started here." He scooped up some lentils with a piece of flat bread. "In fact, I would have been a little kid when he passed. There's a daughter who has visited a few times but she's rarely spoken to me. I got the feeling she disliked me for some reason."

"You? Impossible," said Lynn. "Everyone likes you. Even Matt."

Matt nodded. "I'll admit it."

"Maybe not Maddie Fry's family," said Pat, his voice becoming quieter.

Lynn nodded. "Her husband seems to take a dim view of her coming to yoga class."

"Boyfriend," Pat corrected her. "They're not married. Her mom doesn't think much of it either. I get the impression she thinks yoga is akin to devil worship and not suitable for a Christian girl." A slight smile. "And, moreover, only for pretentious white women."

Matt laughed aloud at that. "She should visit India someday."

"Maddie's trying to find a way to keep it up through the summer. Scheduling, finding a ride—it doesn't look like she'll work it out."

Pat rose. "You finish up here while I go get the pictures I chose, okay? I brought them over with me this morning."

"That's all right with me," Lynn told him. She probably didn't even need to look at them, could have let Pat bring what he would to the gallery. But she might as well act professional about it.

"We can paint some more before we take off, if you want," said Matt, as Pat disappeared into the kitchen. He put an arm around her in a gesture of careless ownership. "He's a good guy. I'm happy for your friend Karen even if she does hate my guts."

And so was she, happy for Karen, happy for Pat. But again, Lynn had doubts it would turn out well.

Thirty-Eight

"LET'S GO THIS way," said Matt, turning left. It was not a suggestion; he had already decided to go east on Springs Road.

"Across the river?" Obviously. Lynn regretted the question as soon as she asked it. Prima Park was passed on their left, a few cars still there, empty boat trailers parked by the launching ramp. Over the bridge, arching above dark water.

The artist had two large canvases to show for the day, both attractive, not quite finished but he would take care of that when he got them to his studio. They might show up at the gallery in a week or two, or he might take them to some other dealer. Lynn knew he displayed elsewhere than *Bayside*, more prestigious galleries.

Her own efforts she felt like heaving from the window of this moving vehicle. Why did she think she could still paint? Or ever paint, for that matter? She knew she would scrape the canvases clean when she got home. Then maybe she would start afresh or maybe she wouldn't paint at all. She just didn't seem to have anything to say today, could find no point to putting pigment on canvas.

"Jay Bruce lives out that way somewhere," she said, gazing across the fields to their right. Here and there, a metal roof caught the glint of the setting sun.

"Yeah? So does old Merriweather, doesn't he?"

That was so. "Karen is looking for a bigger place, a place with some acreage," said Lynn. "Maybe she should check out this area."

"Don't I remember a place upstate?" he asked.

"On the market."

"Oh. It was kind of far away. Is this—yes, we can turn here and loop back into North Tamarind." He turned left at a flashing yellow light. "I know a restaurant over here. We can stop and have a bite before heading out to the beach."

Lynn hoped it wasn't the vegetarian place Pat had taken Karen. She'd had enough of that for the day. "You have to leave early in the morning?"

"Uh-huh." They rode on in silence, as the forested and somewhat swampy terrain gave way to more houses, and roads leading back into subdivisions, the ways disappearing into the shadows of dusk. This area had not been developed nearly as long ago as Tamarind and Consonante Springs.

"Maybe I'll swing by the gallery on Saturday morning," said Matt, after a time.

While on his way to pick up his daughters, Lynn assumed. "We'll be open. Bringing anything?"

"Think not. Maybe I should save anything new for fall, huh?"

"Maybe. We could do a show for you. An opening."

"Ah, you're being ambitious again." Lynn didn't think he meant to be deprecating, despite the slightly mocking tone. It was just Matt being Matt, pretending nothing was truly serious. "Here's the place." He pulled the Savana into a well-lit but somewhat empty parking space. A neon sign flashed *Dante's Italian Cuisine* in green and orange.

Lynn looked the restaurant over and was glad she had brought some dressier clothes along. "Italian's good," she said. Something with cheese would be welcome after their vegan lunch.

"And they have wine," Matt told her.

"Even better." An actual date, at a real restaurant, in public. That was better yet. And about time.

Yet she worried that Matt was being rash. Oh, it was no worse than being seen with her on the beach at Leawood, where he was known, or having her at his house. Surely the neighbors could see what was going on. Maybe she shouldn't go there anymore, at least for a while.

But she should enjoy tonight and not worry about any of that.

Thirty-Nine

"Pat came by the gallery this morning. I almost invited him to come have lunch with us."

"I'm glad you didn't. This is our time."

Lynn nodded. "That's how I felt about it too." And she had realized it might conflict with one his classes at the Springs. "He delivered his pictures. I may hang them this afternoon or tomorrow."

"How did your painting go?" Karen picked up a menu and glanced at it, though both women probably knew it by heart.

"It was a start," was all Lynn was willing to say. Maybe an end, too. She wasn't sure. "Matt worked on a couple canvases."

"Of course he did." Karen paused. "He's a workman, disciplined when it comes to his art. I may not care for the man otherwise but I can see that."

The waitress, the Friday girl whose name Lynn could never remember, brought their usual tea. She didn't bother to ask them anymore. "Ready to order?" the woman asked.

Time to make up for that fattening feast last night. "House salad for me," said Lynn, looking up. 'Donna' it said on the woman's name tag. She should remember that.

Karen sighed rather audibly and said, "Same for me, please."

Once Donna left, Lynn leaned in and asked, "Since when did you count your calories?"

"I'm just trying to eat more healthy," Karen declared.

"Healthful," came her friend's correction. Lynn had been doing that sort of thing since both were kids.

"Yeah, whatever." That, too, was the typical response. "Pat got me thinking about it."

"He's still on to cook for you on Sunday?" An odd sort of date, she thought, but maybe the sort of thing to expect from the yoga teacher.

Karen nodded slowly; almost as slowly, a wide smile appeared. "And I think we both know what else is going to happen."

Oh. Lynn's mind had been so full of her own relationship and all that had happened yesterday, she hadn't been thinking about where Karen's might be going. "He's probably nervous as hell."

"Good! Pat needs to be shaken up a little."

Lynn thought maybe she agreed. The man was a bit too comfortable with his leisurely-paced life, a little too set in his ways. Their salads arrived and conversation lagged for a few seconds.

"I'd like to shake Matt up some too," Lynn admitted, as she squeezed lemon juice on her greens.

"Men don't like to change," said Karen.

Lynn laughed. "Does anyone? I've been stuck way too long."

Her friend did not reply but obviously agreed. "I did get Matt to actually take me out last night," Lynn continued. After a moment's consideration, she had to admit. "Well, I guess I didn't get him to do it. It was his idea."

"And a full day with you at the Springs? He might be thinking of making a decision."

It was possible. "He would still want to be careful," Lynn felt. She had not changed her mind about him being too reckless. "Matt has his daughters to consider in a divorce."

"If there is one," spoke Karen. "Oh, I shouldn't say that. But you're right, no reason to provide ammunition for his wife. For Anne—you've met her, right?"

"Yes," was the only answer she felt like giving. Anne had always been nice to her, had even invited her out to the house in Leawood on occasion. She shouldn't feel guilty; there had been nothing between her and Matt until the couple split.

But she did feel guilty and that was that. The two ate in silence for a minute or so. Lynn found herself staring out the window, once again, wondering about—what? All her thoughts seemed only half-formed, ephemeral. She should paint this weekend, she decided.

Lynn turned back to her companion. To her best friend. "I

scraped the canvases I painted yesterday completely clean," she confessed. "I realized I needed to start over."

"To starting over," said Karen, raising her dripping iced tea glass in a toast. "Always a good idea if you can pull it off."

"I did once," Lynn replied.

Forty

"ACRYLIC, ISN'T IT?" asked Matt. "One wouldn't think it on first glance."

"It is. I couldn't do this with oil. I would end up with a muddy mess." Jason Bruce stepped back from the panel and surveyed it, with an air of detachment. "I know from experience."

He's not the sort to give away too much, thought Lynn. Her eyes went to the small landscape. It was good, wasn't it? Maybe she should give acrylic paint a try.

"I like Jay's paintings very much," said Samson Ibarra, who stood a little aside from the trio. "What we did not know was that he is also very skilled with pen and ink. These we are going to show too, I am certain." He held up a framed drawing for Matt to see.

The slightest of smiles crossed Bruce's face. "Those are what always seem to get the attention. I consider them more craft than art."

"But they have won awards, I have heard."

Matt Stone gave Lynn a barely perceptible wink before stating, "Awards are only advertising, disguised."

"They can be very good advertising," countered Sam. "You have won a few yourself, Mr. Stone!"

"Yes, I am guilty of having entered competitions. But," Matt went on, "I continue to remain skeptical of them."

Jay nodded in seeming agreement but made no comment. "Hang whatever you think will sell, Samson," he said. "Hmm, I should say Lynn too, shouldn't I?" The man gave her a look, an appraising look, and a different sort of look than she had noticed from him before.

Perhaps that shouldn't be surprising. He was comfortable with her now, not trying to sell the idea of showing his artwork to her. As far as he knew, she was single—he wouldn't be aware of her relationship with Matt, of course. Nor would she tell him, not at this point. Best to just be pleasant and not encourage anything.

"Do you consider yourself an Impressionist, Jay?" she asked. "We should write up a little bio and artist's statement for you."

Was there a slight flicker of displeasure? If so, Bruce hid it quickly. "I am definitely not an Impressionist." He took a quick glance toward his own painting. "Oh, I understand why I get that sometimes."

"The broken color," offered Matt. "I can see that. But closer to the Post-Impressionists, aren't you?"

"I suppose so," admitted Jay, "though they are as much a part of the past as the Impressionists. I consider myself modern."

"Or Re-Modern?" asked Lynn. She knew that was a thing, a rejection of the so-called Post-Modern.

"Maybe," the artist said. "I'm willing to leave theory to others."

Matt chuckled softly. "I don't blame you. I get pretty sick of listening to my students babble about that sort of thing." He took another look at Bruce's painting. "Don't hang that too close to my pictures, okay? I think we would both suffer if you did."

Whether he was speaking to her, Ibarra, or both, Lynn was uncertain. But he was right. Jason Bruce's pictures might look gaudy, clumsy even, next to Matt's painterly offerings. But people's eyes would go to them.

"We must hang a couple of Mr. Janson's paintings, too," said Samson. "Over there maybe?" He nodded toward a spot near the front window. "Oh, I shall leave that up to you, Lynn. You are the artist in our partnership!"

It would be a good idea to place at least one of Pat's panels where it would be seen readily from the outside. The mandalas were sure to attract attention. Maybe Jay's work too—hmm, she would think about that and probably move things around a few times before deciding.

"His pictures are interesting," Jay said. "I'll have to meet him sometime."

Samson told him, "You should meet all the artists you can,

whether we show their work or not. You already know Tom Merri-weather, right?"

"I do. We're neighbors. Or almost neighbors." The man took off his glasses, wiping them as he continued. "We don't see each other that often. He's on the other side of Springs Road and I'm not exactly sociable anyway." He slipped the glasses back on and took another look at his painting, head cocked, before shrugging.

"I'll write something up for you if you want, Lynn. Or make up whatever you like. That's probably just as good. I'll see you all later." He nodded toward Matt. "Good to meet you," he said and was out the door.

"He's a bit of an odd one," remarked Matt.

Lynn had to laugh. "You're no one to speak!"

Samson looked from one to the other, shaking his head. "All artists are odd. You two just don't notice it because you are artists yourself. But I put up with you. All of you!"

"And we thank you for it," said Matt Stone. "I'd best be on my way too. Later." As usual, there was no acknowledgment of Lynn in his casual farewell.

Samson watched the artist cross the street to his van. "Your boyfriend should treat you better," was all he had to say.

Forty-One

"Two kinds of legumes," stated Pat. "That's what is needed. I go with lentils and black beans."

Karen peered into the bowl of burger 'meat' he had brought. "I can see some chunks. Those are the black beans?"

"That they are. I leave some texture with them but puree the lentils. I could do just lentil if need be and it tastes okay. You could do sort of a lentil hot dog that way."

Karen wrinkled her snub nose at the thought. "The pans are up there," she told him. "Take your pick."

"Okay. Any cooking oil? Olive, preferably."

"Over there. Oh, just let me be your assistant and I'll hand you what you need."

"I need one of these right now." He leaned down for a long kiss. "Yes, you can be my sous-chef anytime. Then I add some sort of grain to the bean mixture," he went on, as he divided it into chunks with a tablespoon. "Oatmeal is as good as anything else and the quick kind is okay. I wouldn't use it for much else. And then I add some bread crumbs. You could use either one, really, and skip the other. Matter of taste."

"I need another taste of you," said Karen, pulling him to her. His long hair fell around her own face. She rather liked that.

"Mmm, then a couple eggs to hold everything together and seasoning to taste," Pat finished up. "Fry it as burgers or bake it as a loaf."

"Sounds, ah, yummy." She laughed. "I guess I shouldn't be a critic till you serve me." Pat turned on the heat under a large sauté pan, after fumbling with the controls on the electric range for a few seconds. "Do you have any other vegetarian specialties?" Karen asked.

"I do pizza sometimes. Maybe with cheese, maybe without. It's good both ways." He held a hand over the skillet to check the heat, shook his head, and turned back to her.

"Oh, right, you eat dairy."

"But I have some qualms about cheese because they kill calves to make it. For the rennet, you know." Pat's voice was quite serious.

She had a vague idea about how cheese was made but hadn't really thought about it. "So being vegetarian is a moral thing for you? Not about health?"

"Totally a moral question. Meat is perfectly good nutrition."

She stepped back, hands on hips, and looked him askance. "Then you think you're better than we meat-eaters, Mr. Janson?"

"I'd never say that." He grinned. "But I might think it."

"Okay," Karen said. "As long as you never actually tell me you're my moral superior." He probably is, she told herself. She'd never met someone who was so—well, *good*.

But not perfect. Far from that. Pat was slipping his burgers into the hot oil now. "I'll get the salad," she said. There was a vague fear that her effort would not measure up to his. Shoot, she didn't even know if his burgers were edible. She should hardly be worrying.

And the wine. She should get that out too. Karen had no idea what to pair with veggie-burgers but her motto was 'when in doubt, serve Zinfandel.' A bottle was open, breathing and chilling in the fridge. Don't let the boy drink too much, she told herself. She wanted him fully functioning later on.

He did know how the evening would end, didn't he? Oh, of course he did. Pat seemed a bit of an innocent sometimes but he wasn't dense.

"Do we want buns?" she called to him. "For the burgers?"

"If you wish," was his reply. Momentarily, Karen was peeved that he didn't give her a clear yes or no. But it didn't matter, did it? She had bought some whole wheat buns specifically for this evening so she opened the package, arranged them on a serving plate. Ketchup and mustard too, she decided, and placed them on the table—the little Formica-topped table in the kitchen she always used, not the long wooden one in the dining room. No one had eaten there since her father passed.

The little-used king-size in the master bedroom also would see service tonight. Karen had made certain everything was ready there. It had looked so unreal, so unlived-in, when she had gone in to tidy it, like a display in some furniture store.

Pat was flipping the patties. They did smell pretty good. She could almost imagine they were real meat. "Ready in a couple more minutes," he announced.

"I prefer mine rare," quipped Karen.

The young man nodded amiably. "There's a fine line between mushy inside and dried out with these. I don't always get it just right." His tone was not in the least apologetic. Pat was stating a fact.

"If they're dry, we can douse 'em with ketchup," she replied.

"Not fond of ketchup, but a little mustard is nice. There is a pinch in the burgers already." Pat switched off the burner, gave the pan a couple shakes back and forth. "Horseradish is good too. I do like something with a little bite to it."

Karen added it to her mental grocery list. Her father had loved horseradish on his meat but she had not kept any in the house for some time. She looked up to see Pat grinning at her. "Maybe that's why I like you," he said.

"That is one of the oddest compliments I have ever received. I like it." It was no lie. "Are those ready?"

"They are." He began to plate the deeply-browned patties. For a moment, Pat seemed hesitant about what to do with the empty pan, but he slid it onto an unused burner and carried his veggie-burgers to the table.

"Pour the wine, will you?" Karen asked. He glugged considerably more into her goblet than she might have herself, and took a seat opposite her.

"I do usually eat these without any trimmings," Pat admitted, as he slipped one into a bun and placed a leaf of lettuce from his salad atop. "In theory, they already have a good nutritional balance without the addition of a bun." He took a bite and nodded his head in approval. "And I often have some cold ones left over for snacks."

Karen tentatively nibbled hers. Hmm, okay, but not beef. That was for sure! "These will make me fart, won't they?" she asked.

"Undoubtedly," said Pat, taking a sip of his wine and keeping a completely straight face.

But not right away, she hoped. "I should be enough dessert for you but I bought a pie anyway," Karen announced. She didn't mind revealing this. Pat had probably realized she didn't do much cooking.

He lifted his eyes, looked into hers. "Which should we get to first?"

Was there any need to consider that question? She rose and extended a hand to that shy, beautiful man. "Come on."

He glanced at the table before taking her hand and following. He was actually concerned about leaving the dirty dishes, Karen realized, and stifled a snicker. Still, a broad smile remained on her face.

It returned more than once that night.

POSTURE III

vatayanasana
the horse

Forty-Two

KAREN HAD ALWAYS measured herself, and her men, by her father. Like him, she became a successful CPA. And a driven one.

Now she had thrown herself into yoga with that same attitude. Practicing her asanas at lunch time. Doing breathing exercises at her desk. Not smoking.

Proving herself to Pat, as she had to her father. Needlessly, of course. Pat demanded nothing of anyone.

"Will you be able to take a few days off between the spring and summer classes?" she asked him.

It was too dark to read his face but she could hear the hint of hesitation in Pat's reply. "There is no reason I couldn't. I would need to arrange it right now."

"Right now?" she laughed. "Let me finish with you first!"

"What? You still aren't satisfied?" Karen felt him turn on his side, slide closer, his leg brushing hers, then pulling back. "I might manage part of this Memorial Day weekend. Monday maybe."

Of course, the holiday weekend was just what she had in mind. She hoped she hadn't brought it up too late. "Monday could work. We can talk about it later."

"Much later," he murmured. His lips became too involved with her neck, her shoulders, to add more to that. Karen felt his muscular leg again, entwining with her own. Slowly, lovingly, as ever—she did wish he were a little more, well, aggressive. But he was thoughtful and certainly knew his way around a body.

There would be lots of time for them to explore lovemaking. Time to explore many things. Other thoughts, more immediate thoughts, pushed all that from her head, and then she slept soundly, there beside Pat, her Pat, in that big bed that had gone so long unused.

He was no longer beside her when she awoke. A moment's panic—had he left her alone in the night? Deserted her, decided to break it off this way? No, no, of course not. Karen knew those thoughts were ridiculous as soon as they pushed their way into her half-asleep mind. Pat was probably going through his early morning yoga routine out in the living room.

She slipped into the bathroom. Yes, the shower was damp. Not wet; this man was the sort who would wipe the stall down after using it, clean up after himself. Better at it than she was, that was for sure. A quick shower. Briefly she wished Pat would think to join her.

Too late for that, though. She would have needed to rise when he did. Maybe she would do the joining, next time he slept in her house. A whole week? It seemed too long. It wouldn't be right to ask him to move in, no, not yet. It wouldn't be right to put Pat on the spot like that. Karen wasn't sure she wanted it herself.

Maybe after class tonight, or on Wednesday. Oh, any weeknight, really. It was only a few mornings he needed to be at the spa early. A thought brought a smile, as she toweled off. She could even spend a night in his trailer, couldn't she? There was no reason for them always to be here in her house. Maybe he would feel more comfortable.

She was worrying about things when she needn't. She and Pat

had just begun. There was plenty of time to work things out. Plenty of time.

Right now, she wondered what that beautiful man was going to fix her for breakfast.

Forty-Three

"THINGS WILL CHANGE after this week," Lynn pointed out. "Our last class is on Wednesday."

"Yeah." Karen toyed with her half-eaten salad. No reason to say that, her friend realized. Karen knew.

But she went on anyway. "Almost three weeks till it starts up again at the rec center. Pat should be able to find some time off."

Karen gave her a weak smile. "The thing is to find time at the same time." She shoveled some more lettuce in and chewed dutifully for a few seconds before asking, "How about you? We ought to spend some time together."

Matt would have time off too, wouldn't he? thought Lynn. The end of the semester. "I should be able to work something out," she replied. "This coming weekend, then?"

"Uh-huh. It seems like everyone has something to do over the holiday." Karen laughed. "Everyone but me!"

"The beaches will be full of weekenders," Lynn observed. "And the roads. It might not be a bad time to get away."

"You'll see Matt?"

Lynn hesitated. "Don't know. He's busy all this week with the end of the term." And surely would wish to spend at least some of Memorial Day weekend with his family. "At least you'll know where Pat is."

"He may not have to hang around the Springs all weekend. He thinks maybe we will be able to get away." She looked down at her near-empty plate and shoved it aside. "And my real estate agent is going to do an open house on Sunday so I need to be out of the place."

A nod. Lynn knew her friend had listed the house and was not surprised that she was being serious about it. "Are you going to look for a new place out by the beach? Like where we saw the horses?"

"The other direction, I think," said Karen. "Beyond the Springs, maybe. I could get a bigger place for less. Better land, too."

"You could build," Lynn said.

"I've been thinking about it," admitted Karen. "Why don't you come with me and help me look sometime? We can just drive around all day."

"You mean you can drive and I can ride." Not that Lynn minded. "Sure, why not?"

"Good." Karen idly looked at her check, and rose. "I'd best get back. Do try to see if you can take some time off."

Lynn was sure she could work something out with Samson, two or three days off. It wouldn't matter much at this time of year. Oh, they would close Sunday and Monday for this holiday weekend anyway. Perhaps she could extend that. "I will," she promised. "See you at class." The two parted in front of *The Compass Rose*.

Lynn found herself hurrying back to work, though there was no reason. She tended to walk faster when something was on her mind. Should she invite Matt to come along if she took her little vacation? Karen more or less expected him to be a part of the package, Lynn knew. Didn't like it, but expected it.

She said nothing to her soon-to-be partner that afternoon. Sammy departed early, anyway, leaving her to close up. Talk to Matt first, she told herself. And Karen would need to work things out with Pat. It all revolved around the yoga instructor's schedule.

Not that she and Matt couldn't go off on their own. Lynn had a standing invitation to use the farm whenever she wished. She had a key.

As she did to Karen's house. As she did even to Samson Ibarra's house. Why had she and Matt never exchanged keys?

"Memorial Day weekend is on," Karen whispered, as she rolled out her mat beside Lynn's that evening. "Pat already went ahead and arranged his schedule. We're going to drive up on Sunday afternoon."

Lynn slowly nodded. "I'll see what I can work out," she promised.

Forty-Four

"YOU COULD INVITE your new artist to come and paint with us," said Matt.

Was he joking? It was hard to be sure. Maybe the man wasn't sure himself whether he was serious. "Jay's not a *plein air* painter. Works only in the studio." So he had told her when she tried to squeeze some background information out of the artist.

"Okay. But you and I can certainly get away this weekend. I'll be all wrapped up at school and—" Matt seemed reluctant to finish. "And Anne is taking the girls to spend the holiday with her parents."

Oh. A whole weekend of Matt, if she wanted. If he wanted. "I'll be here on Saturday, of course," Lynn said. "But the rest of the weekend is free."

"Great. Then we can take off as soon as you close up on Saturday. We'll talk about it later. I need to head to Sarasota." The artist glanced at his watch. "And out of here before Sammy shows up." He leaned down for a quick kiss. "Looking forward to getting away."

With that, he was headed out the door. A minute later, Matt's van was headed east up Bay Street. For only a moment, Lynn wondered whether he took Forty-One or the interstate north. She had never ridden to Sarasota with him.

Oh, he probably didn't go this way at all, most of the time. It would be easier to go north from his home in Leawood, along the beach and over to the highway somewhere further up. There was a high bridge across the bay up there.

So this coming weekend, the Memorial Day weekend, had fallen into place all by itself. They would go off together to Karen's farm, she and Matt on Saturday afternoon, Karen and Pat the next day. She would paint. Yes. And go out on the lake. Karen said there was a canoe.

It might be her last chance to see the place, to recall the times she had spent there as a teen, visiting with Karen and her father. So long ago! Why hadn't she taken time this past decade?

The back door. That would be Samson. No, voices—who was with him? A moment later, Ibarra came up front, Jay Bruce at his side. The artist was in his work clothes, jeans, tee, a ragged green cap on his head. John Deere, maybe.

"You have not heard, my dear," began Samson, his voice soft but deliberate. "Tom Merriweather passed last night."

Jay remained silent, stone-faced. "A stroke," continued Sammy. "He was rushed to the hospital but it was too late."

"Bayfront," added Bruce. Perhaps recognizing that was unimportant, he said no more.

"Jay stopped out back to tell me," Samson went on, and turned to his companion. "I thank you for taking the time."

"Thought you should know," the man mumbled. "I'd better get to my next job." He nodded in Lynn's direction and, after an awkward moment's hesitation, hurried out the back.

"I don't think Mr. Bruce handles that sort of thing well," said Samson. "He's not used to dealing with it."

"I suppose not," agreed Lynn. The man was a bit of a hermit, she had come to realize. But he must speak with his neighbors or he wouldn't have heard the news about Merriweather. Her eyes went to Tom's paintings, hanging in a group on the east wall.

Samson followed her line of sight. "We must ask his next of kin about those. Best to take them down now."

Contractually, they could leave them up, sell them, Lynn was pretty sure. Still, better to contact the family. Maybe a retrospective show—why was she thinking of something like that already? It seemed callous.

It was also entirely likely similar thoughts were going through Ibarra's mind. Never mind that now. "I'll get onto it," she said. It didn't look like a very busy day. "I can hold things down here if you want to, um, see the family or anything."

"They are surely far too busy for me to intrude this morning.

Maybe tomorrow. But—" He gave her a little smile, his dark mustache tilting up ever so slightly. "I think maybe I would like to go say a prayer for them. And for Tom."

"By all means, Sammy," she said. Lynn wished she could too, but was not quite sure how.

"Yes. I shall pray. And think." Ibarra gave the showroom a quick looking over, nodded, and slowly walked into the back.

Was Sammy feeling his own mortality this morning? wondered Lynn. For a moment, she wished Matt had stayed a few minutes longer. He had liked old Merriweather. She thought he did. It was hard to be sure with Matt.

All the paintings were down and neatly shelved by the time she went to lunch.

Forty-Five

"I WANT TO thank all of you who stuck with this class," said Pat, after the usual opening complete breath. He lowered himself to his mat, taking a half-lotus position. His students plopped down less gracefully.

"Most of you know we shall start up again in a couple weeks, in the afternoons." He gave Jen Carter, standing half inside the kitchen door, a sidelong glance. "June Thirteen, right?"

The recreation director nodded. "Closer to three weeks, Pat."

"Ah, time is but an illusion," he replied, completely failing to keep a straight face. "But try to show up at Three anyway. Let's review some of what we learned."

The familiar faces were there, Lynn noted. There had been some dropouts at the midterm, winter residents who had headed back north. The rest had stayed with it, even Maddie.

The sergeants, too. They had taken their accustomed spot behind Karen and her. Of course, Roger had motivation to come. She suspected that Joe would tag along with his buddy, whether he actually cared about attending class or not.

Lynn still hadn't completely made up her mind about those afternoon classes. She could swing them, yes. That would be no real problem during the slow months of summer. Or she could attend some of Pat's sessions out at the Springs or just put yoga class on hold till fall. Lynn found that she didn't seem to care that much one way or another.

Maybe she would just do whatever Karen chose. Ha, she was being a Joe to her friend's Roger. And like Roger, Karen had a motivation to stay with the class. The fifty minutes passed quickly; Pat murmured a good bye and an enjoy your weekend to his students, and ducked into the kitchen. That was unusual. Typically he would sit while they filtered out of the room and into the night.

"Seeing Pat tonight?" she asked Karen as they rolled up their mats.

"Nah." The woman shook her head. "He has things to tend to. See you tomorrow." With that, Karen was headed to the door.

Roger's subterranean chuckle turned her head in his direction. "You don't know about our instructor giving rides, I would take it."

"I must have looked puzzled," she admitted. Rides?

"To Miss Maddie," said Joe. "He's been doing it for a couple weeks."

"Oh." Karen probably didn't like that. Not that she'd be jealous. Not in the normal sense—but she wouldn't want someone else taking up Pat's time.

"Jen told me all about it," Roger went on. "The girl's, um, boyfriend refused to bring her anymore. I guess she doesn't drive or have a car or something." He shrugged his broad shoulders. "So our instructor offered to give her a ride to class. She lives out close to that Springs place where he works."

Lynn wondered for a moment how Maddie Fry got to work. Or where she worked. "That seems in character for Pat," she said.

"I hope it doesn't get him in any trouble," muttered Joe. "Ready to go, Rog?"

The big man's eyes flickered to the kitchen door and back to his friend. "In a moment."

"Well go bother her. Don't stand here," advised Joe. Roger nodded and headed away. "Jen is going to be way too busy to spend time with him this weekend," said Joe. "I'll have to entertain him somehow." He chuckled at that. "How 'bout you? Any holiday plans?"

"Going out of town. Karen has a country place upstate." She hesitated a moment, unsure of saying more about it. Oh, why not? "Pat is going too." She would not mention Matt, of course.

"And she didn't invite us? You need to talk to that friend of yours!"

Lynn only laughed. She did kind of wish the sergeants could have been invited along. It might lighten things up. As it was, she had unspoken, barely acknowledged reservations about a weekend with just the two couples.

"I'll tell her to do that next time," she promised.

Forty-Six

"Too many folks had plans for this weekend," the slight young woman said, shaking her head. Deloris Merriweather clearly disapproved. "So the funeral will be Tuesday, when everyone is back."

"I shall certainly be there," promised Ibarra. "The morning?"

Deloris nodded. "Service begins at Nine. Then—then out to the cemetery." She stifled what might have been a sob. "Grandpa's last journey. I won't be givin' him no more rides."

This was not the time to say anything about Tom's paintings, thought Lynn. Sammy apparently felt the same way.

"Do you know where this church is?" she asked Samson once Miss Merriweather had slipped out the back door. She was used to bringing her grandfather there; maybe she hadn't even thought of coming in the front.

He nodded somewhat absently. "The AME out just past the river. We can open a little late, if you want to come." Samson sighed. "Bring Stone, too." Another acknowledgment that he knew they were involved. Lynn no longer actively concealed that fact though she never said anything to Ibarra about it.

"He'll be picking you up soon," he continued. A statement of fact or a question? "I might as well get out of here, my dear. Enjoy your weekend."

It was near closing time anyway. Lynn heard the rumble of Samson's Chevrolet as he started up, drove away. She should get her bag and easel out of her car, be ready to go when Matt pulled up. She didn't want to waste any time. Get on the road, on the way, make the most of this weekend.

He pulled his van in behind the car as she was unloading, leaving it in the middle of the way rather than turning into a parking space. Had Matt been waiting for Ibarra to leave? Still being cautious about their relationship? Whatever that relationship was.

Maybe this weekend would help her sort that out. Help them sort it out. It took two, after all. Sometimes it felt more like one and a half to her, with Matt not being completely there. He slid his side door open without speaking and she stowed her kit inside, also without a word. He had come into the alley from the improper direction, from the north, so the door opened toward her and her car.

"Let me lock up," she murmured. Did she even say it loud enough that he heard her? A quick look around. Closed sign in place up front so she knew she had locked up there. Lights out. She latched the door and then the deadbolt behind her. "Ready."

Ready. She'd been ready a long time. "You'll have to navigate," spoke Matt as she settled into the front seat. "I've only a vague idea where this place is."

"You could just get to the interstate and turn north," she replied. "And I'd let you know when to get off."

"That sounds boring."

"Yeah. And probably not the quickest way. You have a map?" She searched the glove compartment for a moment.

"Here." He handed a neatly folded official Florida road map to her. Must have had it in the pocket on the door.

"Mmm. Yeah, go ahead and turn north on the interstate," she decided. "Then we can take Seventy-Two out toward Arcadia."

"Past the Myakka park. Okay." They were following the curve of Springs Road now, heading out of town. "We should be able to miss the worst of rush hour that way. What rush hour traffic there is on a holiday weekend."

"That was the idea," she said. "It's gonna be dark when we get there."

Matt only nodded. He knew that. "Radio?" she asked.

"Okay. Change the station if you want." Lynn had expected him to turn it on but when he kept driving she leaned forward and turned the knob herself. Classical music, as usual. That was probably as good as anything. They turned onto the cutoff before the spa and river, rolling eastward between empty fields, Mozart and then Delibes providing the soundtrack. She didn't care much for Delibes but didn't switch stations. Something else would follow and something after that, as Matt drove on into the Florida afternoon and evening.

A warm afternoon. It was beginning to feel like summer. They might want to run the air conditioning at the farm. "Lots of traffic already," observed Matt as they crossed a busy Forty-One.

Maybe all those people in all those cars were heading somewhere for the weekend too. Everyone wanted to get away from their lives. The beaches would be crowded on both coasts. Disney undoubtedly did big business over Memorial Day. She had never been to the park and had no desire to change that.

The interstate overpass could be seen at a distance. Under it and onto the northbound ramp. Matt was a rather cautious driver, carefully slipping into the stream of traffic, traveling at more-or-less the speed limit, willing to let others hurry past to wherever they felt they needed to be.

There was little to talk about. Lynn might have fallen asleep for a while.

Forty-Seven

KAREN COULD SEE tire tracks on the drive, no more than soft inden-
tations in the dry off-white sand. One could get stuck if not careful.
"And here we are," she announced, as the house loomed before
them and, beyond it, the lake glittering in the afternoon sun.

"Always," replied Pat. She glanced at him from the corner of her
eye. Yes, he wore a crooked grin; Karen was never certain how
serious he was when he said something like that. She still wasn't,
quite.

No matter. Pat was Pat and that was that. She told herself this
from time to time. Her own little meditation mantra.

They had made good time. There would be hours of light yet.
She pulled in beside Matt's van. It seemed strange to have him
here. Oh, it was even a little strange to have Pat come. She wished
for a second or two that only she and Lynn had come.

A look at the man who sat beside her. Maybe it felt a little odd,
a tad jarring, to have him at a place that was so much a part of her
past, a place that felt, well, private. More private than her own
home. But Karen was glad to have him there anyway. "Let's get our
stuff into the house," she said, popping the trunk.

Where were the others? Didn't they see them drive up? Hmm,
all the windows stood open.

And the front door was not locked. Pat followed her in, a bag
cradled in each arm. "Someone is down by the water," he
observed, nodding toward the open French doors, with their view
of the lake beyond. He placed his burdens on the dining table. "I'll
go get the rest of it."

Karen felt only slightly guilty letting him unload the car while
she went out the back. Oh, they had their easels set up. She should
have expected that. The pines cast long shadows across the grass,
across the gentle slope down to the lakeside. Everything looked
more alive than on her last visit, greener, lusher. Lynn spotted her
and waved.

Matt seemed engrossed in his canvas and did not look away from it. Maybe best not to go down and bother them right now. Karen waved in reply and turned back to the house. Her boyfriend had brought everything in, had it stacked on and around the table, and was busy transferring food from the cooler to the refrigerator.

She gave the scene a quick looking-over and announced, "I'm going to get a shower." There should be a towel and fresh clothes in her overnight bag. Yes, there they were. "A quick one," she added, knowing that was enough hint to keep Pat from intruding. Maybe she wanted him to, some, but that sort of thing could wait. "I'll make sure to leave enough hot water for you," Karen called over her shoulder as she disappeared into the bathroom.

What a mess, was her first thought. Sand on the floor, water on the floor. Wet towels in the bottom of the shower stall. It smelled some, too. The small high window above the shower was open; that should help. Karen did not feel like doing anything more right then.

But the place would definitely need some cleaning up before they left, if only because the real estate agent might show it. Had he brought anyone by? He certainly hadn't reported much activity. The hot water beat on her skin, washing those sorts of thoughts away, along with much of the weariness she had worn on arriving. She felt ready to get out and enjoy herself now.

Karen swished the remaining water about with her narrow feet, sending some of the accumulated sand toward the drain. Might as well use those towels Lynn and Matt had left lying to wipe the floor up a bit too. They weren't her towels, were they? No, the couple must have brought them. She would hang them up, out on the porch, anyway. Karen gathered them up, to discover there were swimsuits wrapped inside. Had they been in the lake?

"All yours," she said to Pat. He was already taking possession of their bedroom, laying out his clothes on the rather faded bedspread, a pattern of green leaves vining across a soft yellow field. This had always been her room here, and Lynn's when she

153

came along. She and Matt had apparently taken her father's bedroom. Maybe Lynn recognized that Karen would have preferred that arrangement. "I'm heading down to the lake."

"Be with you in a couple minutes," promised Pat, closing the bathroom door behind him. Karen headed toward the rear doors, holding the wet laundry well away from herself, hurrying so it did not drip too much on her floors. She draped it, none too carefully, over a couple lawn chairs and stopped to survey the yard, the lake, the day.

The canoe was still under its cover. Karen had expected her guests to get it into the water by now. They had been here since last night, after all. She reached for the pack of cigarettes in her waist pack. Not there of course; she had given them up. Just habit. Maybe this place made her feel like falling back into old ways. Memories came of sitting on the dock, smoking, a cane pole in her hand.

Without the cigarettes, she probably couldn't have sat still long enough to fish. God knew it was hard to get through a day at her desk without them!

Matt looked up as she approached, and then toward the sun sinking behind her. "We're losing the light," he stated. "I think I will finish this one in the studio." Karen thought the image on his canvas, a painting of the dock and shoreline, already looked finished. But what did she know?

"I should be enough sunshine for you," she told them. "Having a good time?"

"Great," replied Lynn. "Even better now that you're here." She did sound enthusiastic. Perhaps some of that would rub off on her.

"It is a nice place," Matt added, methodically putting away his paints. "Thanks for having us."

"Anytime," Karen answered. But there would not be an anytime, another time. This place would sell and their lives would go on, played out on other stages. She must have stood there, thinking about that, for a little too long, for she suddenly noticed her friend looking at her, head cocked a tad to one side.

"There is wine in the fridge," said Lynn. "I believe it should be our next order of business."

Karen could only nod agreement.

Forty-Eight

"WE ATE FAST food last night," said Lynn. "This was much better." She leaned in, near-whispered, "Our boyfriends are definitely better cooks than we."

Those boyfriends were finishing up in the kitchen, clearing, cleaning, while the women sat on the dark rear deck, doing their own finishing up of a second bottle of Merlot.

Karen gave only a noncommittal 'hmm' to this. She doesn't feel like talking, does she? thought Lynn. They both sipped wine in silence. Singer Lake could barely be made out, a shimmer beyond the hidden shore. Choruses of crickets and frogs vied in the darkness, and a barred owl called somewhere out across the water.

Were the guys going to come out? Matt had definitely drank too much wine. Oh, they all had, except Pat. Lynn much doubted he ever did anything to excess. But Matt, she knew, could get a little obnoxious when he drank. That is, he would speak his mind.

There they were. Pat settled into the chair beside Karen but Matt chose to sit at the top of the steps, at their feet, gazing out into the dark. "I could stay here all week," he admitted. "I have absolutely nothing I need to do back home."

"I don't really have to get back right away but I do want to make it to Tom Merriweather's funeral on Tuesday morning." Lynn hesitated just a second before continuing. "You could come too."

He nodded, slowly. "Maybe I should."

"I decided not to be in my office till Wednesday," chimed in Karen, "and Pat arranged to take time off through Tuesday. We'll drive back then."

Lynn peered at the yoga instructor, holding Karen's hand, his long hair golden in the light filtering out through the French doors. He would have accommodated Karen, whatever she suggested. She was pretty sure of that.

Karen regarded Matt for a time, as if considering some question. "Matt, if you wanted to stay and paint, Lynn could ride home with us, if she was willing to wait a day. I wouldn't mind you hanging around a while." She stifled a snicker, not too successfully. "Just clean up after yourself."

The man only nodded. Maybe he was thinking about it. Lynn wished her friend hadn't made the offer, hadn't put the idea in Stone's head. Not that it made any difference, really.

She chose to change the subject. "We must take the canoe out tomorrow."

"It's not big enough for us all," observed Pat.

"Three, at most," Karen agreed.

Matt turned and looked up them. "I'd just as soon sit on the dock and fish."

"You brought a rod?" she asked.

"No, but I noticed a barrel full of cane poles in front of that little store up the road. I could drive up in the morning and buy us some."

Karen obviously liked the idea. "I don't think either of these two fish," she told Matt. "Do they have worms?"

"I'd bet on it," he said.

"I guess that puts you and me in the canoe," Lynn told Pat. She hoped he wanted to come. Not that she would mind going out alone. Lynn had always liked sailing by herself.

Pat nodded an amiable agreement to her. He looked half-asleep.

"Any of the red left?" asked Matt.

Lynn dribbled some into a plastic cup and handed it down to him. She sloshed the contents of the bottle back and forth, saying, "Enough for one more refill, maybe. Karen?" Her friend shook her head. So did Pat when she looked his direction. She shrugged and filled her own glass.

"Here's to something or another!" she said, raising it.

"I'll always drink to that," said Matt, lifting his own cup.

Karen giggled and did the same. "To something." She drained her glass and turned to Pat. "Ready to turn in? I'm really tired."

He nodded and rose. Matt and Lynn watched the two disappear

into the house. "I suspect they're too bushed to do anything but go straight to sleep."

Matt laughed. "And we're too drunk!"

Lynn looked toward the lake. "Let's take a walk and get some of the wine out of our system." She gave him a wink. "Then you won't have any excuses later." Maybe she spoke her mind a little too directly when she drank, also.

As it turned out, they walked only as far as the little floating dock. A dim light winked on and off across the lake. A boat? wondered Lynn. Or was it one of the other houses that lined the shores? Matt put his arm around her.

A moment later, they were both reclining and entangled. "An alligator might crawl up and join us," laughed Lynn when her lips were momentarily free.

"Boy or girl?" asked Matt. "Or bull, I should say. Not sure what the girl gators are called. Cows? That doesn't seem quite right."

The dock gently rocked back and forth beneath them. "This is almost like a water bed," observed Lynn. Suddenly, she felt queasy, rolled away, sat up. "I need solid ground."

Matt probably couldn't see her face. He was not much more than a shadow to her. She heard him slap at something.

"Mosquito?"

"Yeah. We'd best not get naked out here, huh?"

"Not unless we were in the water."

"That would really be inviting the alligators to join in."

"The moccasins too! I wouldn't want to mistake a snake for, um, something else."

"You definitely had too much wine," decided Matt.

Lynn giggled and stood up. A wave of nausea hit her and she doubled over, emptying her stomach into the water.

"Well," said Matt, "there's not as much of it in you now. Let's get you inside."

Forty-Nine

"MY GRANDMOTHER WORKED at the Springs as a maid, way back in the Sixties. She said she met my mom's father there but never told anyone who he was."

Lynn continued to rhythmically dip her paddle, a few strokes on the left, a few on the right. Pat could tend to steering them.

"Mrs. Kuenst took an interest in her and my mom, and kept in touch with them," he continued. "I've never been certain why. Maybe she felt responsible or maybe she just liked Grandma."

"She stays there at the Springs in the winter, right?"

"Uh-huh. Usually comes for two or three weeks sometime in the summer too. The off-season." He concentrated on stroking for a few seconds, steering them around a clump of reeds. "She says it's too busy in winter."

"There's the stream," said Lynn, pointing with her paddle. "Want to go down it a little way?" It would be the only opportunity she ever had to explore. Probably.

"Will we be able to turn around? It looks narrow."

Lynn had to laugh. "It's a canoe, Pat. We can just turn ourselves around and paddle the other direction."

"Oh." A pause, silence. Had she embarrassed him? Pat broke into laughter of his own, louder than hers. "I guess that is obvious, isn't it? Let's go on in."

Tea-tinged water moved sluggishly through the opening in the cat-tails. The calls of birds echoed all around. Red-wings? That would be Lynn's guess.

"This flows all the way down to Lake Okeechobee," she told her companion.

"Via the Kissimmee. That's more like a canal than a river down there."

"Yeah, let's not go that far!" Pat must know something of the area down there. She looked at the wall of rushes on either side of the creek. "In fact, I'd just as soon turn around right now. This doesn't look very interesting." Another adventure proving to be a dud. It happened.

As it was, the stream had widened enough that they could reverse the canoe. A few minutes later, they were back on the open waters of Singer Lake. "Want to go all the way around?" asked Pat.

Lynn looked to the far shore and shook her head. "Too long a paddle. And it's getting hot." The mid-morning sun shimmered on the calm lake surface, half-blinding her. "Let's cut straight across instead of following the shore."

She had felt a little unsure about taking the canoe very far out into the lake when they launched. That timidity had disappeared. She must get herself a boat to use on the bay. Preferably with a sail.

As they approached the dock, Lynn tried to make out their friends through the glare on the water. "I don't see them. Maybe they went inside."

"Swimming," was all Pat said, pointing toward two heads bobbing in the lake. There was something in his voice. Disapproval?

"Oh. Matt and I went in a little while yesterday."

"A good way to pick up a parasite or worse." She had never heard Pat speak quite so seriously or so emphatically about anything, had she?

She turned toward him, asking, "Do you really think it is dangerous?"

He shrugged. "Probably not, but I wouldn't go in."

Lynn did feel like jumping into the cool water, at least for a few minutes. All too soon, they would need to think about starting home. She threw off her life vest as soon as the canoe was grounded, ran onto the dock, dove off fully clothed.

She stroked over to the swimming pair. "Catch anything?"

"We pulled in some little sunfish but tossed them back," reported Matt. "Neither of us wanted to fool with cleaning them."

Karen was gazing toward the shore, where Pat busied himself with the canoe. "Is Pat coming in?"

"He thinks we'll all get amoebas in our brains and die, I believe. Then no one could drive him home."

"He'd better worry instead that we'll all drink too much wine again," said Matt, half-floating, half-treading water. Lynn knew Karen couldn't float at all, especially in fresh water. Too little buoyancy to that skinny frame of hers! Lynn rather wished she didn't float quite so well herself.

"We should go in and get some lunch soon," spoke Karen. "We need to get you two on the road." Her eyes went to the shore. "Leave the canoe," she called to Pat. "We might use it tomorrow." She turned her attention back to her companions. "Pat's so damn conscientious he might have washed it and put it back in storage." Lynn could note just a touch of frustration in her friend's voice.

"That boy is too earnest," opined Matt. "Too serious about everything. I'm not sure he actually knows how to have fun."

"I'm not sure you are serious about anything, Mr. Stone," said Karen.

"Neither am I," he replied. "Neither am I."

Fifty

"A GLASS OF wine is like sex," claimed Matt, holding up his cup. "In moderation, enjoyable and good for us."

Karen snickered. "It's possible to have too much sex?"

"It's possible to have too much of anything," replied the artist. "We need to leave room for the rest of life."

He's speaking from experience, thought Lynn. Matt had let his own self-indulgence get in the way of living at times.

Pat observed, "One man's moderation might be another's excess." He seemed a bit hesitant about adding his thoughts, his eyes flicking to his girlfriend and away.

The girlfriend laughed. "You're sounding guru-ish again," said Karen.

"Just like in class," agreed Lynn. Pat blushed and took another sip of his wine, rather than saying more.

"You're more comfortable doing it there, aren't you?" asked Karen, turning to regard the man. "You don't usually spout wisdom when it's up close and personal."

"I suppose so," was all Pat was willing to admit.

Lynn considered this. He plays a role when he's teaching, she realized, being someone else, someone less self-conscious. Not unlike what she did when customers came into *Bayside*. She had enough sense not to say this aloud. "I guess we all agree that wine and sex are both good things," she did say. "Not necessarily in combination." She might already have had a little too much wine or she wouldn't have spouted that.

But Matt was driving them home so it didn't matter. He *was* being moderate. They wouldn't leave for a couple hours yet, anyway. Back to Tamarind, back to whatever it was they had there. Here, it was easy to just see Matt as her lover, her man, and nothing else.

"I think we deserve a little of each," agreed Karen.

Matt practically snorted. "The idea that anyone deserves anything is rather absurd," he proclaimed. "We get what we get."

"Don't get so serious," scolded Lynn. Nor so contentious. No one here wanted to debate him.

"Yes, relax," said Karen, and giggled. "You deserve it."

Matt laughed easily. "Maybe I do!" He gazed out toward the lake, blue beneath a clear noon sky. "For a little longer."

"He's hooked on the place," Lynn told her friend. "You'll have to turn it into a resort after all."

"It would be great for yoga classes too," remarked Pat.

"So, a combination fishing camp, artists colony, and spiritual retreat?" asked Karen. "If it doesn't sell, maybe I'll have to consider it!"

"I can see it," spoke Matt. "Pat can give yoga classes three days a week and I'll take over and teach painting on three others." He winked at Lynn. "You and Karen would have to pose for the live drawing class."

"Is that why you've been eyeing me, sir?" asked Karen. "Just artistic interest?"

"Oh yes, entirely aesthetic." He did not seem overly serious about it.

Pat chortled, not even attempting to hide his skepticism.

"I don't think your boyfriend believes me."

Karen took Pat's hand. "He knows how sexy I am."

Matt suddenly did seem quite serious. "And I would not disagree."

Lynn gave him a sidelong look. "You see Karen sexually? Think carefully before answering, Matthew Stone!"

"I see everyone sexually. It's part of who we are." He shrugged, perhaps a little too dramatically. "No point in denying it."

"That is a valid point," admitted Pat.

Karen looked from one man to the other "Hmmph. Well, don't expect me to pose for you anytime, clothed or not."

"I haven't painted the figure in a long time, not seriously," responded Matt. "Your new artist dabbles, Lynn."

"Jay?" Why would Matt know that and not her? "I would expect to see him tomorrow morning." She paused a moment, unsure. "I'm glad you decided to come."

"It seemed like the right thing." He gave her a crooked smile. "I should try to do the right thing more often."

Fifty-One

"I WOULD LIKE to make a start on carrying things home from here," decided Karen.

Pat looked around. "The furniture?"

"No, that goes with the place. But all the linens, the kitchen items, that sort of thing." She went down a mental check list. "Maybe the canoe."

"You'll need a truck."

"Yeah." That was true. It was also true that there was no point in worrying about any of it until the farm sold.

Part of her would not like to say goodbye to the place. If her house back in Tamarind sold, there would not even be any hurry about it, but she needed the money from one property or the other. Then she could set her sights on a new home, one of her own choosing, one that offered what she wanted. What she needed.

She would rather take Lynn house-hunting than Pat. He would be too agreeable to anything she liked. Karen would have to ask her friend again to ride along with her while she explored.

Would Pat be a presence in that new home? She shouldn't ask herself that sort of thing. It was enough to have him here, now. And preparing their supper, too.

She didn't even mind that it was vegetarian. Karen went to the French doors, gazed out into the darkness. A mosquito buzzed somewhere near her left ear. "I'm going to shut these," she announced. "Too many bugs out there."

Pat had his own announcement. "That's enough time for the pasta." Nothing more, but Karen watched him drain the *farfalle*, toss it with the veggies and shrimp he had been stir-frying. He filled two plates to bring to the little dining table. "Cheese?" She nodded. Pat didn't use any on his serving.

"Good," she said, after a couple mouthfuls. It was the truth. "I'm glad you came, Pat."

"Me too," he replied, his voice as even as usual. Karen recalled Matt's words about Pat not knowing how to have fun. Even making love, he never let himself be completely out of control. Had he truly enjoyed the weekend? She couldn't help feeling he would have been just as willing to do something else.

But he did choose to be with her. After she had initiated things, admittedly.

"I think I like Matt a little better after this weekend," she said.

Pat gazed at her for a moment, over a spoonful of pasta. "I think I like him less." He carefully chewed and swallowed before continuing. "Maybe for the same reason."

Karen cocked her head at him. "And what might that be?"

"We got to know him better."

She needed only think about that for a few seconds before laughing. "You might be right. That doesn't mean either of us actually likes him."

"Probably so," Pat agreed.

Later, they slipped into bed, Karen's bed. It seemed so small compared to the king-sized one at home but that just meant Pat was closer, didn't it? Night breezes sifted in through the open windows; fireflies flickered out among the pines and the ceiling fan slowly turned overhead, another barely audible sound in the dark.

It was a world apart from the one in which she lived her everyday life. She and Pat and their love and nothing else. Was that enough? Could it be enough? For a while, such questions disappeared into the night.

Later, lying beside her lover in the dark, she whispered, "Pat, do you think you'll ever have a normal job?"

She could see his head turn toward her, regarding her form in the darkness for a moment, before he answered, in turn, "Do you think I should?"

"I don't know. It just seems like you could do more with your life."

Pat let out a long slow breath. She knew by now that it was an exercise to calm the nerves. "Karen, you know I would do anything you wanted."

She knew it all too well.

"But this is who I am. Don't ask me to be someone else."

"I won't Pat. Never." She lay her head on his chest. "I'm happy with who you are."

Fifty-Two

SEPARATE VEHICLES. IT seemed silly that Matt still worried about that, but he had brought her by the gallery, after spending the night in her apartment, so she could drive her own car out to the funeral.

She followed his van east on Springs Road now. Lynn didn't need to do that; she knew where the church was. Across the river and—there, to the right, and back a little on a lime-rock road. The clapboard church appeared freshly-painted, shining white in the morning sunlight.

Lynn allowed Matt to go inside before exiting her own car. Samson's Impala was parked near the double front doors. Those were a deep red, almost a burnt sienna, with a frosted glass arc above them. The side windows, too, held frosted glass of an amber cast. They were simple and tall, with arched tops. She felt nervous. How long had it been since she entered a church? This one was filled with strangers.

No, that wasn't so. Tom's granddaughter would be there, Deloris Merriweather. Dee, he had called her. And Matt and Sam, of course, and probably Jay Bruce. A slender middle-aged man in a dark suit pulled the heavy door open for her, murmured, "Thanks for coming, ma'am." She spotted Sammy up front and decided to sit with him. Matt had taken a place on the other side, near the rear.

Oh, there was Maddie Fry. That shouldn't be surprising. Lots of people attended this church. A stout older woman sat beside her, in a purple suit and matching hat. Lynn slipped in next to Ibarra.

An usher was cranking the windows open to let in the air, using a pole with a loop on its end to turn high-set handles. Some squeaked, some didn't, as they slowly swung outward. She turned her attention back to the coffin that rested just beyond the first pews, atop a low riser extending around—what did they call that area, the sanctuary? Maybe not. As she expected, the coffin was closed.

Samson only nodded a greeting to her. A moment later, Jason Bruce sat down across the aisle from them. Lynn inwardly smiled at the thought that all the white folks weren't clumping together and then admonished herself for that thought. We're here for Tom, she reminded herself.

Birds were calling outside the windows. Wrens. Those she could recognize. And that descending whistle came from a cardinal. It was a good sort of music to have wafting in on this day.

They were three rows back, behind the reserved pews. Now an usher removed the tasseled ropes from those, and they began to fill up. Tom's family, she assumed. Yes, there was Deloris. It would be a good guess that the older man and woman she sat down beside were her parents. Tom Merriweather's son. She could imagine a family resemblance, whether it was there or not. Some of the others must be Tom's children and grandchildren, too. She had no idea how many he might have had, nor whether there were brothers, sisters, living in the area.

Lynn knew very little about Tom, truly. Samson would be more knowledgeable.

The pastor said some words. She didn't know his name. A eulogy. A hymn, 'Amazing Grace,' without accompaniment. She could remember enough of the words to join in here and there. Then she realized the funeral was over, and the pallbearers were carrying Tom to his resting place. Lynn and Samson fell in behind those who followed it out.

"I shall go on to the burial," Ibarra whispered to her as they stepped into the sunlight. "The cemetery is a couple miles further out this road."

Lynn nodded. Best she get back to town and open the gallery. Sammy probably expected she would. "I'll see you later," she whispered back, and headed for her little Ford as soon as the hearse pulled out, leading its procession.

Jay wasn't part of it. She could see his truck was loaded for work, his lawn mower on a trailer behind. The man was probably behind schedule already, especially with a holiday weekend to make up for. His clients wouldn't have wanted him disturbing them on their days off.

Maybe he had time to paint, she told herself. Figures, as Matt had mentioned? She should see some of those sometime. Matt—ah, he was already gone.

Best she was too.

Fifty-Three

OF COURSE, KAREN wasn't back yet. "Just me today," she told Jan. "Tea and salad. The usual."

Lynn didn't feel as if she were quite back, either, not entirely. This morning had seemed unreal, Matt, the funeral, the gallery. Matt, especially, in her life one minute, out of it again the next. Had their time together changed anything?

She gazed out at Third Street. The same street she had looked at through this window many times, the same pastel buildings across the pavement, the same coconut palms. Her bowl was empty when she looked down. She had eaten it all? Lynn did not remember doing it.

Few clouds had rolled in; it was still pretty much the dry season. Give it a month. The heat hit her as she stepped out of *The Compass Rose* onto the concrete sidewalk. Nothing Lynn couldn't handle and that would be worse, too, in a month. If she had time, maybe she could swing by the docks, see if there were any boats for sale. Hmm, no, better make that another day. But she wasn't going to forget it. She had made up her mind to sail again.

Lynn fumbled for her key before noticing the 'open' sign was hanging on the front door. Yes, unlocked. Sam must be in the shop. She found him in the back, sipping coffee. Lynn never made a pot this late but Samson surely could if he wished.

"Ah, there you are, my dear," he greeted her. "I trust you had a good weekend."

"Yes, Sammy, I did." It had been good, all in all. "How about you?"

"Oh, I did nothing at all. I was very lazy." Had it been anyone but Ibarra, she might have made a joke about that, something cutting. But not Samson. Maybe it would be better to always keep such things to herself.

"As good a way to spend a holiday as any," she said instead.

"Sometimes," he agreed. A sip from his cup. Black and with

plenty of sugar, she knew. "I spoke to Will Merriweather. He is going to come by sometime later in the week about Tom's paintings."

"Dee's father?" she hazarded.

"He is. I shall suggest a retrospective show in the fall. We can make it our opening for the season, a big event. Something new for us." He set his cup down, fixed his eyes on his assistant-turned-partner. "The sort of thing you have been suggesting."

"Guilty as charged," she admitted.

"This will likely bump your plan for a locals show. We can see about doing that later." He picked up his coffee again and winked at her over the rim. "Of course, I am going to let you do all the planning."

Again, she could think of certain remarks she might make. And again, Lynn kept them to herself. The bell on the front door jangled. "I'll go up," she told Sam.

A solitary browser, a young woman. Let her wander as she will. So, a show of Tom's work—that should be easy enough to mount, and it should draw viewers. All this depended on the son—or maybe some other family member?—giving his approval; for all she and Samson knew, he might take them all home for his own walls or make a deal with another gallery.

It would mean shoving back the debut of the Horley paintings. Lynn had intended them as the centerpieces of her locals show. Ha, Tom Merriweather would have been but another artist in that show, as she had planned it in her head.

The woman came to Lynn at her desk, asked somewhat hesitantly, "Don't you represent that artist who died? The folk painter?"

Already interest! "We do," she answered, "but, ah, his work is temporarily unavailable while we work out some details with Mr. Merriweather's estate."

"Oh." Disappointment. Maybe the woman hoped to get some of Tom's paintings before the demand—and price—went up.

They should definitely raise the prices on his work. "We represent several other local artists," Lynn said. "Jay Bruce was something of a protege of Merriweather." That was very much stretching it but, after all, they *had* been friends.

But it resulted in no sales. Her browser slipped unceremoniously out the door a couple minutes later.

Matt would have to be a part of that local artists exhibition, whenever they chose to mount it. What would he be up to today? He had no classes for another week. Or more? She wasn't sure. She was also unsure whether Anne and the girls were back.

Maybe he was busy in his studio. Maybe he would be bringing in the finished versions of the canvases he had started at Karen's farm. Maybe lots of things.

Fifty-Four

"I'm GLAD YOU offered to feed me," Karen confided. "I would have collapsed if I'd gone straight home." She snickered. "And then woke up later and devoured ice cream."

"Ice cream has a bad rap," stated Pat. "There are far worse things."

"But they don't serve it here."

"Afraid not. They don't even have yogurt." She knew Pat made his own and always had some in the fridge in his trailer. "Anyway," he continued, "it was best I check in here so they know I'm back."

"Oh, I know they can barely get by without you. There would have been a collective sigh of relief when we rolled in!"

Pat wasn't listening. He peered out into the dusk. "Hey, Jag," he called through the open door to the kitchen, "there's a light on in the Kuenst house. Is something going on?"

The cook leaned against the door frame and turned his eyes toward the old mansion. "Not sure. Mrs. Kuenst is supposed to be coming in a few days. Maybe someone is getting the place ready."

"Oh!" Pat turned to his companion. "Another reason it was a good idea to stop here. I would have missed out on all the gossip."

"There's more," said Jag. "I hear she is selling her place up north and moving here permanently."

The yoga instructor considered this. "Then it is unlikely she is putting the spa on the market. Despite what her daughter wants."

"She has property somewhere?" asked Karen. She had pictured the old woman in a condo, for some reason.

"In eastern Tennessee. It's hill country, pretty from what she has told me."

"Springs country, too," said the cook. "There are old resorts there, just like this one."

"Older than this one," replied Pat. "Some over a century."

"I am tempted to ask if it is good horse country," said Karen. "Maybe just a little too far away though!"

Pat laughed. "She's set on having a place with horses," he explained to Jag. "We kept stopping and looking at fields on the way back here."

"Miss Caroline used to ride." Jag shrugged. "Maybe she still does."

"That's the daughter," Pat told Karen. "She's married and lives somewhere down the coast. Naples, isn't it?" He directed this to Jag.

The cook nodded and said, "I'd better get back to work." He slipped into the kitchen but exotic smells continued to waft out to the couple.

Pat, in a lower voice, confided, "It might be she is selling her estate in Tennessee to help keep this place afloat."

"Her daughter wants her to sell?"

"Yes, to developers. I assume it will happen when Agnes passes."

Karen disliked that possibility, even while recognizing the likelihood of it. "Lynn told me about your—grandmother, right? You've never mentioned that to me."

"It just never came up. I don't know much about your past either."

Neither had talked much about the past, Karen recognized. "We're still strangers, in some ways."

"But less so every day." Pat stood and picked up their empty plates. "Are you ready to go?"

"I'd like to sit here a little longer," she replied. Karen waited on the patio, now fallen into night, while Pat carried the dinnerware into the kitchen. She could see the light he had mentioned in the house. "Could we see Mrs. Kuenst's house?" she asked when he again sat beside her.

"Right now?" She was going to say that wasn't what she meant, but he continued. "If someone is in there, it would be as good an opportunity as any. Come on." He rose, she followed, out between the banyans. "Not that I don't have a key," Pat said. "I could give a tour anytime."

"Not when Mrs. Kuenst has taken up residence."

"That is so. Anyway, if Verna and Carl are back here, I want to hear what they have to say."

The porch light was on, and a fainter illumination shone from one of the interior rooms. Pat came to a sudden halt, staring toward the dark Mercedes pulled up beside the house, barely visible in the shadows. "That's Caroline's car," he said. "Tour canceled."

He spun around at once and headed back toward the spa. Certainly it wouldn't do to barge in if the woman had just arrived, but there was something more going on, Karen was sure. "You don't get along with her, I take it?"

He slowed down, took a breath. "She dislikes me for some reason. I avoid her."

"Hmmph. Then I dislike her! Let's get to my house." She took Pat's hand. "I'll make sure you feel welcome."

He stopped, turned toward her. "Thank you for that, Karen."

Rather than answer, she brought her lips to his. That should be answer enough! But she could not help adding, "You have to go anyway. Your truck is there."

But it would go in the morning. After that? Who could know?

Fifty-Five

"You know Mr. Bernhard, don't you? Roger?"

She looked up from her chore of dusting picture frames. How would Samson know the sergeant? "I do."

"Sometimes I see him at church. At Saint Francis."

Lynn was fairly positive that was the Catholic church in Leawood. "I didn't know he was Catholic." Not that there was any reason it would come up. "Does he bring his girlfriend?"

"Not so far. Ah, here is Mr. Merriweather." Lynn turned to see a dark older sedan pulled up on the far side of Bay Street. A Taurus, wasn't it? Her own dad used to drive one. "Deloris is with him. Good. The girl knows far more about all this than her father."

Lynn was aware of this. "She's helped Tom for years." Started young, too. Dee couldn't be more than twenty or so. The pair crossed to the gallery.

Both were rather dressed up. Were those the same suits they had worn to the funeral? She was pretty sure Will's was. After greetings, Will Merriweather looked to his daughter, wordlessly turning things over to her.

Deloris got down to business. "You know we set up a trust for my grandfather and his art a couple years back." Lynn did indeed. She had made out checks to it. "And I was named to administer it."

That must have been as soon as Dee was considered old enough, when she turned eighteen maybe. Maybe it had even been her idea. Something seemed different about the young woman today—oh, her voice. She had dropped her country accent in favor of a generic businesslike one.

"So she can go right ahead and do what she wants with the pictures," proclaimed Will Merriweather. His daughter nodded. She seemed a bit pleased with herself.

"I know this means all the contracts Grandfather and I signed would still be in force," Deloris admitted.

"That does not mean we are not open to a new deal," said Samson. "I have no doubt there are more paintings available."

"And you would like to have them? Exclusively maybe?" The girl couldn't help grinning. She was enjoying being a businesswoman, it seemed!

"I am quite certain we can work something out," Lynn assured her. "I think we—" She gave Ibarra a quick glance. "Will not show any of Tom's paintings for a while so we can mount a retrospective show in the fall."

"But will folks still be interested?" asked Will. "I don't want 'em forgettin' my dad's work." He gave a sheepish smile. "Not that I ever understood why they liked it."

"If it's not too long," said Samson. "Right now, many of those who might buy are gone for the season."

"So, September maybe?" asked Dee. "That *is* pretty long."

"Three months," muttered Will Merriweather.

"Closer to four," admitted Samson. "Things don't really pick up till late September." Many winter residents did not show until after Thanksgiving but there was no reason to bring that up!

"Then we have lots of time to figure things out," decided young Miss Merriweather. She chuckled. "And I'll have more classes under my belt so I can make a better deal!"

Will beamed. "Dee is on her way to bein' somebody. Just got her college diploma!"

"Only an Associate degree, Daddy," she objected, though it seemed she might be a bit proud of it herself. "I need to get my Bachelor's at South Florida now."

"Oh, that was my school," Lynn told her. "But art, of course." She assumed the girl was studying business.

Whatever her major was, she didn't seem inclined to divulge it right then. Samson broke into the moment of awkward silence. "Again, I offer my condolences for your loss. Tom Merriweather was a fine man and I shall miss him."

"Me too," breathed Lynn. She wasn't sure if the Merriweathers even heard her.

"Thank you, Mr. Ibarra," said Deloris, in very formal tones. "I don't think there is any other business we need to discuss right now."

"Later, then," agreed Samson.

"Didn't you want to say somethin' about your friend Maddie?" Will asked his daughter.

Lynn guessed the young lady had decided not to. She looked discomfited by her father's words.

"And that boyfriend of hers. What they call him, Race?"

"Yes, Daddy. His parents named him Horace but everyone calls him Race."

"Fool name, either way. I wouldn't call no boy Horace."

"It was the name of a great poet, long ago," spoke Samson. "But I do not think I would saddle a young man with it either."

Dee made no comment on this but asked, "Miss Lynn, you know Maddie Fry, don't you?"

"Not well." She had never actually spoken to the girl. "A friend of a friend, you could say."

"Meaning Mr. Janson, right?" For a brief moment Lynn was amused by that name. Pat. Hardly anyone ever called him Mr. Janson. Not seriously.

"Yes. Others, too." Roger. Maybe Karen. Had she gotten to know Maddie?

Miss Merriweather nodded. "Race Hadley is not happy about her continuing that class, after he wouldn't take her no more. Any more." She had corrected herself without hardly stopping for breath and went on. "He is saying things he shouldn't about Mr. Janson. About Maddie too. I thought maybe your friends should know." Lynn was sure there was more but Deloris was giving them the condensed version.

"I'll see Pat's girlfriend in a few minutes," she said. "I'll tell her."

Fifty-Six

SAMSON IBARRA STARED out into the dark Monday morning. "I think we should close up," he said, "and stay closed tomorrow."

Lynn was inclined to agree. "At least until we know which way the storm is going."

"What are they naming it?"

"Colin." That was what they said it would be on the radio. She was not sure whether it was powerful enough to wear the name yet.

"Wherever it goes, we are in for lots of rain," said Sam. He turned from the windows.

"Some wind, too. Maybe you should get on the road before it gets too strong."

"You too, my dear." He glanced outside again, nodded his head, and locked the front door. "Perhaps we should have put boards up."

"Too late," Lynn felt. The storm was not expected to intensify to an hurricane, anyway.

"I suppose so." Ibarra turned the 'closed' sign to the outside. "I'm going," he announced. "Don't you wait too long."

No, there would be no point in dawdling—but none in going home either. The day was not so bad, yet, bands of rain, some modest wind gusts. It looked worse out there than it actually was, maybe.

Still, she was glad she had chosen to drive rather than walk. It was not bad at all when she went out to her car a few minutes later. And close to lunch time. She might as well drive over to *The Compass Rose*.

She hoped Karen would have enough sense to do the same, if she showed at all. Ah, yes, there was her red Lexus parked up the street. Lynn pulled in just ahead of it, to glimpse her friend getting out in her rear view mirror. With an umbrella—Lynn suspected she had one somewhere in her own car but had no idea where it might be hiding.

"I wasn't sure you'd make it," said Karen, as the two hurried into the restaurant, beneath the scant protection of the dark blue fabric.

"Same with you," replied Lynn. "We've closed for the day. I'm not going back to the gallery."

"Maybe I should too." They took possession of their usual table. "We could sit here and let Jan serve us coffee all afternoon."

Lynn only nodded and peered out the window. "I think I might go look at some boats if the weather doesn't take a turn for the worse." She smirked at her friend. "I should make you ride along like I did yesterday."

"You enjoyed every moment," asserted Karen. "Iced tea," she said to Jan.

"The same," spoke Lynn, "and salad. I don't suppose you made up your mind about anything."

Karen shook her head. "Lots more properties out there to look at. And I still need to sell one of my places. Thanks, Jan. I'll take a salad too, okay?" She poured sugar into the tea the waitress had set before her. "I still think we should have stopped and bothered your artist friend."

They had driven past Jay Bruce's house on their Sunday afternoon explorations. "He's too private to just drop in on, unannounced," said Lynn.

"I like his place. That might be a good area for me."

Lynn had no opinion on that. "Did you get to spend time with Pat?"

Karen tasted her tea before answering. "Nah. He was too busy with Mrs. Kuenst arriving."

"Just in time for the tropical storm."

"I suspect she has seen quite a few of them. Pat promises to introduce me to her."

"Probably after the daughter has gone home."

Karen laughed. "Probably!"

"Matt plans to paint out there again. He's at loose ends with no

181

classes to teach for a while." She paused before adding, "I don't know if I'll be able to join him."

"You're better off painting on your own," asserted Karen. "And not comparing your stuff to Matt's."

There was a lull in the rain as they left the restaurant, and even a little sun breaking through. Lynn chose to drive down to Bay Street and then turned south. The bay waters were gray and choppy. No boaters were foolhardy enough to be out on them.

But plenty of boats were tied up to docks along the waterfront, rocking and swaying, rising and falling. She cruised slowly down the near-deserted rain-shiny way, past the dark *Bayside Gallery*, looking out at them, no particular purpose in mind. There were some little marinas down further, toward the southern end of town. She would go check them out. If the weather held.

The parking lots were mostly empty. A few people were hauling their boats out of the water, just in case, though they might be every bit as safe afloat as on a trailer. She pulled into a space and ambled down to the water. The wind was brisk, with just a touch of dampness to it. Lynn could handle that.

Indeed, it made her feel alive, reminded her of long-past days on boats. She progressed along the weathered board dock, eyes out for any 'for sale' signs. Not that Lynn intended this as any sort of serious shopping effort; no, not even as much as her little trip with Karen yesterday.

"What's a nice girl like you doing in a place like this?" came a familiar voice. Joe Gill.

"Do you use that line everywhere?" she laughed.

"Stick to the tried and true, I say," replied Joe. "But it isn't the best of days to be out here, Lynn."

She shrugged. "We closed the gallery and I'm killing time." Lynn swung an arm toward the docked vessels. "I'm thinking of buying a boat."

"Yeah, me too. I mean killing time, not boat shopping. Our

place is back that way 'bout a block." He motioned vaguely inland with his head. "I walk down here when I got nothing better to do."

"Roger isn't around?"

"Off with Jen again. They're getting serious." He did not seem to consider this a good thing. "Spending all his days with her."

"Nights too?" She knew she probably shouldn't ask that.

"Nope. Jen is one of those Christian girls who waits for marriage." He snickered. "She's been waiting a pretty long time!"

Lynn couldn't help laughing. She knew she probably shouldn't do that either.

"My fear is that they really will go ahead and get married," continued Joe. "That will pretty much ruin things."

"For you."

"Yeah, for me." The former sergeant gazed out over the wind-tossed bay waters. "Reckon that storm is gonna hit?"

"Who knows. Life in Florida is like that."

"Ain't that so?" agreed Joe.

Fifty-Seven

"MAYBE WE SHOULD set Joe up with someone," Matt felt.

"I am not completely sure he is straight," replied Lynn. "I've seen the way he looks at Roger sometimes."

"Oh. But not willing to admit to it, huh?"

"Or I could be all wrong," she said. "Not much damage here."

Colin had brought a few branches down and little else at the spa. The tropical storm had gone ashore somewhat further north on Tuesday and crossed the state. Only a memory now for Florida, one of a long list of storm names.

"Want to go in first?" asked her boyfriend. It could be the last time both found time to paint together, Matt with classes starting up again soon, Lynn intending this to be her last full Thursday off as she moved to a new schedule.

"Sure. Pat might be around but we should probably pay anyway."

Matt chuckled at that and followed her into the reception area. He surveyed a group of paintings along the far wall as she paid for their day.

Was he waving her over? She had never thought them that interesting, some portraits, some very old views of the resort. Matt had his head cocked at a portrait of the spa's founding father, John Prima. A rather handsome man but not an interesting picture otherwise.

"Look at him," whispered Matt. "Does he remind you of anyone?"

Hmm, the dark blond hair, the high cheekbones and wide brow. He did look sort of familiar. "Pat!"

"Okay, it's not just my imagination. I guess we know who got his grandmother pregnant."

"And he has never figured it out?" She gazed up at the picture. It would not be a good idea to say anything to Karen. Not right away. They could be all wrong about this.

"Nor anyone else around here." He chuckled. "Maybe it takes an artist's eye."

"Maybe. Let's use our artists' eyes around back today."

"Not the banyans. I've painted enough banyans out at the Horley place."

"There's always the river. Or the solarium. Or the house."

"Not to mention lots of oak trees. Okay."

Shortly, they were set up, their easels close but facing opposite directions as Lynn chose one of the big oaks as her subject and Matt tackled a view of the Kuenst residence. "It's nice to work in the shade," he commented. "We didn't have much at Karen's place."

"Have you finished the paintings you started there?" Lynn asked.

"Pretty much."

She shouldn't have expected more than that from Matt. He would bring the finished work by the gallery when and if he felt like it. The man had never once invited her into the studio at his house. Maybe it was crammed with unfinished pictures.

"A spectator," spoke Matt, only loud enough she might hear it. A dark-haired, deeply tanned woman in red shorts was headed their way. "She could pass for you from a distance."

"A very long distance," Lynn sniffed. But he was right.

Older than her, maybe forty-ish, she guessed. The woman gave her a friendly nod and a perfunctory scan of her canvas, before moving on to Matt. There she stopped. "That is excellent work," she stated, and held out a hand. "I'm Caroline Dunhill."

"Matt Stone," he replied, taking that hand. Being left-handed, there was no need to transfer the brush he held. "And thank you." The name apparently did not mean anything to him. Lynn, however, knew it—this was Agnes Kuenst's daughter. "And this is Lynn," he went on. "Lynn Devinne. Co-owner of the Bayside Gallery. They show some of my work."

"Oh." Sudden recognition from Caroline. She must have heard of them—and their connection to Pat. Plenty of people here would gossip to her. "I must come by your gallery sometime," she said, addressing neither directly. "But I am leaving tomorrow. Must spend some time with the husband!"

Lynn thought Caroline did not resemble John Prima in the least. But a portrait of Abraham Kuenst hung in the lobby as well and she could see the similarity there. "Is your mother well?" she asked.

"Settled in," came the reply. "I'll be back to visit her in a week or two." Another look at Matt's painting and quite possibly at Matt as well. Lynn did not think she was imagining that. "Take care." With that she strolled off in the direction of the kitchens.

Matt's eyes followed Dunhill a moment before he turned back to Lynn. "You know her?"

"That's the owner's daughter," she informed him. "The one who dislikes Pat. I think maybe we figured out why, eh?"

"Maybe we did," agreed the artist.

Fifty-Eight

"WERE YOU EXPECTING Jay to stop by?"

Lynn looked toward the street. She couldn't see much from her position behind the counter but that was certainly Bruce's truck across the street. "No, but I'm not surprised." It was a Saturday, after all.

"Someone with him. A girlfriend, maybe?"

This she had to see. Lynn went to stand beside Samson. "Why, that's Maddie Fry. A little young for Jay, I think!" And she has a boyfriend—or was that *had* a boyfriend?

Fry seemed hesitant about accompanying Jay into the gallery but he held the door open until she stepped in. Her eyes darted from side to side, taking in the showroom and its treasures.

Bruce gave the pair a friendly nod. "Maddie Fry, this is Mr. Ibarra. I think you know Lynn."

"Pleased to meet you, Miss Fry," said the courtly Samson.

"I'm giving Maddie a lift into town. She lives just down the road from me. Um, her mom does." He gave the girl a sidelong look.

"So do I." Maddie sounded quite firm about this. "I'm lookin' for a new job today." She clutched what was probably the want ads, shifting the paper from hand to hand.

"Not that Saturday is very suited to that but I was available," said Jay. "Sold all my pictures yet?"

Samson seemed unsure what to say. Had he taken the question seriously? Lynn jumped in. "We had to reduce them to a Dollar-Ninety-Nine each," she announced.

"Ah, whatever it takes. Overpriced at that, I reckon."

"Undoubtedly. I hear you do some figures. You should bring some of that work by."

"Um, yeah, maybe." Obviously, he wouldn't. Change the subject.

"My friend and I drove past your house last weekend. She's looking at property out there."

That, he seemed willing to discuss. "Karen, right? I've heard about her from Maddie. And from Pat. She wants to raise horses, right?"

Lynn nodded. "You know Pat?"

"Met him when he started giving Maddie a ride." He winked at the girl. "I think she has a crush on him."

"That's mean," Lynn told him. "And all the women in his class have a crush on him."

Maddie laughed at that. "There must be *loads* of jealous boyfriends!"

In addition to hers. Lynn wasn't sure of a response to that. "I hope it doesn't get him into any trouble," said Jay, lowering his voice.

"You think it could?" asked Sam. "Pat does not seem like a fighter!"

Jay nodded. "You and I know Pat is about as nonviolent as they get but he looks impressive. His muscles would make a lot of guys think twice about starting anything."

"Mr. Bruce was a Golden Gloves champ," Maddie blurted out.

The man looked a tad embarrassed. "That was half a lifetime ago, kid." He laughed. "I'm an artist now, or so they tell me. My stuff's over there." He gestured toward the hanging pictures. "Look around. It's okay."

The young woman wandered off. "I am going to drop her off so she can walk to a few places while I run errands," Jay confided. "She just lost her job."

"That is too bad," said Samson.

"It was a shitty job, working in a convenience store." He glanced toward Maddie, who had found her way into the antiques section. "The girl is hellbent on bettering herself. What she sees as bettering herself. I think maybe she caught it from her friend Dee Merriweather."

"Miss Merriweather will go places," Samson felt. "But Maddie is not in college, is she?"

"No. Her family hasn't exactly encouraged her. Moving in with a man didn't help things."

"It rarely does," said Lynn. Perhaps she put a little too much sarcasm into her tone.

"And it will always happen anyway," Bruce replied. "Ready to go, Maddie?"

Miss Fry hurried back to the three and then turned to survey the gallery. "This place sure is neat, Mr. Ibarra. I didn't know anyone had older furniture than my mom!"

Fifty-Nine

"AGNES WANTS TO meet you."

"Mrs. Kuenst?" Why would the old woman be interested in her? "I guess I could visit sometime."

"We were thinking more like dinner tonight."

"Dinner." Karen could think of nothing else to say.

"At her house. It wouldn't be any different than what we might eat right here. Jagadish will be cooking."

"I would rather you cooked for me, Pat. At *my* house."

He sighed. "I'll tell her some other time if you wish."

"No, of course not. But you will need to make this up to me, Mister." She rose from her poolside lounge. "I should shower and change then, shouldn't I? Do I need formal wear?"

"Of course. But wear the small tiara."

"Never travel without it." What she actually had with her was slacks and a loose blouse. Good enough, Karen decided, especially with no advance notice.

Not that it would have taken long to pop back to her house for something else. "How soon?" she asked, emerging from the dressing room.

"We could start now," Pat said, "but we needn't walk fast."

"Good. I need you for myself a while." It was no more than mid-afternoon, but dark beneath the great spreading trees. The pair strolled in the general direction of the river, with no particular intention of reaching it.

Yet reach it they did, and stopped there to hold each other. That had happened several times already, and lips had met lips. Karen looked out over the stream. "It would be nice to have water of some sort at the new place."

"Your farm has quite a bit of water," Pat observed.

"But I would have to move there to get much use out of it. Don't think I haven't considered it! Best to sell the place and move on."

"One may be happy anywhere," said her companion, and chuckled. "More guru-isms from me."

Or unhappy, she thought. "Let's go get fed."

Karen looked more closely at the Kuenst house than ever she had before. It might or might not be called a mansion; certainly it was large, far larger than one old woman needed. Two stories rose, white stucco with a red tile roof. Amid the shade of the tall trees, it did not look quite right. Such a house should stand in the sunlight.

Cracks ran up the sides, here and there, and rust-colored stains showed around the ground level, the result of years, decades, of dowsing from sprinklers. There was a broad, tile-floored porch.

A slim figure, wrapped in a yellow silk sari, met them at the door. Even for a woman in her seventies, she was handsome.

"Come in, come in. Karen, right?"

"Yes, ma'am."

"Call me Agnes. You met in yoga class, I understand?" They followed her down a wide hallway. It was practically wallpapered with paintings, some of them Pat's.

"The one I teach in Tamarind," explained Pat. "That starts up again tomorrow."

"As if we don't keep you busy enough! Do you drink, Karen?" They had stepped into the dining room, a tall, well-lit space with a long table of dark wood. Walnut maybe.

"I've been known to, Agnes."

"Good. I need someone to help me drink my wine. Pat will never take more than a little glass or two."

"Don't I know it!"

Their hostess chuckled. "Jag, is dinner ready?" she called.

The cook popped into the room. "Give me a quarter of an hour, Agnes." He popped out as quickly.

"No reason why we can't start on the wine anyway," stated Mrs. Kuenst. Karen quite agreed. Fifteen minutes later, the dinner did indeed appear and, as Pat had said, it differed little from what they might have been served in the spa's dining room. Or on the back patio, for that matter. But the wine was very good.

The trio sat at one end of the big table, which Karen had decided was mahogany. There was small talk, gossip of things that had happened at the Springs during Agnes's absence. Things of which Karen knew little. Then, Mrs. Kuenst stated, "If I am going to stay here from now on, I should have a maid just for this house. No," she decided, "more than a maid. A companion. Someone who could live here."

"I know someone who might work," said Pat. "Not any experience, of course."

"Good, then she wouldn't have to unlearn anything. Send her to Verna or someone."

Karen didn't know whom he meant, nor did she much care. This house was, to say the least, eclectic in its furnishings. She liked it. Lots of oriental touches, Indian mostly, but also old fashioned furniture, harking back a generation. Maybe two generations. She wasn't absolutely sure how long a generation was.

"Your husband built this house?" she asked.

"He did. Dad was always willing to live in the main building. I grew up there, in hotel rooms. But Abraham thought we needed a real house." She might have laughed; there was little sound. "Plus it gave him room to expand the space for guests."

She shrugged. "My father was a visionary. My husband was a businessman. I loved them both. My own daughter grew up in this house. Your friends met her the other day."

"Lynn told me," Karen said. "She's home now?"

"Uh-huh. Lives in a condo down in Naples, with my grandson and her husband. Plays golf." She shook her head in mock solemnity. "I went wrong somewhere."

"Golf courses are a great waste of land," opined Karen.

"They should be used as horse pastures, right?" Pat asked.

"Absolutely."

"Caroline was curious about your friends," said Agnes, bringing the conversation back around to that topic. "Especially the artist."

"They are both artists," maintained Karen. "However, Matt Stone is also an ass."

Agnes smiled faintly. "Well, that's good to know. I'll pass it on."

"Matt sort of comes along as part of the package with Lynn," said Pat. "I don't think either of us would be friends with him otherwise."

"But he can be a charming guy," admitted Karen.

Pat continued, "Lynn, on the other hand, is a lovely person."

"You really think so?" asked Karen. "You've never said anything like that before."

"Didn't want to make you jealous."

A joke to hide behind, thought Karen. We all do that. "I don't mind you saying it one bit. I agree with you."

"Then I must meet this lovely Lynn someday," said Agnes. "Desert?"

Sixty

"THAT IDIOT CAME to where we work and raised a ruckus and got her fired! So I decided to quit too."

"In protest?" asked Samson Ibarra.

"It wasn't a very good job anyway," Deloris stated. "Maybe I just wanted an excuse." She wrinkled her nose. "I'll need to find work up in Tampa soon, anyway."

"When you head off to USF," hazarded Lynn.

"That's right. Though I could take a lot of classes at the Sarasota campus. I can drive there."

"Even the main campus isn't that far," Lynn said. But she had chosen to stay in a dorm. Karen too. Roommates.

"I 'spose not. I'm going up to see if I could fit a course or two in this summer. Depending on whether I get a new job and what my hours are!"

Already enrolled at South Florida, then. Moving on from community college was fairly painless.

"I shall wish you good fortune with your job hunt," said Sam. "Miss Fry, as well."

"Oh, Maddie has a job—Mr. Janson got her one at the Springs. I just took her by there on my way into town, and they got it all worked out. She's even gonna live there!"

Lynn wondered if Karen knew anything about this. She would have to bring it up at lunch. In fact— "I'm about to head off for lunch with Miss Fairfield. Would you like to join us? My treat." Maybe she shouldn't have added the last. Dee probably had more than the usual share of pride. "Consider it a start on business networking."

"Networking, Miss Lynn? I suppose that's a good idea." The girl grinned. "And I won't turn down a free lunch anytime. Take my car?"

"We walk."

"Um, okay. Let me get those pictures out of the car first so Mister Samson can look at them. That's why I stopped by here."

"Miss Devinne needs to see them too," came Sammy's immediate response. "We are partners." Lynn silently thanked him. People would continue to see Samson as the boss here, she knew, and she probably shouldn't resent it.

But of course she would! There must have been nearly twenty panels on the rear seat of Dee's old Nissan.

"There's more at home," the girl cheerfully informed her. Too many. They should not make them all available at once. A few minutes later the pictures were stacked in the back room and the pair was hiking up Bay Street.

"I'm not a business major," said Deloris, "but I need to know about it. I'm going into media." She looked up the street. "How far?"

"A couple blocks over. We'll turn at the corner." Media? Like television? Lynn decided not to ask. She feared she might not understand the answer. Things had changed in the dozen years since she went off to college.

Dee chatted on. "Maddie and I both worked at the convenience store up the road a bit, up Springs Road, 'cept it isn't called that out there. Up at the corner where you can turn back toward North Tamarind. I was late night shift. I'll tell you, that can be scary!"

"Overnight?" She knew the store but had no idea whether it was open around the clock.

"Just till Midnight. That's late enough."

"I agree," said Lynn. "I think I would fall asleep."

Dee had to stop and give *The Compass Rose* a good looking over before entering. "Never eaten downtown before," she murmured. "Never spent much time in Tamarind at all."

It would be convenient for those in her neighborhood to drive over to one town or another on Highway Forty-One. Dee would have gone to college in one of those towns. North Port or Venice maybe.

Karen was at 'their' table. Her eyes went to Lynn's companion, as she scooted in beside her. "Have you met Deloris Merriweather?"

"No, but Maddie has mentioned her." She extended a hand across the table. "Pleased to meet you, Deloris."

"Dee will do," responded the girl.

"So call us Lynn and Karen," said Lynn. "None of this Miss Whoever stuff."

"Three teas?" asked Jan. "Or am I going to have to learn the quirks of a new customer?"

"I'd just as soon have a Coke, ma'am," said the young woman.

"Tea for me. And a BLT." Karen chuckled. "Once again making up for eating vegetarian yesterday."

"Salad," ordered Lynn. "How about you, Dee?"

"Um, I guess I'll have a salad too." She giggled. "That's a businesswoman's lunch, isn't it?" She perused the menu again. "Is the chef's salad different?"

"Try it and find out," suggested Karen.

"Okay." Jan nodded and left them.

"Did you know Pat got Maddie Fry a job at the Springs?" asked Lynn.

"Oh, so that's who he was talking about last night." Karen considered this fact for a moment. "She might do. Personal maid for Mrs. Kuenst."

"I haven't met her," admitted Lynn. "Just the daughter."

"I like her a lot. And she seems to really care about Pat."

Lynn knew it was not the right time to say anything about what she and Matt suspected. Maybe it never would be.

"I hope Maddie gets along with her," spoke up Dee. "Now I'm the one who needs to find a job."

"Why, you're networking with two high powered businesswomen," Lynn told her. "You should just go on to success after success now."

Karen snickered. "But first, eat your businesswoman's lunch," she said, as Jan set their orders before them.

Sixty-One

THERE WERE EVEN more students than in the spring class. Maybe an earlier start was more convenient. Lynn looked them over. Older, mostly. Some she recognized. Some were new.

No Maddie. There would be no point in her coming if she could take one of the classes Pat taught out the Springs. Her job was likely to keep her there in the afternoons anyway.

She took more-or-less the same spot she had for the previous class. Why change? Lynn was a tad disappointed when Roger and Joe settled down further forward and to her right.

Three in the afternoon. Lynn could actually get back to the gallery after class if she wanted. But closing time was Four so there was no point. There was not even any certainty that Sammy would wait until Four. Would Karen show up, leave her office in Allie's hands? She, too, could take take one of Pat's classes out at the spa. But she had promised.

There was Jen. The woman made a circuit of the room, flipping the switches for the overhead fans. No need to pay her for class. Lynn had done that online last week.

Jen and Roger. She did feel a little for Joe. This was the first she had seen of him since Colin blew through, since she went to look at boats. She had not gotten back to that. Don't forget, Miss Devinne, she told herself. Don't let things get in the way.

Pat slipped into the room and went to whisper with Jen. His eyes swept across the room every now and again. Looking for Karen? The recreation director nodded and came to the front of the room. "Welcome to yoga class," she said. "We'll be meeting ten weeks through the summer, until August Seventeenth."

"You get July Fourth off," called out Pat. He would never have done that only a couple months ago, would he?

"Right, Pat, we know that," laughed Jen. "This is our instructor, Pat Janson." He nodded toward his assembled students. Some were still filtering in, or loitering by the entrance.

"If you have not paid, see me after class," Jen went on. Lynn glanced to her right to see Karen settling beside her. Others were choosing spots, taking places, also. "So I'll turn it over to Pat," Jen finished, a tad awkwardly, hesitating before she walked over to the kitchen door. Her favorite spot, half in and half out. Maybe she liked to feel that she could duck out of the way if need be.

"We will start with the complete breath," announced Pat.

Karen leaned in. "I'm giving Dee a job," she whispered. "Filling in for Allie when she goes on vacation."

Lynn nodded. Three summer weeks. That would be good. Ideal, almost. "No sense in hiring from a temp agency," added Karen, and turned her attention to Pat.

There was nothing new over the next fifty minutes. Pat pretty much began the same beginners' class over again each season. Maybe she should have checked out one of those at the Springs. Lynn felt it was time for something more advanced.

Not that she couldn't enjoy these familiar moves. That was the whole point of it, was it not? She did not need to learn anything new, just follow Pat's lead through the yoga postures.

"Are you going back to the office?" she asked as the session ended.

Karen shook her head of auburn-brown hair. "No point." Her eyes went to Pat. "In fact, we will actually have more time to get together on these class days now. Pat only does an evening session on Tuesday and Thursday."

"I considered taking those classes instead of this one. They charge like twice as much at the spa!" That, really, was what had made Lynn decide to stick with the rec center.

"Unless you pay for the pool too," Karen pointed out. "A membership might be nice. At least for a month or two."

Lynn frowned at her friend. "You get in free anyway! I need a boyfriend who works there too."

"Jag isn't taken."

"Jag? The cook, right?"

"The top cook. Not a bad looking guy but I don't think he is too interested in girls." Karen rose to her feet. "Not gay, maybe, just not the relationship type."

Lynn rolled up her mat and stood. "It might be easier to steal Pat."

Karen gave her a long look. Had she taken her seriously? A small smile. "Right now, the class is stealing him." Students were clustered around Pat. "I'll see him later. Heading home now."

"I might as well too." Lynn would have plenty of time to soak in the little pool back at the *Neptune Apartments*. "Who is yelling?"

Something was going on in the parking lot. A man was shouting. She couldn't quite make out the words. Madeline Fry's boyfriend. Ex-boyfriend.

"I'll whup that sissy boy!" Race had both hands up, as if he were ready for a fist fight. "He can't steal my girl!"

Roger had moved forward. "No one stole your girl, young man," he rumbled. "You don't need to be making any trouble here."

Hadley looked at the towering ex-soldier and glanced at the less impressive Joe Gill standing slightly behind him. "What's it to you, old man?" Lynn was fairly certain he backed away a little as he said this.

"Just trying to keep you from getting into trouble, son."

That seemed to infuriate Race. "I ain't your goddamn son, you mother-fuckin'—" He couldn't seem to think of a proper insult to finish his statement, so he stepped forward. Then he thought better and stepped back. Roger stood a head taller and a good bit wider than he.

The young man wheeled and walked toward his car, a large old Buick with rust-eaten doors and fenders. It had probably been green once. He turned back to them and shouted, "It's not over! I'm gonna make that asshole pay!" With that he practically leaped into the driver's seat. If the Buick had started right away rather than needing to grind for more than a few seconds, the exit might have been more dramatic.

They watched him motor out of the parking lot. "Pat should probably know about him," commented Roger, rather matter-of-factly. He faced both women but undoubtedly meant Karen.

"It's a good thing you were here, Roger," said Lynn. "There was no way he wanted to mess with you."

Roger only shrugged his wide shoulders. "He's lucky Joe didn't get involved. My friend can be a very dangerous man."

POSTURE IV

chakarasana
the wheel

Sixty-Two

"Caroline brought her husband along this time."

"The woman we met a couple weeks ago?" asked Matt. He turned to Lynn. "Wasn't she going to stop by the gallery?"

"Lots of people say things and then don't do them," she replied. "Her husband, Pat?"

"Yep, Eric Dunhill. *Doctor* Dunhill. There's a teenage boy too but they left him at home. We should all be grateful."

"I'll bet you were a sweet boy," said Karen, and laughed. "The sort I would have ignored!"

Pat only gave her a little smile and shrugged. "She rolled in on Friday evening. I think she plans to stay on when Eric goes home. Not that she tells me anything!"

"So maybe she will be able to stop by the gallery," noted Matt. "I'm not likely to have any time for that, myself."

Matt would return to teaching tomorrow. Lynn knew he had been back and forth to Sarasota all the previous week, preparing for the new semester. "I'm going in," she announced, and plunged into the pool.

She stayed in the cool blue depth as long as she could, swimming underwater to the far side before pushing off the bottom, to reach up and grasp the tiled edge. She turned to see none of her friends had followed her. Their loss, thought Lynn. Leisurely back-stroking along the pool's side, she gazed up at the afternoon sky, filling with clouds. There would be rain later, maybe. The summer weather pattern was settling in.

And things were settling back into their same pattern in her life. Not that she minded so much but it all had to change *someday*.

Matt dove in. Lynn wondered if the life guard was giving him a dirty look. There were signs admonishing one not to dive, after all! With no one there but the two couples and the girl on her high canvas-backed chair, it was unlikely she would say anything. But Lynn wished she would blow her whistle, just to remind Matt to behave. He swam to her side; both treaded water for a few seconds.

"We could go someplace later, if you want," the artist said, with no preamble. "It might be our last opportunity for a week or so."

Not really, Lynn told herself. Matt wasn't that busy, even with classes starting up again. He just didn't want to be bothered with it, with having to do more than necessary. She understood this. She might act the same, given the same circumstances.

"Sure," she said, and dove again, down to the deepest part of the pool. Let him decide where to go, where to take her. She didn't care. Lynn touched her hand to the bottom and shot back up. Pat and Karen were sitting on the pool's edge, legs dangling in the water, not talking. Where was Matt?

Ah, briskly swimming toward the shallow end. Maybe he meant to do a few laps. A man stood beyond him, watching. A guest who hadn't checked out yet? Most were gone by the middle of a Sunday afternoon.

Pat waved toward him, then tilted his head down to say some-thing quietly to Karen. She nodded and looked toward the visitor, ambling their direction. I might as well get out and see what's going on, thought Lynn. She had pulled herself out the water beside Karen by the time the man reached them.

Matt climbed the risers at the end of the pool and headed their way. He could be as curious as anyone else.

Spindly arms and legs protruded from the immaculate chino shorts and polo shirt. A short sandy beard attempted to make up for the lack of hair atop the stranger's head, which thrust forward, giving a stooped appearance on first impression. He crouched beside Pat.

"So this is the rumored girlfriend?" he asked, raising his eyes to Karen. He gave her a friendly grin.

"Hi, Doctor Dunhill," spoke Pat. "Yes, this is Karen."

"Caroline isn't around. It's safe to call me Eric. Pleased to meet you, Karen."

"And this is my friend Lynn," Karen said, "and that is Matt." She nodded in the general direction of Stone.

The doctor rose and extended a hand to Matt. "The artist, right? My wife's been telling me about you."

Matt had to laugh. "I must have made a good impression." Lynn was a tad surprised—but pleased—when he added, "Lynn is a painter too." Her boyfriend didn't always think to say things like that.

Eric only nodded. Probably not interested. "I think Caroline plans to stop by your gallery this week. She's staying on with her mother while I go home." He turned back to Lynn. "You have something to do with the gallery, don't you?"

"Part owner," Karen stated before Lynn could get her mouth open. Not quite true yet. Soon. "She discovered Pat's artwork and put it on exhibit."

Eric gave Lynn a long look before turning to Pat. "I didn't know your paintings were being shown. Congratulations."

Pat gave a wry smile. "Congratulate me when one of them sells."

"I'd buy one and hang it but Caroline wouldn't approve." Eric returned the smile. "Maybe I shall anyway! Ah, well, I'd best be on the road to Naples. Nice to meet you all." He wheeled around and headed toward the parking area.

"Must already have the car packed," mused Pat. "He came out here on purpose. Maybe to meet you," he said to Karen.

Undoubtedly, Lynn told herself. He didn't even know who I am. Aloud, she said, "Naples isn't very far." Mostly just to have something to say.

"A couple hours at most," felt Matt. "I'm surprised they don't come more often." He dove back into the water and the lifeguard once again frowned.

Sixty-Three

"Now THERE IS something I haven't seen in a while," remarked Samson, peering out the front window. "They only built that Volvo sports-car-turned-station-wagon for a couple years." He furrowed his brow. "In the Seventies? Hmm, yes," Ibarra asked and answered himself.

Lynn went to stand beside him and watched the little white wagon ease into a parking space along Bay Street. Plenty of those were available on this Monday afternoon. "I've seen that car at the Springs. Mrs. Keunst drives it." But it was not Agnes Keunst who emerged from the driver's seat. "Oh, her daughter is at the wheel. But there's Keunst." She assumed the older woman exiting on the far side was Agnes.

"The Volvo is garaged while Agnes is away," she continued. "I didn't know it existed until a couple days ago."

Samson nodded politely at this bit of trivia. "We shouldn't be waiting at the door," he noted. "They'll think we are preparing to pounce on them." He made a pretense of being busy with a chest of drawers while Lynn returned to the counter.

Caroline opened the door for her mother. The older woman at once turned her attention to Lynn, without looking at any of the displayed merchandise. "You must be Pat and Karen's friend," she said.

"And Matt Stone's," added the daughter. "You're all friends of his, right?"

Lynn nodded. She had attempted to be in the company of Pat and Karen when she and Matt went anywhere as public as the Springs, so it would not look so much like they were a couple. Or had Matt been the one to suggest that sort of thing?

Anyway, Caroline would be unlikely to know they were more than friends. "Mrs. Dunhill, Mrs. Kuenst, this is Samson Ibarra." Sammy had ambled over to stand beside her.

"Agnes," spoke Mrs. Kuenst, extending a hand. "Pleased to meet you, Samson." Caroline only gave the man a noncommittal nod of the head before turning her eyes to the paintings covering the walls.

Lynn was a bit disappointed Agnes was less exotic than Karen's description had made her. Both women looked like they could have just come from a round of golf at some country club.

"I like this," said Agnes, standing before one of Jay Bruce's land-scapes. Her gaze moved on to Pat's mandalas. "And naturally I like Pat's pictures. It's good to see his work in a gallery."

Her daughter looked over Jay's painting and seemed to show some grudging respect for the work. But she was obviously more interested in seeing Matt's pictures. That was what brought her to *Bayside*.

"I had hoped to meet Mr. Stone again. Do you see much of him?" she asked.

Of course, Lynn had seen Matt just that morning when she woke up beside him in her little apartment. That she was not going mention. She did not even intend to mention she had seen him the previous afternoon and he had met her husband.

As far as this woman knew, her relationship with Matt Stone was professional. She would just as soon keep her thinking that. "He stops in from time to time," Lynn said. "He'll be busy with his teaching this week. Classes just started up."

"And Stone does not show exclusively with us," admitted Ibarra.

Caroline did not seem surprised by this. "There is another gallery somewhere in town, isn't there?"

"Indeed there is," said Samson. "The *Antiqua*."

"I'm sure you've driven by it," Agnes told her daughter. "The place is right on Tamarind Road. Near where the Piggly-Wiggly used to be." She smiled, but shook her head. "We used to shop there. All that area is becoming gentrified now."

"It seems like a better spot. You're somewhat out of the way here," felt Mrs. Dunhill.

"I prefer to think of us as more exclusive," came Samson's amiable reply. "The *Antiqua Gallery* tends more to the tourist trade than we do. Louise and I do sometimes send stuff to each other that doesn't seem quite right for our own shops."

"Or doesn't sell," Lynn couldn't resist adding.

Samson laughed. "That too!"

Agnes wandered through the antique section, chatting with Sam, while Caroline continued to scrutinize paintings. Matt's paintings, mostly. Lynn was sure she actually grimaced at some of the other work; Dunhill did not seem to have a high opinion of their art or their establishment.

She did choose to purchase one of the Matt Stone landscapes, and not one of the smaller pieces. Lynn wasn't sure she liked Matt's work when he went that large. It lost something. Focus, maybe? But people did expect big paintings. Real artists, serious artists, turned out large canvases.

"You can deliver it to the Springs," she told Ibarra, largely ignoring Lynn's presence. "*Bayside Gallery*, right?" She scribbled the name on a check.

"Oh," said Agnes, "that one, too." She pointed to a Jay Bruce painting, a modest lake scene. "I like it. And," she added, "my Maddie has been telling me about Mr. Bruce."

Sixty-Four

THESE AREN'T AS bad as I thought, Lynn told herself. I had something then, something I've lost. She picked up another painting, held it at arms' length.

Maybe Karen was right. Maybe being around Matt kept her from being the painter she could be. The painter she was. Or maybe that painter was gone.

She carried the paintings to her car, stowing them in the back seat. The boxes of paints and pretty much everything else that had sat so long in Karen's garage were already in the trunk. There was still plenty of time to get to class.

Lynn would keep painting. Maybe with Matt, maybe not. It wasn't fair to blame him, really, was it? She had called him with the news of their sale—it was a pretty pricey piece of art—and he had made some vague suggestion they should celebrate. Not this week. Sometime soon.

Mrs. Kuenst and her daughter were barely out the door when Ibarra had remarked, "Mrs. Dunhill felt she was slumming, coming to our little gallery."

"She didn't hide it very well, either," Lynn had agreed.

"I'm not sure she even tried." He turned to his young associate and spoke seriously. "Agnes knows all about you and Stone but I do not think she has said anything to her daughter." It did not surprise Lynn at all that Kuenst had revealed this to her partner. Nor did it surprise her when his Tuesday morning delivery of the paintings kept him away for several hours. All he would admit was that he and Mrs. Kuenst had talked for some time. And had lunch.

He also mentioned that Caroline was off somewhere. Sammy thought that was a good thing. "Agnes has many interesting things in her house. If she ever plans to sell any, I hope she thinks of me!" he had said.

Back into Tamarind she drove, straight across to Bay Street and the rec center. There was Karen's car already in the lot. Empty; her friend was undoubtedly inside trying to monopolize Pat.

That friend had a mysterious smile when she joined her, unrolled her mat next to Lynn's. "There is going to be some interesting news after class," was all she was willing to say. The class went as most of Pat's classes did, smoothly and over too soon. Lynn always felt they were just a little too short, anyway, and maybe they were. Did he go longer out at the spa?

"Before we come to an end, some announcements," Pat spoke, following the usual mediation pause. About three minutes it ran, normally, Lynn thought. She didn't wear a watch to class but she had tried counting the seconds. That, of course, was not at all what she was supposed to be doing during that time.

"First," he continued, "I am sure you all know next Monday is a holiday and there will be no class. I wish you all a happy and safe Fourth." He gave Jen a sidelong look, where she stood at her favorite spot, in the doorway to the kitchen. Was she reddening up? wondered Lynn.

Pat smiled rather enigmatically. He was good at doing that. "Second, our director here at the Tamarind rec center has just become engaged to her boyfriend." Lynn's eyes went to the retired sergeant. Why, he was blushing too! "I hope you will all join me in congratulating Jen and Roger."

Would Pat have made an announcement like that once, even a few months ago? Being around Karen had made him more open, hadn't it? Maybe even being around her had helped. Lynn suspected the yoga instructor really had no close friends before.

Applause. "I'll see you all in a week," announced Pat, rising and walking to where Roger had already joined his fiancee. A small crowd was gathering around them.

"Give 'em a moment," whispered Karen. "Did you suspect? You know Roger better than I."

Lynn shook her head. "Joe said some things but, no, I had no idea this was coming." Thinking back on those things Joe had said, she thought perhaps she should have. He stood a little aside from the couple now, not talking with anyone. "I don't think he's very happy about this."

"Jen Carter is stealing his boyfriend," said Karen. "Yeah, I can see that too."

"But he'll be happy for his friend." He would be. Joe would not begrudge the couple's happiness. "Let's go on over."

Pat put his arm around Karen as she joined them. Lynn chose to stand next to Joe, gave him a bit of a smile. An encouraging one, she hoped.

"It was time for the next stage in my life," Roger was saying. "We haven't set a date yet."

Jen chimed in. "Maybe around Christmas. I'll take my two weeks of vacation and we can have a real honeymoon."

Karen suddenly stated, "Lynn has an announcement too," and turned to her friend.

For a moment, Lynn wasn't sure what she meant. Oh, of course. "As of this Friday, I shall officially be a partner at the gallery."

Karen, of course, had know all about this, having been involved throughout. The final decision had come only a couple weeks ago. "Why not now?" Samson had asked. "We're as ready as we would be in three months." This was true; the audit had been made, all the papers were ready. All the papers had been signed—it was really going to happen. It *had* happened.

"We're going off to my place upstate to celebrate it," said Karen.

"And the holiday weekend," Lynn added.

"Just the two of you?" asked Roger. His eyes went to Pat and back to the women.

"Pat is too busy at the Springs to come along," Karen said. Her boyfriend nodded in acknowledgment of this. Matt would be busy too, spending the weekend of the Fourth with his family.

"I'm always gonna be way too busy on these holidays," Jen told them. "I'll have to leave Roger to his own devices all weekend."

Karen pondered the big man for a moment. "Why don't you come along with us, then?" she asked. "Joe, too."

The two sergeants exchanged a look. Joe shrugged. "It's all right with me," said Jen, when her boyfriend turned to her. Probably glad not to have him underfoot this weekend, thought Lynn.

"Then we're in," said Roger.

Sixty-Five

SHE RECOGNIZED THE sergeants' over-sized truck. Did it belong to both of them? wondered Lynn. Joe always seemed to drive.

Everything was squared away here and Sammy was already gone. Might as well go out the front, as that was where the silver pickup was pulled to the curb. Lynn went into the back to get her bag and her easel. For a moment, she looked toward the paintings she had stowed in a corner of the storage space, her old paintings. They wouldn't remain here but they could sit for now.

She saw something in those paintings that wasn't there anymore. Oh, maybe she was just feeling nostalgia for another time in her life. Maybe she couldn't recapture what was in the pictures any more than she could those lost days.

Lynn checked the back door. Locked, as was her Ford out in the alley. No one would bother it over the long weekend.

Out the front and to the truck. Karen and the men had decided to take their vehicle at some point, rather than tuck them all into her sedan. There were fishing poles in the bed, hanging over the tailgate. She could barely see over its edge.

Roger stepped out onto the running board. "Okay if we put your easel in the back?" he asked. She only nodded and handed it up to him. The big man reached back and slipped it in, then pushed open the smaller door that gave access to a commodious rear seat. "You and me can ride back her," he said, lifting up her bag, "and let Joe and Karen sit up front. They both like to be in the command position."

"You know the way to her house?" Lynn asked. Karen wouldn't be at the office on a Saturday afternoon.

Rog slammed the doors shut and settled beside her. "You can show us the way."

"No need," came Joe's voice from the high-backed driver's seat. "I got a map from Google." He snickered. "I could drive all the way up to her farm without asking directions."

"Oh, we could just leave Karen at home then," laughed Lynn. "I do have a key, after all."

Roger leaned in and confided, "Joe knows all that internet stuff. I would have no idea how to get directions somewhere."

"No need," she whispered back. "Pretty soon, you'll have a wife to tell you what to do."

A few minutes later they pulled into the drive at the Fairfield residence. The 'for sale' sign, bold red letters on white, still stood near the street. "It's nice out here," rumbled Roger, glancing at it. "Jen and I may be house-hunting soon."

Joe made no comment on this so neither did Lynn. She had assumed Roger would move out of the little cottage he shared with his fellow retiree. As for Miss Carter, Lynn had no idea where she lived.

Joe did blast his horn to inform Karen they had arrived. She sauntered out, after a while, obviously not intending to be hurried. How do I get this window down? Lynn wondered. I'd tell her to get a move on. Best they be on the way so they could unpack before dark.

Well, it would stay light quite late at this time of year. But the bugs would be out.

Roger stretched forward to unlatch the front door and take the bag Karen handed up. Her friend settled herself in the front seat. "Are we going to be listening to that all the way?" she asked. Her tone was neutral but Karen obviously did not care for the country music station someone had chosen. Joe, perhaps.

No, not Joe. "That's Roger's music," he said. "Dial in whatever you want, Miss." The truck's throaty exhaust rumbled as much as Roger's voice as he backed it out onto the street. "He can't stop you from back there."

Joe apparently knew he could take a short cut to Springs Road, for the truck pointed east. Maybe the man was just good with maps. If he had been in combat, it was a useful skill to have, thought Lynn. Not that she knew anything about the military.

"Let me guess," Karen was saying. "Hard rock? No?" Joe had shaken his head. "Not classical?" She moved the tuner on to the next station.

"He'd listen to talk radio all day if I let him," Roger commented. "Never saw any entertainment in it myself."

Karen left the radio tuned to smooth jazz programming. There were worse choices. It would have to be tuned to something else in an hour or so. They pulled out onto Springs Road and then off it again just before the resort, heading out toward the interstate. "South on Seventy-Five, I think," muttered Joe.

"That would be my choice," said Karen, "and then north to Arcadia before turning east."

"But it's prettier the other direction," Lynn objected. Not much, she had to admit to herself. As long as they got there, it didn't matter at all.

Then all day tomorrow at the 'farm' and most of Monday, the Fourth. They wouldn't need leave until late. Why had Karen invited these two? Lynn had rather looked forward to just the two of them. There had been too many other people getting in the way lately.

The last time she visited, she had actually wished the sergeants had been invited. Lynn had some doubts about just Karen and her and their boyfriends going then, thought maybe having someone else along might lighten the mood. But that weekend had gone well enough.

Oh, Joe and Roger were good guys. It might be fun having them at the lake. Hmm, where would they sleep? She would share Karen's room, she supposed, like when they were teenagers. Neither would mind.

It was unlikely the guys would feel the same way. And Roger wouldn't leave enough room for anyone else!

Up through the flat pasture land, and fields of beans and of melons, they passed. The AC was good in this truck. Too cold, really. Lynn had anticipated—she slipped on the sweater she had packed.

It was nice enough to sleep outdoors maybe. She might like that instead of closing herself in the air conditioned house. Karen would definitely turn on the air. Darn, she should have brought a tent.

Roger snored gently as the jazz station came and went and Karen fiddled with the controls before settling on some sort of soft rock. That would put anyone to sleep, thought Lynn, before drifting off herself.

Stopping? We aren't there, are we? No, Joe had pulled in for fuel somewhere. This truck must use a lot. A large lake shimmered off to their right; the sun lay low on the left. They must have turned north again while she napped. It wouldn't be long, then. Not long at all.

Sixty-Six

KAREN WATCHED HER friend move her easel again. The shade of the tall pines kept shifting around, sometimes leaving Lynn in shadow, sometimes in the sun. It would be too sunny to paint soon anyway, too hot, she was sure. Lynn had set her easel up early, while the others lazed over their breakfast.

Early risers, all. Was it ingrained in those two ex-soldiers to be up at daylight? There had been a cot for Joe, stored in the utility room; he already had it folded up, in a corner of the main room, when she had wandered out in search of a morning meal. There hadn't really been space for it in the room Roger occupied, the one Karen's father had always used. She thought maybe Joe preferred it that way.

The two of them were carrying the canoe down to the water now, as she trailed after. Supervising, she told herself.

"Go ahead if you want," she called to them. "Maybe I'll paddle around later." She wanted to spend some time with Lynn right now.

That looks different, thought Karen as she approached. Different from the canvases Lynn was working on the last time she was here. Exactly how, she wasn't sure.

"Some of the oils I stored were still good," Lynn said, stepping back from her work. "They sat an awful long time."

No one to blame but yourself for that, thought Karen. "There were other supplies too, weren't there?"

"Yep. Like this." She held her long-handled brush up, before dipping into a pile of yellowish paint on her easel. "I missed having a good bristle brush these last months. Just junk and synthetic stuff at the craft stores."

"You could buy online."

"Oh, the place that does our framing has good art supplies. We even get a discount. I just haven't found the time to get to Venice."

Lynn considered the panel on her easel for a few seconds. "Sammy usually deals with them."

Karen felt her friend was far too lackadaisical about this. "Remember you're a partner now. You need to make yourself known to all these businesses."

"Uh-huh." Lynn's attention was back on her painting, and on the scene she was trying to capture. It was a view toward the south end of Singer Lake, where the outflow disappeared into the marsh. She daubed, she looked, she sighed. "The light has changed too much. It's time to stop." She began cleaning her brush. Is that mineral spirits? wondered Karen. It didn't smell like turpentine.

No matter. "I think I'll swim," she said.

"Sounds good." Lynn peered toward the lake. "Did they take their fishing rods with them?" The canoe floated near a brushy area on the shore, a bit north of them. "They aren't likely to be back very soon."

"Good," felt Karen. "I'll need their muscles later, though. I can carry some of the stuff here home in their truck."

"Oh, so that's why you invited them!"

Karen chuckled. "Not really, but I might as well put the guys to use. I just thought some company might be nice."

A nod from Lynn. She wiped her brush dry on a rag, stowed it in her box of paints. Still just a cardboard box, Karen noted, nothing sorted out in it. "You miss having Pat here?"

"Yeah, some," admitted Karen. "But it's also a relief to get away from him sometimes."

"Too attentive?" Lynn understood her.

"Yeah. Pat is not demanding at all. And he's good for me, I'm sure, but sometimes I get, oh, itchy maybe."

Lynn folded her easel and tucked it under her arm. She attempted to get a grasp on the still-wet painting with the free hand, while holding her box.

"Let me help you with that." Karen took the painting. It is better work, isn't it? she thought. But Pat—they were talking about Pat. "I think he wants to please but isn't always sure how."

"You knew he wasn't strong on social skills," Lynn reminded her.

The rest of the morning they spent in the water, followed by a leisurely lunch with their guests. Karen had to admit to herself she was getting a bit bored. Itchy, as she had said to Lynn.

"How soon do we want to take off tomorrow?" she asked them. "Afternoon?"

Joe objected. "Rog and I brought fireworks," he announced. "We have to wait till dark and launch a few rockets across the lake."

"We've been saving them a while," added Roger. "Bought 'em on our way south."

"There will be a fireworks display back home," Lynn said. "Out at the beach, I should say."

Karen knew this. She also knew they would all be too tired by the time they got back to go out to Leawood. "I'm willing to stay for our own private show." And she wouldn't have to drive on the way home, after all.

"Good enough," said Joe. "So what does one do for excitement around here?"

Roger shook his head. "I thought we came for some peace and quiet."

"I get enough of that already." Joe turned to the women. "Didn't I see a bar up the road?"

"I don't know how exciting that would be on a Sunday night," answered Karen. "But I'm up for finding out."

Roger shook his head again. He probably did that a lot, hanging around with Joe. "Not me. I'd rather sit on the dock."

"Me too," spoke Lynn.

Wouldn't a redneck bar be Bernhard's sort of place? wondered Karen. He's the one who likes country music. She could put up with it—and maybe a few cowboys too. Just for a little fun, maybe some dancing, tonight.

"Then it's you and me, Joe." *The Corner Bar* it would be.

Sixty-Seven

"JOE GOT VERY drunk." Karen poured herself a cup of coffee. It was the second pot Lynn had made that morning. "I had to drive that monster of his back here."

Lynn had heard the couple come in late. Couple? Well, there were two of them. That was a couple, her half-awake mind had told her. A couple of people. She had fallen asleep again without even bothering to look at the clock.

"Roger and I paddled out onto the lake in the dark," she reported. "I think he would like to live in a country place like this. But no way he could talk Jen Carter into it!"

"I wouldn't think so. Where is the sarge now?"

"Down casting off the dock. I don't know where the other one is." Joe's cot had apparently not been used.

"I left him sleeping it off in the truck. Maybe he's still out there." Karen took a gulp of her brew. "Joe's not much fun to hang with. Fortunately, there were other people there. Not many on a Sunday, of course, even if it is a holiday weekend." She giggled. "I got more than one invitation to a cookout today."

"We could do that here." There was a grill out back, not used in ages.

"We would have to go buy some charcoal. And maybe some steaks too. Pat's not here to disapprove." Karen pondered something for a moment. Whether cooking or Pat was on her mind, her friend wasn't sure. "Yeah, as long as we're staying till dark, why not?"

The sound of a truck door slamming—Joe must be awake. Was there enough coffee? He would probably need it. And where was he? It must have been a couple minutes before the door opened, not the front door but the one from the utility room, connecting to the carport.

Lynn poured a cup and handed it to the man. "Thanks," he mumbled and collapsed into one of the chairs.

"Sleep well?" asked Karen. She sounded quite innocent but Lynn knew better.

"Not the first time I've sacked on that rear seat. But it was mighty hot last night!" A hoarse laugh, a cough, and Joe continued. "I tried rolling down a window but there were too damn many mosquitoes."

"Well, why didn't you come on in?"

"I didn't want to come blundering into the house in the middle of the night and disturb everyone. And I would never have managed to get the cot open in the dark."

"I think I would have slipped in anyway and slept on the floor," said Lynn. She remembered her thoughts about a tent. "A screen house here would be nice. A place you could sleep outside at night."

Karen gazed out through the French doors for a few seconds before commenting. "That was one of Dad's projects for the future, a permanent screened-in room down near the water. For picnics or whatever." A project that would be pointless now.

"I remember him talking about it," said Lynn. "A boathouse, too."

"And rental cottages eventually. Maybe someone else will do that here."

There was silence. Joe drained his cup and stood. "I'll come back and find some breakfast. Gonna go check on the fisherman right now." He stepped out through the French doors and sauntered down the slope toward the dock.

"The sergeants are much lower maintenance than our boyfriends," remarked Karen. "Maybe we need to trade up."

"I get Roger," was Lynn's immediate response.

Karen's laugh was just as immediate. "There's enough of him for both of us!"

But no one wants Joe, Lynn thought. It was a bit unfair. "We'll have to send them to the store," she said. "Or better, I'll ask one to drive me."

"You don't want to take the truck yourself? It's quite an experience."

"I'll bet. Steak? Chicken, too, I think."

"Or just hamburgers," said Karen. "No need to make it complicated."

Maybe so. Things were already complicated enough.

But she did come back with more food than they needed, no doubt. Plenty of charcoal, too; Roger had been set to cleaning up the grill while she and Joe made the run to the little store up the road, just down from the bar. No one over there on this morning. Karen would have to fill her in on any cowboys she might have met some other time.

Enough now to enjoy an impromptu picnic, the launching of holiday rockets. Anything more could wait.

Sixty-Eight

"I HAD MY daughters on Monday," Matt said. "We swam at the Springs and then drove out to the beach to watch the fireworks. They were very sleepy girls by the end." His voice grew just a tad wistful; one might not notice it if one didn't know him. "It was the first time they slept at my house in months."

He looked over the parking lot. "Okay to leave your car here?"

"Sure. It won't be overnight, after all." It was only late afternoon. There would be people in and out of the rec center all evening.

"Class was good?" Matt was just being polite with that. But class had been good. Now it was time for that celebration he had mentioned last week.

She nodded. "Where to, Mister Stone?"

He fumbled with his car keys. "Have you ever been to *The Palms Cafe*?"

"I have. Not in quite a while." Not since she had Easter morning brunch there. "It's okay. And close. We could walk."

"Oh." A pause while he considered this. "Sure, why not?" Matt closed the van door he had just opened and locked it.

Lynn was glad to be able to stretch her legs. "Four blocks over," she told him. "We can go right across on Fifth."

The rec center fronted on Fifth Avenue. She started off and Matt fell in beside her. "You're decisive this evening," he remarked. He tried to make it sound like he was joking. Lynn smiled but gave no other response.

"I met Caroline while I was out at the Spa. Dunhill," he added, as if she didn't know who he meant. "She headed back to her home yesterday."

Then she would have seen Matt's daughters, thought Lynn. I wonder if he told her about Anne.

"She has gallery connections in Naples. She may introduce me." He glanced into a window they passed. Auto parts? That gentrification Agnes had mentioned had not reached this far up the street. "There are some prestigious places to show down there."

Lynn knew this. Knew it well. "So Dunhill will be coming back?"

"In a couple weeks, yeah. Hmm, make that a little more than a week now."

Silence for half a block. "How was your weekend?" asked Matt.

"It was fun." It had been. "I think Karen may even be having second thoughts about selling the place."

"Oh, Pat and I can open our art colony slash yoga retreat after all!"

"She's a better businesswoman than that," Lynn informed him. "We turn right here." They had reached Tamarind Road, Fifth Street. "Joe and Roger brought fireworks and we had our own display. There were other folks shooting off rockets around the lake too."

The restaurant would be about a block and an half south. Across the street she could spy *Antiqua Gallery*, in a vaguely ranch house-like building with wooden posts out front, supporting an overhanging metal roof. What used to be there?

Matt followed her eyes. "The competition."

"Friendly competition." A hardware store. That was it.

"A serious art gallery would be another matter," he observed.

Lynn didn't think there would be much incentive to open one in Tamarind. "You'd have to help me burn it down," she told him.

He nodded knowingly. "But first, make sure it accepts a bunch of my paintings and we insure them for double their value."

"Triple. No sense in being cautious."

Matt put his arm around her shoulders. "I love it when you talk sexy to me like that."

She had to laugh. "It's true," he continued. "That sort of thing is why I fell for you. Anne is so—so humorless."

Anne took him seriously. More seriously than he was willing to. That was part of their problem, wasn't it? Lynn recognized that the man was full of—well, all sorts of things. Not the least of them being himself. They crossed Fourth Avenue. "Here we are." The cafe was to their right, a brightly-lit 'family' restaurant. There would be kids this early. Kids and the elderly! "They don't do alcohol, you know."

Matt apparently didn't know. "I'll survive." He looked around the dining room, decorated in yellows and pale blues. Did he wrinkle his nose at the color scheme?

"Table for two?" asked the hostess. A kid, in Lynn's eyes; the whole staff looked like youngsters. She didn't wait for an answer but started away.

"By the wall, if you can," Matt told her. So he could watch the room. Just like Karen, there, but probably for different reasons. Matt liked to observe things.

But there came a point when one needed to stop observing and begin acting.

Sixty-Nine

"Roger and Jen eat there a lot," said Pat. "He hangs around until she gets off, more often than not, and then they go somewhere together."

And what about Joe? wondered Lynn. Where does he spend those evenings? "I'm not inclined to go back soon," she stated. "Honestly, I'd rather come here and eat your vegan meals."

She could hear a mower somewhere. "The groundskeepers must work a lot at this time of year."

"Non-stop. You should come and paint the flowers." Beds of flowers were in bloom all around the spa. "Or even come across the road and paint the organic vegetable garden." He smiled broadly as he said this.

It might be as good a subject as any. "If I'd known Karen was going to run so late, I would have brought my easel."

"Agnes would like that." He smiled rather radiantly. "She likes you."

"Should I call her Agnes?" Lynn had her doubts about this.

"You had better. But I'd stick to Mrs. Dunhill for Caroline." Pat stopped and gave her a serious look. "For some reason, I don't think she likes you any better than me."

Maybe she suspects my relationship with Matt? No telling. Not worth worrying about, either. "And how does she feel about Karen?"

"I don't believe they have interacted but—well, if I weren't part of the equation, I suspect they would like each other."

Lynn was inclined to agree. "I hope Mrs Kuenst, Agnes, that is, likes Karen." They resumed their stroll through the grounds, headed nowhere, killing time until their friend arrived. Karen had some sort of meeting with her real estate agent this Saturday afternoon.

"Well enough. But it's not like they are going to be best friends or something." He laughed at the thought of that, and Lynn had to join him. Agnes and Karen besties? Pretty unlikely.

"I do want Agnes to like her. This is my world, you know?" The young man sighed. "Sometimes I don't feel like I'm doing enough for Karen. She doesn't seem—content."

Lynn had noted her friend's recent restlessness. She had seen it before. "There's her car," she announced. The deep-red Lexus was pulling into the parking area.

"She could have parked back by the house," noted Pat. "Not a big deal." He started forward, but Karen was already out of her vehicle and striding their direction.

"I cut my asking price a tad," she announced at once. "It probably makes no difference. Ready to go?"

Pat hesitated, as if he had meant to embrace her and changed his mind. "Sure."

The moment had been spoiled when she immediately started talking business. Lynn wondered if Karen realized that. Or if maybe she intended it.

"That's Jay Bruce's truck," she suddenly realized. The pickup was pulled in beside the Kuenst house. "Was he invited too?"

"Not that I know of," came Pat's reply.

Karen snickered. "Maybe you're his date, Lynn."

"He's a friend of Maddie, right? More likely that's it."

Pat nodded in agreement. It made sense. It was Maddie who opened the heavy forest-green front door to them.

"Come in, folks," she invited. The girl was wrapped in the same sort of sari Agnes favored. Lynn hadn't actually seen her in one but Karen had reported. This sari was green and, she was pretty sure, silk. "Mr. Bruce is already here." Maddie leaned in close. "Miss Agnes really likes Mr. Bruce's pictures. I think maybe she likes Mr. Bruce too!"

Said Mr. Bruce was in the dining room with Agnes, sipping wine at the long mahogany table. "Welcome," called their hostess, not bothering to rise. "Dinner will be ready, um, sooner or later! Sit and have some wine." Their young guide seemed to hesitate as they found seats. "You too, Maddie. You're eating with us."

"As long as Caroline isn't here?" asked Pat.

Maddie came to the woman's defense. "Oh, Mrs. Caroline don't mind me sitting down with the family. I think she growed up with that sort of thing."

"That is true," stated Agnes. "Caroline has her faults but she's neither prejudiced nor a snob. By the way, she'll be back here next weekend."

Pat nodded gravely toward his employer. "Then I apologize for thinking ill of your daughter."

"Oh, you may think ill of her. She's way too ruthless when it comes to getting her own way." Agnes laughed. "Takes after her father!"

"I kinda like Mrs. Caroline," said Maddie, to no one in particular.

Jay Bruce had sat quietly with his glass of wine through all this. Lynn noted that Jay's glasses sat crooked on his nose. Oft-broken, she guessed. Hadn't Maddie said he used to box?

"Everyone knows everyone, right?" asked Agnes. "If you didn't, you do now."

Lynn had to think whether Karen had ever met Jay. Hmm, Pat had become acquainted with the man, so probably she had. She wouldn't know him well. Did anyone know him well? He was pretty private.

"Jay and I were discussing, of all things, Zoroastrianism. He has an interest."

"Only in the basic good versus evil concept underlying it," said the man. "I'm certainly no follower of the religion."

"Hmm, my late father claimed to be a Zoroastrian and maybe he was, at heart. But he never belonged to any sort of congregation." Agnes held out her glass and Jay refilled it. They seemed to have a bottle of their own up at that end of the table. "He was a bit of a crackpot, it has to be admitted—sometime nudist, vegetarian, dabbler in astrology. I never paid much attention to the stars, myself. Ha, not unless I had someone beside me to watch them with."

"The best kind of star-gazing," agreed Karen, lifting her glass in salute.

Lynn joined her in it. "But you're not a Zoro-whatzit, right?" she asked, glancing about at the many exotic items in the room—many of them certainly religious in some sense. "Buddhist?"

"I'm not Buddhist. Nor Hindu, though closer to that." Agnes's enigmatic smile rivaled Pat's. "Just a seeker after purpose in life."

"The purpose of life may be to keep hoping that there is a purpose to life," averred Jay.

He out-gurus Pat, thought Lynn. She didn't know Jay Bruce at all, did she?

Seventy

"MY MOTHER DIED while I was a teen," said Agnes. "Daddy lost interest in things and was willing to let Abraham run the hotel when I married him."

The dinner—vegan, naturally—had come and gone. A different cook, not Jag, had prepared it in Mrs. Kuenst's kitchen this time. It tasted the same to Karen.

Agnes then looked at Pat and said something no one would have suspected. "I could see you running it one of these days."

Or Karen didn't think anyone would have suspected it. Lynn had a sort of smug expression, as she did when she knew something no one else did. But Pat—he looked surprised and maybe even scared.

"You have been helping run things around here for almost six years, even before Verna and Carl took the reins. They won't be staying forever, you know."

Pat regained his composure. Probably used every trick in his yoga arsenal. "I didn't think I would, either," he said.

"One never knows," was all Agnes would say. "I knew his grandmother, of course," she told her company. "We were friends when she worked here and I always felt a little responsible for her."

Pat nodded. He knew this.

"A pair of hippie chicks, that's what we were." Agnes smiled at the memory. "Yes, I was a little older, but not too old to be a part of what was going on those days. Even in this backwater!"

"And she got pregnant," said Pat.

"That she did. How is your mother these days?"

"Doing okay, it seems. I don't hear from her very often."

"She was a wild kid. You don't mind me saying that, do you?" Pat shook his head. "And not much better as an adult."

"An addict," said Pat. "She had my grandmother's free spirit but not her self-control."

"You're a lot like your grandmother. She raised Pat after his mother, ah—"

"Disappeared? Abandoned me? It's all right to say it, Agnes."

The old woman nodded. "And his grandmother got him onto the right track. He was a troubled boy. Yes, I know that, Pat."

Why didn't *she* know this? Karen asked herself.

"She introduced me to yoga," he said. "That was the start."

"Discipline," spoke Jay, just the one word and no more.

Pat nodded. "Exactly."

"When I heard that she passed, I at once offered you a job here," Agnes said. "I was aware you knew how to teach—had been teaching over in Fort Pierce."

"And I assumed you had kept tabs on my grandmother," replied Pat and then, with a ghost of a wink, "and undoubtedly sent her those checks. Those were a mystery when I was growing up."

"I could imagine," came her dry response. "Enough about our Pat, hmm? We should put someone else on the spot. And open another bottle!"

Maddie at once rose to fetch the wine. She had learned her employer's ways quickly, it would seem. But she brought it to Jay Bruce to open.

Karen didn't quite approve. Probably no woman at that table did. But as long as the bottle got opened, no one was likely to complain. Bruce had been opening all the bottles, hadn't he?

Acting the host, in a way. He poured for Agnes and himself, handed the bottle back to Maddie, who tended to everyone else. Yes, definitely acting the host.

Was something thumping somewhere? Yes, someone was banging on the door. Yelling, too? "That's Race Hadley," said Bruce. He seemed rather matter of fact about it.

"Oh, what is he doing here?" wailed Maddie. "I'm sorry, Miss Agnes. I'm sorry." She seemed on the verge of bursting into tears.

"Been drinking, I reckon," Bruce went on, rising. But so had the rest, Pat ahead of all of them, already opening the door by the time they crowded into the hall. Yes, it was Race Hadley standing there, still shouting. Something about Maddie was all Karen could make of it.

Pat spoke quietly to the young intruder, but seemingly to no avail. Race's voice became louder, his invective more menacing.

"Enough of this," muttered Jay, shouldering his way through the group to face the man. "You're making a fool of yourself, Race. Get on home."

Race had no intention of doing so. "You gonna make me, lawn-mowin' man?" He stepped across the threshold, into Mrs. Kuenst's house. That was further than Jay Bruce was apparently going to allow.

A jab landed square on Hadley's chin, backing him up. Not meant to hurt the kid much, just to warn him, Karen suspected. It didn't work. He swung wildly at Jay, who stepped inside to land a solid right to his gut. Race buckled and sank to his knees. "Don't you bother this girl any more, Race Hadley," came Jay's steady voice. "You hear me?"

The young man nodded weakly, staggered to his feet. He looked around, seemingly bewildered, before his eyes seemed to focus on Maddie, staring at him. "Sorry, Maddie," he mumbled, and stumbled off into the dark. Karen hoped he could find his car. It wouldn't do for him to be wandering around the grounds all night!

Bruce turned back to those gathered at the front door, gave a small smile, a slightly grim smile. "You might have talked him down, Pat, but I'm impatient."

"My parties haven't been this exciting in years," commented Agnes. "Come back in and we'll finish that bottle of wine before calling it a night." She laughed then. "And if Maddie will go find us another one, we'll finish it too!"

"Sounds good," said Jay. He put an arm around Maddie's shoulders and followed their hostess in. "It'll be okay, kid," he told her, barely loud enough that Karen could catch it. "Mrs. Kuenst knows how these things go."

But Pat lingered out there on the porch, gazing into the darkness, before turning to her. "I am sure Agnes knows who got my grandmother pregnant. Whether she'll ever tell me—" He shrugged.

"I guess you'll just have to wait and see," said Karen. For a moment they embraced, before following the others in.

Seventy-One

SHE WOULD NEVER see Jay Bruce the same way. Lynn had to give Samson the entire tale on Monday morning. She had already told it to Matt the previous night. If anyone else were available, she might have told them too.

Lynn did hope Jay was right about it not bothering Agnes Kuenst. She would hate to see Maddie losing her job. The girl already had a sort of hero-worship thing for Jay, didn't she? Maybe a crush, even. This could only make it worse!

"Jay is a surprising fellow," was all Ibarra had to say.

He was, and a far more confident fellow than the one who first stopped at the gallery on that Saturday morning. Surer with his fists than with his words, that was for certain.

"I wonder if that ex learned his lesson," she said to Karen at lunch.

"He learned one lesson for certain—not to mess with Jay!" came her reply. "It's a good thing he was there."

"Good for both of them. Any other night, someone would have called the police on Hadley."

Karen only nodded agreement to this, and sipped her iced tea. Then, "I have an offer on the house. A pretty good one."

"You'll counter-offer?" asked Lynn.

"Uh-huh. Whether we make a deal or not, I need to get serious about finding a new place."

"We don't want you moving into Pat's trailer."

"I've avoided sleeping over there so far! He really needs a new place too." Karen smiled. It was a sly smile, almost a smirk. "I bet Agnes would let him stay in her house."

"But he wouldn't agree to it." Lynn felt pretty sure about this.

"Probably not. I don't quite get what is going on between those two." Karen frowned at her friend. "And I think maybe you know something you aren't telling."

Lynn looked out at the street for a moment, gathering her

thoughts, before answering carefully. "It's something I shouldn't tell. I'm not even certain about it, to be honest." But she knew she and Matt were right in suspecting that Agnes Kuenst was Pat's aunt. It wasn't for Lynn to reveal that to anyone.

Even though she would love to tell Karen. Yes, she would love to divulge that secret.

"Okay," said Karen, and nothing more for a while, sipping her tea. Lynn scraped up what remained of the salad in her bowl. She should order something else now and then, but hot food didn't appeal to her in this mid-summer weather.

"Maddie's friend will be coming to work for me in a couple weeks."

Lynn looked up. "Dee Merriweather. I haven't seen her recently."

"She has dropped by the office. Wanted to familiarize herself a little, I think." There seemed to be approval in Karen's voice. "Allie will be taking off for three weeks in the mountains. It's a good time for it, she says."

"You could have just closed up and gone somewhere too," said Lynn. "I know you're not busy this time of year."

"Not very busy. There's always something," Karen replied. "I'd rather spend some time at the beach, maybe after Labor Day. The east coast, maybe."

Lynn was immediately suspicious. "You could get Pat to show you where he grew up." Was that what her friend had in mind?

"Fort Pierce? I don't think there is much there for him to show me. Just his grandmother's house. His early years were spent over by Lake Okeechobee. When he was with his mom." Karen's bark of a laugh ended almost as a sigh. "It took some work to get any of this out of him!"

She drained the last of her tea and leaned back. "I remember riding to Pierce with one of those surfer boys when we were in high school. Skip. Remember him?" Lynn nodded. She had a vague picture in her mind of a lanky bleached-blond boy.

"He surfed at the jetty there. The north one—" Her brows knit in a brief frown. "I think. Yeah, of course, I remember which side the waves were breaking on."

"The north, obviously," said Lynn.

"Yeah. Along the left side of it. Left side facing out to the ocean. I guess a surfer would see it the other way around!"

"I heard Skip became a photographer."

"Really? I haven't heard anything about anyone from high school in ages. I wonder if he still has all that hair." Karen gazed out of the window for a long moment. "Time to get going."

Seventy-Two

"YOU'RE CERTAIN?" ASKED Karen. "Absolutely sure about it?"

Pat slowly nodded. "And he saw me."

Oh. That changed things. "So Matt knows you're onto him." She considered this. "Then we'll let him stew. He won't know whether we told Lynn or not."

"Shouldn't—shouldn't she know?" Pat looked pretty unsure about her idea.

"She already knows what Matt is like," she reminded him, "but if we see him cheating again—no hesitation!" Karen scooted her metal chair a tad to one side so she was facing him more directly. "Give it all to me from the start. Like a story."

"Um, okay. This morning—no wait, I should begin with Saturday. Caroline had barely arrived yesterday when she drove off again. Gone out, was all Agnes knew." His eyes went to the Kuenst house, out beyond the banyans, before turning back to his girl-friend.

Karen wondered if Maddie had seen anything interesting. She should ask the girl. Or ask Dee to ask her.

"Gone all day, as far as I know. I'm always pretty busy on Saturdays." He laughed, a bit self-consciously. "You know that. Anyway, I saw her Mercedes pull in a bit after dusk and didn't think any more of it. Then I noticed Matt's van in the parking lot hours later. Way after guests would normally leave."

"Ah, the plot thickens!" Why did I say that? Karen wondered almost immediately. That was an expression her father would have used.

Pat continued his tale. "But that's not a big deal, of itself. He could have been invited to dinner. Agnes does invite artists, after all."

"True," admitted Karen. "And Dunhill did buy one of his paint-ings. An expensive one, I hear." I wish she'd invited us over this evening, she thought. I could use some wine. She scraped up another spoonful of yellow peas as Pat went on.

"When the van was still there early the next morning—"

"All your detective instincts were aroused," Karen laughed. Maybe she shouldn't have; this was kind of serious. She knew Pat would have come across the road from his trailer before daylight to lead his sunrise yoga session and the walk around the spa grounds.

"Yeah. I had things to do but I tried to keep an eye on the van." A pause and a shrug. "Didn't need to. As I was gathering my group out here—" He waved an arm toward the grounds. "Caroline and Matt came slipping out." Pat craned his body forward. "Right over there," he said. "The back stairs to the second floor."

"Just rooms up there, right?"

"Right. I saw them. They saw me."

"So Caroline knows her secret isn't secret, huh?" Karen had to think on this a moment. "And she has a husband. Mrs. Dunhill might be pretty worried right now."

Pat grinned. "You should help me write my blackmail demand. Anyway," he went on, "I ran into Carl later and he told me Caroline had asked to use one of the rooms last night. A lot of them are empty this time of year. He figured she'd had a fight with Agnes or something. It wouldn't be the first time."

"Matt probably didn't want her Mercedes parked at his house overnight," Karen felt. Or at all, for that matter. And Caroline would have had a hard time smuggling him in and out of her mother's place. That sort of thing might get out.

Especially with Maddie in residence. Now she wanted to talk to the girl all the more.

"Finished?" asked Pat, picking up their plates. "I'll take these on in. Hey, Jag, have you been listening to all of this?" he called.

"Some," came the response from the kitchen. The cook stepped out onto the patio. "None of my business, I know." He shook his head. "But I've known Miss Caroline since she was a girl. I've a mind to give her a good talking to!"

And I'd like to do the same with Matt, Karen said only to herself. Let it go for now. See how things work out.

"Let's get over to my place," she whispered to Pat. "I don't feel like hanging around here."

All she wanted was for Pat to hold her.

Seventy-Three

"DEE?" THE YOUNG woman was seated across from Karen. Lynn slid in beside her.

"She's been at the office getting last minute instructions from Allie," explained Karen. "Thought I'd bring her along." She turned her attention to Dee. "None of that next week. You'll be at your desk when I go to lunch."

"Miss Allie brown bags her lunch," said Dee. Wondering if she should do the same, perhaps.

"No need for that." Karen snickered. "Allie isn't conscientious. Just cheap!"

Dee didn't seem to know how to respond to that. "You can go out if you want," Karen continued. "Before or after I do."

"Okay, Miss Fairfield."

I'd save a lot of money if I didn't come to the *Rose* almost every day, thought Lynn. I'd miss it. I'd miss seeing Karen.

They had actually seen a lot more of each other these past few months, hadn't they? More than they had for a long time. Pat was undoubtedly a factor in that.

Maybe Matt was too. He had been avoiding her all week. Lynn was not sure why. Not sure at all.

The waitress set her salad in front of her. Not Donna. No sooner had she remembered the name of the Friday waitress than the shifts were shifted. She had told herself to order something different some times, hadn't she?

Lynn turned her attention to Dee. Better dressed than either of the older women. She probably wanted to make an impression. Of course, it wasn't hard to look classier than Lynn; she dressed pretty casually to work in the gallery. Slacks usually. And she was the boss now. She could wear what she wanted!

"Have you heard from Maddie lately?" she asked. It seemed that the bump with her ex-boyfriend hadn't hurt anything.

"She's doing fine, Miss, um, Devinne." Lynn glanced at Karen.

Her friend looked like she was containing a desire to laugh. As long as Dee was working for her, maybe it was just as well she used both their last names. Let the girl try to be businesslike. In three weeks they would go back to being more familiar, right?

"Maddie is older than you, isn't she?" asked Karen.

"A couple of years, yes. She was like a big sister to me when we were growing up." Dee turned her attention to her grilled cheese for a moment, cutting off a piece and eating it with a fork. Lynn didn't think she had ever seen anyone do that. "She told me all about what Mr. Bruce did for her."

"He could just as easily have gotten her fired," commented Karen. "The man's a little too quick to use his fists."

Lynn laughed. "I thought you went for macho guys."

"Nope. Big peaceable lugs like Pat. Or Roger."

"Okay, then I relinquish all claim on Roger and will take Jay. When we ditch our current boyfriends, of course." A—look came and went quickly on Karen's face, before she smiled at the quip. Lynn didn't have time to think about it.

"I think Miss Jen might object to that," opined Dee, popping another piece of her sandwich into her mouth. "She gonna—she says is going to send me a wedding invitation."

"I suspect we'll be getting those too," spoke Karen. "They're not in much of a hurry, it seems."

Lynn knew why, via, of all people, Samson Ibarra. "It's going to be in the Catholic Church. They require a long lead time on marriages."

"Ah. Lots of time to pick out a present. What the heck would one give that pair?"

Lynn shrugged. "The usual stuff, I guess. Kitchen appliances."

"Is Jen domestic at all?" Karen wondered.

"Doesn't matter. Roger is." He did the cooking in his and Joe's house. And the big man had been involved in something of that sort in the military, hadn't he?

"Okay, maybe china," said Karen. "I'll think about it." She

looked at Dee sawing her last piece of grilled cheese sandwich in two. "Or silverware."

"I have to ask, Dee," spoke Lynn. "Why are you eating your sandwich that way?"

"Why, so I don't have greasy fingers, Miss Devinne. I wouldn't want to get spots on Miss Fairfield's papers!"

"That does make sense," admitted Karen. "Not that I ever worry about it myself."

"I learned to be careful about that sort of thing in my classes. We handle some delicate equipment."

"Well," said Lynn, "I've learned something. I guess it pays to be nosy."

Karen observed "If you keep painting, you're going to have watch out for that too. You always have stuff on your fingers!"

And maybe that's a good thing, thought Lynn. She should have stuff on her fingers more often.

Seventy-Four

"MATT BROKE UP with me last night," Lynn told her.

Her best friend had been crying. Karen could tell that. All cried out now, maybe, or at least for a while. "Sit down," she said. "We can cancel our drive."

"Oh, no, no. I need something to do."

Karen took a seat beside her on the sofa. It had been the longest couch in the store when her father had bought it. He claimed he needed room to stretch out, though he was not particularly tall. She should offer Lynn a drink.

But first. "Tell me about it." Get it out of her system.

Lynn's voice was leaden. "It was just out of the blue. He and Anne are going to give it another try." Then it took on a little edge. "Or so he says."

Not out of the blue. Not for Karen. And hadn't Lynn said the man had been avoiding her?

"And he didn't offer any other reason?"

Lynn shook her head. "I don't know why he suddenly made this decision. Not really. Maybe he found someone else. Maybe he's been sleeping with one of his students." Frustration. There was frustration, for sure. Maybe resignation too. "Oh, I don't know."

And it would be best if she didn't. Surely Matt's activities of the weekend past had played a part in this.

"At least I'm not in limbo anymore, wondering where we were going." A sigh. "I have resolution at last. Just not the resolution I was hoping for."

Was she truly? Lynn had expressed her own misgivings about the relationship more than once. "Would you like some coffee?" She hadn't made any, but could.

Lynn shook her head. "Had enough already." A bit of a smile, at last. "Especially if I'm going to be stuck in a car all day."

"Not all day. And we'll stop someplace nice for lunch." She considered this. "Or go swim at the Springs."

"Okay." Lynn stood, apparently ready to take off right then. "How did the offer on this place go?"

"My potential buyers weren't willing to deal. Or I wasn't!" Karen had to admit there was stubbornness on both sides. "They wouldn't meet my minimum anyway. Doesn't matter. Someone else will." She picked up her bag. "Let's head out."

"Which way today?" asked Lynn, as Karen locked her front door behind them. Maybe it should have been repainted. Karen never actually cared for that red.

"Out east. I've pretty much decided on finding a property out there. Five acres minimum."

"How much maximum?"

It was not a serious question, only banter, but Karen responded. "Maybe up to twenty. I've actually thought about it. And I would like water. A pond, a stream. Something."

"Oh, maybe a swamp!"

"That might do. A cypress pond is not such a bad thing." A few minutes later they were on Springs Road, cruising past the spa and over the river. Lynn became subdued again. This was going to weigh on her for more than a few hours. More than a few days.

"There's the church Dee and Maddie attend," said Lynn.

"And Jay Bruce lives further out that road. Let's go that way." Karen turned up the lime-rock road. The grass around the clapboard building was packed with vehicles. "I clipped some listings. Would you look in my bag for them?"

Lynn perused the pieces of paper she found. "Hmm, I don't know where any of these addresses are. We need a map. Oh." She spied the one Karen had tucked into her tote. "Prepared, aren't we?"

"I've been carrying that around for weeks," admitted Karen.

The side roads were mostly plain dirt. Some had signs naming them, some didn't. "There's a cypress pond for you," said Lynn, pointing to their right. The grove of moss-hung trees lay at the bottom of a long, shallow slope, cleared and planted with something or another. It wasn't very good agricultural land, really. Karen knew this. Just sand.

But it would grow a pasture. That was all she wanted. She slowed to a halt and looked down toward the cypress trees. Karen could imagine horses galloping across that slope. A place like this would do just fine, were it for sale.

"What's the closest property?" she asked Lynn, who was studying the county map spread in her lap, and consulting the listings.

"We, ah, could have turned left a couple roads back—hmm, go ahead for a while. There's a place right on this road."

Rows of gravestones, to their left, behind a metal fence. "Tom was laid to rest there," murmured Lynn. Tom Merriweather. Forgotten by most of the world already, but the paintings would keep his name alive for a while. Then Jay Bruce's house. He only had a couple acres. Neat, well-manicured acres.

"Doesn't that car belong to that boy? The one he hit?" asked Karen.

"Hadley?" Lynn leaned forward to get a look. "Yep, that's it." The old green sedan was parked next to Jay's truck.

"I hope he's not causing any trouble. Maybe—oh, I don't know. Maybe we should call someone."

"Or we could just go in and find out what's going on," said Lynn.

Yes, they could. Karen turned up Jay's long driveway. Over there, under a spreading live oak—two men fighting. She should grab her cell and call the police.

Lynn laughed. "Why he's teaching that kid to box," she said. Karen looked again. Both were wearing gloves and, at the moment, were only standing looking toward the car. She let out a long breath. Why had she let herself get so flustered?

Jay was peeling off his boxing gloves and walking their way. "We might as well get out and say hello." Karen knew her voice sounded a little weak. Shaky.

247

"More students?" asked Bruce. "My fame must be spreading."

Race had removed his gloves too and now came up to stand beside him. "I'll be going, Mr. Bruce, and let you tend to your guests." He took the older man's hand and shook it. "And I thank you, sir." A minute later, he was only a dust cloud on the road.

There would always be lots of dust on these country roads. "We were out looking at property," Karen explained. "And, um, thought we'd stop and say hello." Her heart beat was returning to normal, her adrenaline rush subsiding.

"Always welcome to stop," Jay replied. "Want to come in? Have a cold drink?"

It was Lynn who answered. "Sure. You look like you need one yourself."

"It is getting hot. I'm kind of glad you showed up so I didn't have to spar with Race anymore."

"So there's no—trouble between you now?" asked Karen.

"I've known that young man most of his life. He just does stupid things, like most young men."

"Even you?"

"I suppose I was young once, so I must have." He opened the screen door for his guests. No air conditioning running here. "The boy had actually come to terms pretty much with Maddie leaving him, but then he went out and drank too much and, well, ended up where he ended up. Maybe Maddie moving there drove in how final it was. He was truly sorry and came to apologize to me the next day." Jay gazed out toward the road for a moment and then chuckled. "He asked me to extend an apology to Agnes—and asked me also if I could teach him to punch like that."

"Is that wise?" asked Lynn. They were standing in a large paneled room that extended all the way to the back of the house. The furniture seemed nondescript and a bit shabby.

"He has promised to use his new powers for good," Jay dead-panned. "I don't think there will be more trouble. Lemonade?"

"That would be great," said Lynn. She took a seat in one of the roomy armchairs, looking around. "Built on sort of a basilica floor plan, isn't it? I like the clerestory." Karen looked up at the rows of windows set high on the walls. They were kind of nice. This cavern of a room would be gloomy without them. She found a chair herself.

"It is," came Jay's voice from the kitchen. "I designed it." He returned to them with pitcher and glasses. Mismatched glasses. "There wasn't any house here when I bought the land. I lived in my barn for a couple years while it was going up."

The house was a bit of a barn, too, thought Karen. Still, she could see living in a place like this. She tasted her lemonade. Tarter than she would have preferred.

"I hear Deloris Merriweather is working for you," said Bruce.

"For three weeks, until my secretary gets back from vacation. She and her family are probably in the Appalachians by now."

"Family?" asked Lynn.

Karen had been listening to the woman chatter about her family for years. But Lynn didn't know anything about Allie, did she? "Yes, complete with husband and kids," she told her. "I do let Allie go home to them now and again."

A spouse and children. Something none of the three of them had. A trio of old maids! Karen had to keep from laughing out loud at the thought of Jay Bruce being so labeled. Where was his easel? He must paint here somewhere.

"You should come by the Springs and paint," said Karen. "We're going over this afternoon."

"I only paint in the studio," Jay told her. "Or mostly."

"By artificial light, right?" asked Lynn. She turned to her friend. "He told us he prefers the consistency." Bruce only nodded agreement to all this.

"Well then, come and swim. You can swim, can't you?"

"After a fashion." He gave her a rather frank looking-over. "I suspect neither of us floats very well."

But he said no more on the subject of visiting the resort and the topic gave way to others, before they made their goodbye and continued the tour of properties.

"I don't think I want to go out to the Springs this afternoon," said Lynn as they drove past another unsuitable place. "Do you mind if I go on home after lunch?"

"No, of course not. There will be other days."

"Yes. Yes, there will."

Seventy-Five

LYNN DIDN'T FEEL like sitting in her apartment, nor by the little pool. There were too many people in it on this Sunday afternoon, too many children. Visiting children, mostly. The cozy apartments at the *Neptune* were not suited to families.

Walk. That's what she needed to do. Activity, physical activity. The afternoon sea-breeze could be felt these miles inland, coming in across the bay. It wasn't so hot when it blew and if it rained later, that wouldn't be a bad thing. She had walked many miles in Florida rain over the years.

She should go to the bay. It was close. Even if she just went over and sat by the docks, it was something. Maybe she could sort things out. Two blocks west to Bay Street; that was the way she went when she walked to work, and then up to the gallery.

But Lynn didn't turn on Bay Street, not either direction. Across to the docks. She hadn't been here since that storm day, the day she had run into Joe. Maybe she should drop in on the sergeants. Lynn had looked up their address. It was only a block east, on Second, and north a little way.

Not that either was likely to be there. She was curious about their house, though. Maybe there were other places like it in the neighborhood. She needed to get out of that apartment. She was exceedingly tired of it and its memories.

Ah, who was she kidding? Any house, even a tiny one, would be too expensive in this area. They would be eventually torn down, giving way to luxury homes or condos. Her own *Neptune Apartments* would go, too.

The docks were busy, boaters coming and going, or standing and gossiping with each other. Power boats, mostly—it was sails that Lynn wanted, not a motor. She'd had a dinghy as a teen, had learned to sail on it.

It sat waiting for her while college and career took her elsewhere, when other winds filled her sails. At last, her parents had asked if they could sell it when they moved to Clearwater. What could she say but 'yes?' Lynn couldn't expect Mom and Dad to haul the boat to their new home.

Ah, but she wished she had it now. Or something a little bigger maybe. Not that she could afford much—if she had the money, she'd get one large enough to live on. That would sure beat apartment living!

Enough daydreaming, Lynn. There were 'for sale' signs here and there. She wandered down the sidewalk to another small marina. Were there more places beyond it? It all looked to be private homes down there, their docks extending from the seawalled shore. Small sailboats sat at the front of the parking lot, trailered, a row of trim little hulls. All white, but with varied markings. She walked over to look at them. Hmm, not for sale, but apparently people did sail from here. The launching ramp seemed a tad steep to her.

What was that? A Snark, right by the marina store's windows. She remembered Snarks. Did they still make them? And it was for sale. Different from her dinghy but not much larger. She walked all the way around it. Ten foot? Perhaps a little longer.

"You sail, Miss?" came a voice. A stout man, bearded. The faded red polo shirt had a 'Franklin Marina' logo on it, so he must work here. Or run the place.

"Used to," she was willing to admit. "Might again."

The man broke into an easy laugh at that; Lynn had to, too. "Jerry Franklin," he said, extending a squarish hand.

"Lynn," she replied, shaking. "Lynn Devinne."

He seemed mildly surprised by this information. "Now I remember a little girl by that name who used sail a dinghy all over out there." He waved an arm toward the bay. "This wouldn't be a bad step up if you were thinkin' of gettin' back into it."

I am, she said to herself. Yes, I am. And it's about time. "Let's talk price," she said to Jerry Franklin.

Seventy-Six

"You actually came!"

"Nothing better to do," muttered Jay Bruce, looking about. "Is Lynn with you?"

"Ah, no, she didn't feel up to it." Should she let him in on what had happened? He knew about Lynn and Matt, right? "Getting over a breakup with her boyfriend."

"Stone." He sank into one of the poolside chairs. "For the better, I'd say."

Me too, Karen silently agreed. "Pat will be along shortly. He's finishing up some chore or another."

A couple kids were splashing at the other end of the pool. His eyes went to them for a moment before he replied. "I was coming over here anyway. Mrs. Kuenst asked me to."

"Maybe she plans to buy all your paintings!"

"If only. I suspect she wants to talk about Maddie. About her future."

Karen knew nothing of that so she chose not to comment on it. Children's voices arose behind them. She recognized them at once. "Matt and his kids," she whispered.

Jay's eyes flickered their direction. "His wife too, I would suspect."

Well, that made sense. They were together again. Maybe the little girls had asked to come and swim here; she couldn't think of any other reason Matt would show up.

She rose and turned to greet them. Anne was gorgeous. Karen had to admit that. She had never actually met the woman before, spoken to her. Nor had Jay, apparently.

"Hello, Karen. Hi, Jay, never expected to see you here. Say hello to Miss Karen," he told his daughters. They murmured a greeting but their eyes were on the beckoning swimming pool. "This is Anne, my wife. Karen Fairfield, Jay Bruce."

The woman might assume they were a couple. Karen wouldn't

bother' to say anything about it. "Pleased to meet you," Anne Stone breathed. "Are you artists?" She glanced toward her husband, perhaps wondering how he knew them.

"Jay is," replied the man. "Karen sits at a desk and counts things all day."

She had to smile despite her anger toward Matt. It was a fair description.

And was she really angry? Not as she had been when she heard of him cheating with Caroline Dunhill. The breakup with Lynn had been anticlimactic, something she had kind of expected all along. Something, if she was honest, she had hoped for.

While Anne shepherded her little ones into the water—she was even more striking in her bathing suit—Matt sat down beside them. He said nothing for some time.

"Things that happened recently made me reevaluate," he spoke finally. "Having the girls out at my house, sleeping there—that was a part of it. And, well, you know what else." He wasn't going to say anything about Caroline in front of Bruce. "I regretted that almost at once."

Or as soon as Pat saw him, Karen felt like saying. "Lynn knows nothing of it," she informed him.

He slowly nodded his head. "That's good. But whether I was with Lynn or—or someone else, I was cheating on my wife." His eyes went to Jay, who had been attempting to act as if was not hearing any of this.

"I think I'll go visit Agnes," said Bruce, getting to his feet. "Maybe I'll see y'all later." He ambled off.

Good man, thought Karen. She turned to Matt. "But you had a relationship with Lynn. This Dunhill thing—a one night stand, right?"

"It is now." He shrugged. "Whether more would have followed, I don't know. I decided not to take the chance."

"You have a new chance now," she told him. "Don't blow it."

Seventy-Seven

A WEEK MAKES a difference. Maybe not a lot of difference, but things do move on. And she had sailed. Yes, Lynn owned eleven foot of used sailboat now and intended to be on it as much as possible. Who needed a guy, anyway? she asked herself, and chuckled aloud at the memory of Georgia and Sandy saying something like that.

Good thing no one else was in the *Bayside Gallery*. But then, people expected artist types to act oddly. She looked across Bay Street to the sparkling water. Saturday meant she could close early and get out onto that water. It would be crowded, of course, on a weekend, powerboats running up and down and across the bay. She had rediscovered a deep hatred for powerboats!

There was Jay. He had phoned, saying he would drop by this morning with some new work. Alone? Yeah. He came around to the passenger side of his truck, pulled out a black trash bag. The same way he had brought those first paintings by.

They had sold two of his pictures so it was good he was bringing new ones. Jay Bruce had been a find, no denying. Except he had found them. "Hi, Lynn," he called as he came through the front door, carefully turning his awkward package. It was not a cheerful greeting, not really. Jay never sounded particularly cheerful.

She returned his hello. "I'll just set this down here," he said, leaning his paintings against the counter and turning to her.

His eyes lingered on her breasts rather too long, Lynn thought. Oh, men did that, she knew. She knew it well. She hadn't expected it from Jay, for some reason.

"My eyes are up here." Lynn attempted to sound more peeved than she was.

"And the rest of you is down there," was Bruce's amiable answer. "It's all you, right?"

She had to laugh, though she knew she shouldn't. "I guess so!"

"But sorry if I made you uncomfortable, all right?"

He was serious, wasn't he? "Apology accepted. I'm just assuming it was artistic interest. By the way, I still want to see some of your figure work. Sometime."

"Mmm, well, I am not bringing any of those paintings here." He turned and began slipping the new ones out of their trash bag. "But I wouldn't mind getting your opinion on them. Sometime."

"Let's look at these ones first." Three acrylics. "No drawings?" Lynn was slightly disappointed. Those had sold better than the paintings. She considered suggesting Jay have prints made of them.

"You know I hate to do those."

"Even though you're good at it."

"Maybe because I'm good at it. There's no discovery, like with painting."

Lynn understood exactly what he meant. Why hadn't Matt ever talked seriously about art to her? Really serious, not just about technique but about what it all meant. Well, don't start thinking about Matt, she told herself.

"Isn't that at the Springs?" she asked, pointing out a picture of a spreading oak. "I thought you didn't paint outdoors."

"From a photo. I take pictures, maybe I sketch." He shook his head. "But paint? No." Then a sly smile. "Wanna know why?" A dramatic pause. Lynn figured he didn't expect her to actually say anything. "Because acrylics dry waaaay too quickly outdoors. Especially if there is sun or wind."

"That's all?" She was rather disappointed.

"No, but it is the main reason. So, you want these daubings in your fine establishment?"

She looked over all three. Lynn couldn't say one stood out more than the others. "Sure. Let's write up a receipt thingy for you."

"That the technical term?"

"It is here. I'm the boss, so what I say goes." She gave the paintings another look. "I'll need to get them framed. Take them up to

Venice next week, maybe." She should do it herself, instead of letting Samson take care of it. As Karen had told her she should.

He nodded. "Good enough." A moment's hesitation. "I was serious about you looking at my other work. If you want."

"At your place? I didn't see a studio when I was there."

"It's in one of the side rooms. I'll be there most of the afternoon. Most of tomorrow too."

"I'm sailing this afternoon," she informed him. Nothing was going to get in the way of that. "Probably tomorrow too!"

He digested this, nodded. "Any time then. I'm home by four or five most afternoons. Drop in if you want."

Maybe I shall, she thought, as his yellow pickup disappeared up Bay Street. Sometime.

Yes, sometime, Lynn told herself later, as she sped across the bay. She could do what she wanted. Just as she did in this boat, dependent only on the wind and herself.

Maybe she would drive out to Jay's and look at his paintings some afternoon this week. Maybe after yoga class. There would be lots of time. Or next weekend. Whenever.

She adjusted her sail and tacked to starboard.

Seventy-Eight

"HE'S SO GOOD for me," she told Lynn. "So sweet, so gentle."

"I've seen how happy you were these past months. I know he is good but is he also, well, *good*?" She giggled over the question. Why would she ask that?

Karen smiled. "I don't think he had much experience before me. I'm trying to make up for that! And he's in such good condition—that counts for a lot. Still," she continued, with a touch of hesitance, "I wish he were a little more aggressive."

Lynn immediately sobered. Was there trouble?

"It's not a big deal. He's just different from the men I've known before." She pulled out a pack of cigarettes, turning it over and over, waiting to step out of the *Rose* before lighting up.

Her friend eyed her but said nothing

Karen seemed to feel she needed to, that she should explain herself. "Pat doesn't care."

"You know he does. He just wouldn't say it, right?"

"No. He never says it."

But there was no sign of problems at yoga class that afternoon, no seeming tension between Pat and Karen. Just a bump, maybe thought Lynn. She hoped it would work itself out, more for Pat's sake, perhaps, than her friend's. Hadn't she worried from the first about their yogi's involvement with Karen? Karen, who could grow restless, who could be demanding. And liked men who were demanding, too, men who pushed back. Maybe she had it all backwards. Maybe it was Karen who truly needed the relationship to work.

That was up to the couple. They would be together this evening, going somewhere, doing something. And Lynn? No plans for her. It was still light out, still early. Why not make this the day to go visit Jay? She was curious to see his studio. To see that whole house he apparently designed and largely built himself.

Less than an half hour later she halted in the road and surveyed that house. It still looked like a barn from the outside. Only Jay's truck was there, parked well back by the actual barn. No sign of the man himself as Lynn drove up the entry lane. She was tempted to turn around and pull back out. Surely he had better things to do than entertain her after a hard day in the sun. He was probably relaxing now, maybe soaking in the shower.

Hmm. She had a quick vision of Jay in the shower. Cut that sort of thing out, girl, she told herself. You came on business! And Bruce had invited her. She made a decision and turned off the engine.

As Jay opened the front door and waved her direction. It would have been too late to make a run for it anyway.

She should have changed after class. Lynn suddenly felt self-conscious about wearing a pair of shorts pulled on over a leotard. Especially in that Jay looked so neat and clean. Wet hair—he *had* just been in the shower.

"Welcome," he greeted her. Jay was only wearing a tee and shorts himself, and flip-flops, none of his outfit looking too new. She needn't have felt ill at ease. "So you made it. I wasn't sure you would follow through."

"Neither was I!" She stepped through the door he held open. Still no air conditioning but she thought she heard a unit running.

"I have Zinfandel in the fridge. Want some?"

"Sure." She was about to plop into one of the comfortable chairs as he disappeared into the kitchen. Well, didn't disappear. She could see him across the bar. She decided to go sit on one of the slat-backed stools there instead. "I'm told you and Agnes were plotting Maddie's future," she said.

He poured out glasses of red for both. "She and Pat both think she is a rather apt yoga student. Maddie may become a fixture at the Springs."

Apt? Every now and again this seeming redneck, this lawn-mowing man, used language that sounded more like it came from a book than the Florida countryside. But Jay Bruce didn't speak to much of anyone all day as he worked. He lived alone. Maybe most of his interaction was with books. Quite of a few of those lined the walls in this room.

"Assistant guru maybe?" she joked. But if Pat moved up to manage the spa, others would have to take over his teaching. Some of it, at least.

"So it seems."

It wasn't bad in here, even with no air running. There was a row of ceiling fans down the room, slowly turning, and the house was well-shaded by trees. Maybe Jay had planted those.

He hesitated after handing her a glass, and then came around the bar to sit beside her. Jay's bare toes gripped the rung around his stool—he had kicked off his thong sandals at the door. For outdoor use only, apparently.

He noticed her glancing at his feet and laughed. "I'm kind of lax about what I wear, since I'm the only one here. And no neighbors close!" He sipped his wine and nodded approval. "Feel free to kick your shoes off too."

Self-consciousness suddenly rushed back in. Jay had a great body, lean, hard. Lynn had to admit that. She was much less confident about her own.

But it wouldn't hurt to slip off these loafers. She did at yoga class, after all. Yes, it was better. "So do I get to see your studio?"

"Sure." He rose, glass in hand. He gave the wine a look. "Just a gulp left," he said, and gulped it. "Come on."

Lynn had already drained her glass so she followed him across the room. "This is the work side of the house," he announced, and looked around before opening a door. "Have to make sure the cat doesn't slip in."

She had seen no sign of a cat but was willing to believe in its existence. There had been a certain odor that she could now place. "He tends to wreak havoc in the studio." Not a studio but apparently Bruce's home office was beyond the door. "And in here too."

Lynn could see the light flashing on his old-fashioned answering machine. Jay ignored it. "Back here." He led her into a much larger room, a long room, flipping on the bank of overhead fluorescents. A large easel stood at the center.

I think he built that, she told herself. Unframed paintings crowded the walls. Some not very good—and not very new, Lynn realized when she made out the dates. Why that one was twenty years old!

And there were figure paintings among them. Men, women. Most of them nudes. Who poses? she wondered, and remembered at once that he worked from photographs mostly. "You were right," she admitted. "Not for our gallery. I think." Though that woman in the dress there—hmm, or that one. "But some are good. You might investigate another dealer."

He chuckled. "Sending me to the competition?" Jay turned to survey the pictures himself. "I never carried these to any of the outdoor shows so they kind of piled up." He went to a rack and extracted a pair of canvases. "These are newer."

"And better," she had to say. Matt should have seen these. She would never suggest that now, though she would see the man from time to time. Gallery business would go on, however their personal lives turned out. Ha, Mr. Bruce had let her into his studio the first time she visited. Why couldn't Stone have been that welcoming? Why couldn't he have opened up, committed? Something. She suddenly realized she was sobbing.

Jay didn't know what to do, obviously. He awkwardly put an arm around her and accompanied her back to the living room. A large orange cat darted away when he caught sight of a stranger.

"Maybe I should go," Lynn said. She had regained her composure, for the most part.

"You don't have to. Maybe—maybe we could go have some dinner."

She smiled at that. "Not in these clothes." It was as good an excuse as any.

"Then stay here. I can boil pasta with the best of them."

Lynn almost said yes. "Make it a rain check, Jay, for sometime when I'm not such a wreck."

He shrugged. "Okay. But you've promised now. I'm holding you to it!"

Seventy-Nine

"JAY SEEMS TO like Lynn. She thinks maybe he has all along."

"I'd call that trading up," observed Pat.

Karen agreed. "I haven't seen Matt in a while. Not since he brought his family here."

"Me neither." Without Lynn, he had no place in either of their lives. "How about Mrs. Dunhill? She ever say anything to you?"

"Caroline hasn't been around for a while. Avoiding the Springs. Maybe avoiding me." He stopped walking, turned around to look toward the Kuenst house. "I think Agnes knows something happened but she won't ask."

"The woman should be grateful to you for saying nothing." And Karen was grateful she would not be with them this evening.

"I am not holding my breath. But maybe it did earn me some good will."

"Or she might want to get rid of you all the more."

"Anything is possible," admitted Pat. "So Lynn and Jay are, um, dating?"

"Not yet. Maybe never!" She knew nothing might come of it, that Lynn might not be ready. "But it would do her good, don't you think."

"That depends on just what sort of a relationship they would have, doesn't it?"

"Well, a little sex wouldn't hurt her any."

"I don't quite see her, ah, using Jay." They both had to chuckle at the thought.

"No. Lynn is not the sort who would even think of having a one-night stand." She wasn't, was she? Karen suddenly felt not quite sure of it. Lynn changed. They all changed.

Pat gave her a quick look but said nothing. Karen could guess his thought, his unvoiced question. Guys always wondered about things like that. "Yes, I have had some. An awfully long time ago." He didn't think less of her for it, did he? No, not Pat—she almost wished he would, that it would arouse something in him, at least a tinge of jealousy.

"It's sprinkling again," observed Pat. "Let's get on over and drink Agnes's wine."

"No one but us, right?" Karen hoped the evening wasn't going to grow into another dinner party.

"And Maddie." A quick smile. It seemed almost a smirk. "Agnes thinks I should dump you and take up with Maddie. She likes that girl."

Was Pat being serious? She couldn't tell. "Way too young for you, Grandpa." Karen did the figures quickly in her head. Eight years difference? Maybe even nine. "It's nice to know Agnes likes me, though." Karen thought she had.

"She does. Just not for me, it seems." He stopped and turned to her. The rain dripped down through the thick canopy of the oaks, falling noiselessly onto the leaf carpet. "Don't be bothered by Agnes's quirks."

"It does bother me. Don't tell me it shouldn't!"

He looked at her with mild surprise. "Okay, Karen."

Pat wasn't going to engage. She felt like throwing something at him. Well, almost. A handful of leaves wouldn't make much of a point.

Okay, she shouldn't be bothered by Agnes. Chances are the woman was just joking too. It was more Pat's attitude that had set her off. Why couldn't he assert himself more?

Maddie opened the door to them. "Is that my dinner guests?" called Agnes. She slipped into the hall to greet them. "Just the four of us. Maybe I should have invited some of your other friends. The artists."

"Oh, Miss Lynn and Mr. Jay are already going out somewhere this evening," Maddie informed them. She eased the door closed, after looking out into the gray of a rainy late afternoon.

"Together?" asked Agnes.

"Yes, ma'am!"

The girl would know more about Bruce's doings than any of them, Karen realized. They were neighbors. Used to be neighbors. Maddie was moving further and further from that life.

And she looked it, wrapped in a sari to match Mrs. Kuenst's. Where had that country girl gone, the hesitant student who walked into Pat's class back in the spring?

Maybe Pat *would* be better off with someone like her. Karen shook that idea from her mind. "I'll be sure to get a report on their date tomorrow, and gossip about it to everyone," she promised.

They followed their hostess, not into the dining room but what could only be termed a library, across the hallway. She turned to them. "There is a special remembrance for me on this day," spoke Agnes. "Twenty years ago my Abraham passed. The Seventh of August, Nineteen Ninety-Six.

Her eyes swept across the tall bookcases. "Right here in this house, stricken down with a heart attack. Right here in this room." She shook her head. "He was gone before the medics ever arrived."

Pat asked, very quietly. "Was your daughter here?"

"No, Carrie was in Europe, on summer vacation." Kuenst smiled, perhaps at the memory of the Caroline who had been. "She had just finished her freshman year at college."

Agnes turned from them, still speaking as she opened a cabinet. "Abraham was a man in his prime, by most reckoning, only a little past sixty. But he was taken and that is that." She set a tray, with bottle and glasses, on the glossy reading table. "I would like you all to drink a toast to his memory today."

She picked up the bottle, blew away some of the heavy dust. "Abraham's favorite Scotch. It has sat here untasted a very long time." She dribbled a bit into each glass. "And when I pass, I expect you to come and raise a toast to me, too." Agnes lifted her glass. "To Abraham Kuenst. My husband."

It was exceedingly good Scotch. Karen wished she could get close and wipe the dust from the label. That would be pretty gauche. A single malt, most certainly. Agnes slid the tray into its cabinet. "We can wash those glasses and put them back later," she said to Maddie. "Now let's go eat."

Eighty

ALL THE WAY to Punta Gorda Jay had driven, first on back roads leading eastward from his home. The cab of his truck smelled of fresh-mown grass.

It was a low, unassuming tin-roofed building near the docks, but Bruce swore by the seafood there. Lynn was ready to swear by it too, once they were served. Dingy, as low inside as out, the thick rich smell of fried fish permeating the dining room's atmosphere—she didn't know there were still places like this.

"They sell fish out of the other side of the building," Jay told her. "Buy it too. The fishing boats can dock right there."

"I want to see it," she told him. And they did, went down and watched sun-burnt men in overalls tossing fish into bins, and then strolled along the docks. There were some real sailboats here, the sort one might, indeed, live on. How wonderful would it be to wake up on one, to have nothing to do all day but paint and sail?

And maybe have someone to share it with? She glanced at the wiry tanned man walking at her side. Maybe. Maybe someday she would want that.

But she still ached. Her heart still would sometimes pound without reason as she thought about the end of what she had with Matt. Why? Why not move on?

She walked a little closer to her companion. He could put his arm around her, couldn't he? That might make things better. And he did put his arm around her and perhaps things were a little better.

There was still a ghost of the sunset when they returned to Jay's Barn. She had named it this in her head. He didn't ask her to come in nor did she ask; they simply went in together, wordlessly, his arm again around her.

Then both arms, as he drew her to him, put his lips to hers. They remained together for some time.

"Like something to drink?" he asked, once they returned to earth. "I could make coffee."

"Coffee would be nice." It would. She watched him fill his coffee-maker from a jug of bottled water.

"The well water here is atrocious," Jay informed her. "Full of sulfur."

"I could fill buckets at my apartment and bring them out to you," she offered.

"You're welcome anytime, with or without buckets. Hey, Joe." What? Oh, he was talking to the cat. It perched on the back of a chair, regarding her with steady green eyes. The machine began chugging. "Hmm, back in a minute," said Jay and disappeared into one of the rooms. The ones on this side of the house, not where he worked.

"Had to turn on the AC unit in my bedroom," he explained. "It's all I ever run. Hard to sleep when it gets really hot, this time of year."

Lynn nodded. Sensible. And a good night's sleep was worth having. She should head home soon and get one herself. Turn on her own air conditioning!

Not too soon, though. She liked being here, right now, and she liked being with Jay. Maybe she liked Jay too. Such a strange mix he was. So competent, in so many ways, but not showing it off to anyone. "Have you ever been married, Jay?" she asked. Lynn had wondered about his bachelor existence.

"Nope. No one was ever willing to stick with me. Coffee's ready."

He wasn't going to talk about it. Okay. Mmm, that was good coffee. Lynn hadn't noticed the brand. Colombian, she suspected. No one would stick with him? Maybe because he seemed so self-sufficient. No one would feel needed.

Stop trying to analyze the man, she told herself. But she would like to feel needed. Matt hadn't needed her, not at all. Matt had *liked* her. He pretty much said so. She was the epitome of friend-with-benefits. It was good that it was over.

Jay had turned on music somewhere. She zeroed in on the source—a radio over on the counter. Some public station, broadcasting folk music. That was all right with her.

And she hadn't needed Matt, had she? He had been the path of least resistance, the easy way that demanded little of her. If he hadn't broken with her, if he had divorced Anne, they could have had a comfortable life together, sharing their painting, making amiable love, keeping out of each others way. It didn't seem very desirable, now.

Jay was sitting, watching her wool-gather. He was smart. He could probably guess what preoccupied her. Or he could simply think she was tired.

Tired of the life she had lived, that was what she was. Things were going to change. They already had. Matt gone. She was sailing again. She was painting. The past was broken so she had broken with the past.

She leaned forward on the bar, resting her chin on her hands, and looked at her host. "I'll bet you would be painting if I weren't here."

"I might," he admitted. "No telling when the urge will arise."

"Any sort of urge," she giggled.

"Um, yes."

"Let's sit on the couch." Joe bounded away as they settled onto the sofa. Lips again met; hands strayed. Things were going to happen. Lynn knew this. Let them. Let them.

"Are you sure about this?" Jay suddenly asked.

"Because I'm on the rebound? I don't care!" He seemed hesitant anyway. "You're not taking advantage of me, Mr. Bruce." I'm taking advantage of him!

It did not take long for him to make up his mind. "Come on," he said, taking her hand. "I know a place with air conditioning."

Eighty-One

MATT WAS THERE. It was to be expected, sooner or later.

And it didn't bother her. Not really. They would both ignore all that had happened, all there had been between them. Still, she was hesitant about coming out of the back room, seeing the man, and being seen.

He only nodded a greeting as she came in, and turned back to his conversation with Samson. "So we have decided to sell the house," Matt was saying. "Anne likes her job in Saint Pete, but not the commute. I'll be closer to my teaching in Sarasota, too." He glanced at his watch. "Which I'd best be heading to."

Matt turned to her, his face betraying no emotions, his voice seeming purposely carefree. "Bye, Lynn." With that he was out the door and headed to his van.

"We may lose Mr. Stone as an artist if he moves," remarked Sam. She didn't know what to say to that. "Ah, yes, I know, I know. You have already lost him. But I would say that was Matt's loss. He was not good enough for you."

"Maybe none of us are good enough," Lynn said. Exactly why, she wasn't sure.

Samson shook his head. "That does not matter. God gives and forgives anyway." He paused, smiled. "Sometimes we humans are able to do the same."

Maybe I have, she told herself. But Lynn only nodded at Ibarra's words and went back to her paper work.

Almost, she called Karen's office to cancel lunch. Dee would still be answering the phone this week, wouldn't she? The young woman didn't actually have much else to do at her temporary job. Tell people Karen was too busy to talk—which none would believe, of course. But she found herself walking north a little after noon, her head crowded with thoughts, thoughts of today, thoughts of yesterday.

There was a lot to sort out about what had happened with Jay.

Lynn didn't think she would tell Karen anything. Karen seemed to be having her own problems.

Which she seemed willing to talk about. Or wanted to talk about. "I wonder if I'm good for Pat," she said, between mouthfuls of her hamburger. "If I am right for him."

Lynn had to think a moment before coming up with an answer. One she thought was appropriate, that is—other possibilities were rejected first. "He didn't have anyone before you," she pointed out. "Maybe never." Not that Pat was any sort of innocent, she knew, but Karen might well have been his first true, steady girlfriend.

"So I'm just his training wheels," said Karen. She did smile as she said this, but Lynn suspected she believed something of the sort. "Maybe it's time for him to take them off."

"And what about you? No one has ever made you as happy."

Karen replied only, "For a while."

Don't get angry, Lynn told herself, but she definitely felt like giving her best friend a piece of her mind. Couldn't she work at the relationship? Couldn't she try to meet Pat partway? He certainly had been giving it his best.

But no sense in saying things like that. "Try to be happy again," was all she said.

"I could tell you the same. So—last night?" Oh, so it was going to come around to her date with Jay after all.

"Jay drove us down to a great seafood place he knows in Punta Gorda," said Lynn. "I should give you directions."

"Sure. And after? Any fireworks?" Karen leaned back, mischief and curiosity mingling in her expression. "At least a kiss good-night?"

"Uh, yeah, we kissed." I am *not* going to tell her anything more than that, vowed Lynn. "He kisses well." Oh, did he kiss well! Jay did many things well. She realized she had slipped away into a daydream for a few seconds.

Karen's look now held all sorts of suspicion. But, "That's good," was her only comment.

Eighty-Two

"I AM FAIRLY certain she and Jay had sex." She had been thinking about that possibility all week. Off and on.

"Things happen," was all Pat seemed willing to say. He wouldn't gossip about something like this.

"They do. It seems–abrupt." He only nodded to that. But Karen was concerned. Jay Bruce seemed a good enough sort but she didn't want her friend hurt.

Her phone buzzed. Normally she would have ignored it on a Sunday evening but she noted the number and answered. Allie. Back home. Karen thanked her for calling and letting her know. She would have expected her to be at her desk in the morning anyway.

"Allie's back," she informed Pat. Not that it would matter any to him. She wasn't even sure he had ever met her–and she wasn't a typical topic of conversation.

"Dee did an okay job while she was gone?" he asked. Just the sort of question she should expect from the man.

"Sure. But I'll be glad to have things back to normal." Whatever that was. Oh, she had meant to ask him something. "You'll be tied down by your job over Labor Day, won't you?"

"I will," he admitted. "And we'll be ramping back up for the season quite soon. Really, we need to begin on it right after the holiday."

And he would be starting up a new class downtown too. Only a week left in the summer class now. It would be a good time to get away, a good time to think things through. "I believe I will go up to my place on the lake for the weekend. Just me."

He digested this. "We all need some time to ourselves." A gentle smile. "But not tonight, I hope."

No, not tonight. Maybe she should forget all her misgivings about a future with this beautiful man, this good man. Maybe she should ask him to move in at last. After Labor Day. After she thought about things.

"I smell supper," she said, deeming a change of subject suitable. "Is it ready yet?"

Pat peeped into the oven. "No, but I should take off the lid and let it brown for the last ten minutes or so." Steam rose as he reached in with oven mitts and removed the glass cover. Karen refilled their wine glasses. Refilled hers; Pat's was still half-full.

He continued to surprise her with cooking skills. Lasagna tonight. With eggplant. She had never cared for its bitterness but Pat assured her he had a way to subdue that.

She only hoped he was the one to wash that casserole pan later! He returned to his seat beside her, took a sip of Merlot. "Tell me about when you were a kid," she suddenly said. "Agnes claimed you were troubled."

He let out a breath, slowly, and began. "I had problems, sure. I acted out. Some of it I could lay at my mom's feet but I won't—that's the past. I was just a wild kid running around, getting into trouble but not causing trouble, you know? Skipped way too much school. I was never comfortable there."

"Not comfortable?" Learning difficulties? Bullied? Karen could think of a host of problems.

"Anxiety. Probably depression too. No one got around to diagnosing that but I definitely had serious anxiety attacks. So I would disappear, go hide out, camp, boat. Easy to do there along the Okeechobee shoreline. And my mom wasn't paying much attention.

"Then it was Mom who disappeared, when I was fourteen. Oh, I didn't want to go live with my grandmother. I considered slipping away, trying to live off the land. I didn't know what to do, I'll admit it—I was just a kid. So, in the end, I went to live with her in Fort Pierce, where she taught yoga and ran a little shop."

"That must have been quite a change." Anxiety attacks? Did he still have those? Had be been hiding them? She could think of occasions—

"It was. And she taught me yoga and its philosophy, and to turn to it to deal with my problems. I remade myself, in a sense, while searching for spiritual answers."

Karen had no ready response for that. The timer sounded and Pat went to again look into the oven. "I'd say that's ready," he announced, setting the casserole pan atop the range. "But it needs to rest a few minutes to firm up."

She could say the same about her thoughts. They needed time. But no more thinking tonight. That's an order! Enjoy your meal, enjoy your man, and let the rest wait. Wait and firm up.

Eighty-Three

"I wish to thank all of you for sticking with me through the summer," announced Pat.

"Thanks for sticking with us!" someone called from the back of the room. Was that Georgia Miller's voice? Her friend Sandy—and the hutch she had bought at *Bayside*—had gone north in the spring.

"You are quite welcome," he replied. "There will be another class starting in the fall. Not until September Twelfth."

"In the evening?" someone else called out.

"Yes, we will return to an evening class. Once again, thank you. Namaste." Pat rose and walked toward the kitchen.

"That's almost a month," Lynn remarked. Karen gave an absent-minded nod. She probably knew all about Pat's schedule.

"You two going out tonight?" she asked.

"No, he's going to be monopolized here for a while." A crowd had gathered around the instructor. "I must share Pat with his admirers." Karen's smile was crooked. "How about you? Have you been seeing Jay?"

"No. Not for a while." Lynn had avoided him, ever since they had been together, uncertain about—about everything. A week and an half. That was wrong. That was unfair. She needed to talk to the man.

Yes. She did. She had spent enough time trying to make sense of what had happened. Lynn watched her friend's red sedan roll east on Fifth before starting her own car. She would head east, too, but had a different destination.

No one but Jay again at his house. She had not expected otherwise. Lynn walked toward the front door, ready to knock boldly, confront him, say what needed saying. Someone called to her.

"Back here!" He was out by the barn, hosing off his lawn maintenance equipment, in jeans. A soaked tee shirt hung over the tailgate of his yellow truck. Jay had a bit of a 'farmer's tan,' his torso a shade or two paler than the bronzed arms, face. That hadn't been so obvious indoors, by dim artificial light.

Ah, what was she doing? Was this the right way? She liked this guy, but—best to say what she had intended.

He looked as if he might have all sorts of things he wanted to say, himself. He chose only to greet her. "Hello, Lynn."

"Hi, Jay." What now? "I'm sorry I've been—been—ah, I might as well say it outright. I've been avoiding you."

"I figured that out," he replied. Nothing else.

"I spent the weekend sailing up and down the bay, thinking about things. Trying to decide—something."

"It was too soon, wasn't it?"

Exactly. He put it into words better than she did.

"We'll forget it happened, if that's what you wish." Jay did not sound enthusiastic about the idea.

"I'll never forget," she promised. "But we need to step back." She needed to step back. "For now, anyway," she continued, trying to sound firm about it. "I need more time to sort my life out."

"And I'll give it to you. As long as you want."

"Thanks, Jay. Right now, I just need a friend."

What a cliché! But he didn't call her on it. "Always and anytime. If you need to talk right now—"

Lynn shook her head. "No, I shouldn't hang around. I promise to take you up on it some other time." They both needed to sort things out in their heads first. Damn, she was already feeling regrets, wondering if she had chosen the right course.

But it was the course she had chosen. And she might have said, 'for now,' but Lynn knew better. What she and Bruce had, briefly, was unlikely to rekindle.

She returned to her little white Focus, gave Jay's 'Barn' one more long look, and started toward home.

Eighty-Four

"HAVE YOU VOTED?" asked Samson Ibarra.

"Before I came to work," Lynn answered. Her precinct cast their ballots at the rec center. Sammy had obviously voted too—he had an 'I Voted' sticker on the front of his shirt.

"I ran into your friend Karen. We vote at the same place, the firehouse out Springs Road."

"Probably for the same party, too," conjectured Lynn. "I'm not seeing her as much since our yoga class ended." Karen had canceled more than one lunch recently, too.

But Lynn had not been very sociable lately herself, had seen little of any of her acquaintances. She had needed to listen to her own voice, and that of the wind in her sail.

"She is going away for the weekend, she tells me. Alone."

Lynn nodded. She knew all about that. Maybe she should go out and keep Pat company. He would be busy, sure, but a friendly face might help both of them.

Or not. She might just sail again, all this Labor Day weekend. And then— "Things will start to pick up quickly next month."

"That is so," agreed Samson. "We should talk to Miss Merriweather about her grandfather's paintings one of these days. Before she goes off to college and is too busy."

"I'll make a note to call her," promised Lynn. "We'll need to have dialogues with many of our artists."

"Yes, Lynn. If it is awkward for you to deal with any of them, tell me."

"It won't be." It wouldn't. Ibarra knew something had gone on between her and Bruce, but hadn't pried. No one but she and Jay knew, and she was pretty certain it would stay that way. And all of Matt's water had flowed under her bridge long ago.

Today, Karen did not cancel lunch. "I'm leaving the office at noon," she informed Lynn, "and sleeping at the farm on Friday night." She also had an 'I Voted' sticker. Maybe everyone who went to the firehouse got one plastered on them.

"Maybe after the holiday you and I can go over to the East Coast for a weekend," her friend continued.

"It would have to be before things started getting busy," said Lynn. "The season will be on us before we know it."

Karen nodded. "September, then. Ha, maybe we can find a surfer boy or two to come along."

Lynn had to laugh. "There are plenty of them already over there," she pointed out. "I guess it would be easy enough to drive over for a day anytime." Neither would have thought anything of that once. Fun didn't require so much planning when they were younger.

"True enough. But I need to get away first. I need to think, Lynn, and make some choices."

"Make the right ones," urged Lynn. "Some can't be changed later."

"And some should be made sooner than they are."

"Things come when they come," was all Lynn could think to say. It was something she could almost believe.

Eighty-Five

It was a weary drive up here. At least the holiday traffic had not been bad yet. That was why she had chosen to come early, avoid Saturday's crowded roads.

And she wanted to be here as soon as possible, to get away, to think. Pat. Karen knew she could end things and go on. She knew it would hurt him terribly.

But she wasn't good for the man, was she? Not for the long term. In his way, Pat was just as driven as she, just as focused on his own life. If she pulled him away from that life, he would resent her, in time. Forget until tomorrow, she told herself. You need sleep now. She slipped into the bed in her old room, a bed almost forgotten a season ago, but grown again familiar.

Karen dreamed of horses. She hadn't done that in some time, not that she could remember. If she had believed in omens she would have believed this was one. Karen didn't know what she believed. She wasn't sure she believed anything.

It was early when she had awakened from that dream. Too early. She tried to return to sleep but couldn't. Too many thoughts. Her hearing, her attention, became fixed on the creak of the ceiling fan, and she could not shut it out. Three AM? Ah, what was the point of lying there?

Karen rose, showered, made coffee. She couldn't get Pat out of her thoughts. But that was what she was supposed to be thinking about, wasn't it? She had to decide where she and Pat were going. No, she wasn't good for him, she told herself again. She wasn't even certain he was good for her, at least not any longer. It would be best not to let their relationship deteriorate, fall apart. It would be best to make it clean.

He would never be completely hers. Too many people wanted part of that man and he was altogether too willing to hand those parts out. Karen wanted all of him. She wanted him to want her the same way. That, too, she knew wouldn't happen.

Could she get the canoe down to the water? It would be nice to paddle around the lake a little. She could think as well out there as anywhere. Maybe better. Karen was pretty sure she could drag it down. If not, maybe she could go up *The Corner Bar* and recruit some cowboys. Now there was an idea!

No, she wasn't going to any bars. She had come to be alone, to shut out other voices for a few days.

She would think and she would come to a decision. She had all weekend.

But Karen already knew what it would be. She went to uncover the canoe, lighting a cigarette as she walked down the slope, the rising sun before her.

Eighty-Six

IT WAS GOOD to sail at dawn. Oh, it was good to sail anytime. The bay was calm, almost mirror-like, as the sun rose. She could forget everything, the turmoil of her life on solid land.

Jay. Pat and Karen. Matt. The gallery, her art. There was a long list of people and things that had weighed on her. Think of the good, she told herself. You broke out of a deep rut this summer, a rut you had worn in your own road.

It was good to sail again. Boats were to her what horses were to Karen, a sort of freedom. She hoped her friend would have those horses soon, whatever else happened in her life. And it was good to paint. She felt more confident there every time she picked up a brush. Lynn knew she was still not doing that often enough. Not nearly often enough.

It was even good to be partner in the gallery at last, not that she was sure she actually wanted that. Better than standing still, maybe.

A flight of pelicans skimmed along the glassy surface, their reflections keeping pace. Could she catch that in paint? Perhaps not. It did not matter that much; her mind had caught it. Her soul had caught it.

Things went on. She did not regret Matt; no, not one bit. Lynn suspected he had been what she needed at the time. Shoot, maybe she had even been what he needed. She liked to tell herself so, anyway. Start a turn here. Ah, that breeze is fickle at this time of morning. She would like a strong wind to drive her on.

Yes, things went on, whatever wind drove them. She might find herself blown into some port soon, find there what she desired. Or she might sail on, searching.

It was good to know she could.

Eighty-Seven

LYNN PULLED INTO the rec center parking lot. It wasn't too dark, yet, but they had returned to the evening schedule for fall. Another ten weeks of yoga class, geared for the beginner. As before, she didn't mind that. Just having the class to go to was enough. And Pat to teach, once again.

Pat would be heartbroken, was heartbroken, of course, but he would have turned back to his meditation and his asanas, and kept an even keel, hiding it. His inner turmoil would not be evident but it was there.

He feels deeply and has learned to control his powerful emotions, she told herself, or at least attempt to. And so he may seem too cool and uninvolved at times. She knew better.

Enough daydreaming. She entered the center, the familiar room with its beige walls, chose a spot to unroll her mat. Some familiar faces, some new ones. No Karen. She hadn't really expected her.

Pat entered. "We will begin with a complete breath."

Karen's retreat had not been so much to decide things, perhaps, as to calm herself before she did what she had intended. She had needed to focus herself, to shed her fears and doubts.

"I want to welcome you all to yoga class," Pat was saying. The same introduction as always. She knew the words now.

Why did she break it off? she had asked her friend. Lynn pretty much knew, though. She had seen this coming. She had seen Karen pull away from the man who loved her, the man Lynn was sure she had loved. Almost as soon as she returned from her retreat at the lake, Karen had told Pat they were through. No explanations to him, just that it would be better for both.

But to Lynn, she attempted to explain herself. We didn't have much in common, was the excuse. It *was* an excuse, even if true. I wasn't good for him. I didn't want to hurt him but—well, it's for the best.

It was for Pat's best, Lynn would agree now. Maybe she would

Stephen Brooke

have agreed all along. For his best in the long run. Poor wounded Pat would go on, would heal in time, better for no longer being with a Karen who always longed for more, who had to believe she *deserved* love from a man, had earned it.

Pat could never be that man. He demanded nothing of anyone but himself. His love he gave freely.

The class was rising, following Pat's lead, stretching upward, reaching toward the sky.

Maybe a man like Pat was just what she needed, Lynn thought. And, maybe, just maybe, Lynn was what he needed.

An Afterword

I hope you have enjoyed this novel. Although it is intended to stand on its own, there just may be a sequel some day.

Neither Tamarind nor Leawood are real places. They are, however, inspired by various small towns that lie between Fort Myers and the Tampa Bay area in south-west Florida. Nor is there a Consonante Springs, but it, too, has its real-life models. Most of the other locales, roads, landmarks mentioned in this book are actually to be found in Florida.

I actually taught yoga classes in a Consonante Springs-like resort at one time in my life. However, I would have to admit that I have little else in common with Pat Janson.

Stephen Brooke

www.ingramcontent.com/pod-product-compliance
Lightning Source LLC
Chambersburg PA
CBHW030033030726
47500CB00001B/82